Praise for Lindsay Maracotta:

TURNAROUND … YOU'RE DEAD

'A sparky whodunnit … Maracotta's handling of the murder-mystery plot is skilful enough, but the best thing about the book is its satirical portrayal of the film-making community of which the author herself is a part'
The Times

'A gleeful spin – packed with laugh-aloud zingers – through the family lives of filmdom's rich and famous'
Publishers Weekly

THE DEAD CELEB

'Sly, witty Hollywood send up'
Guardian

'Smart, sarcastic narrative voice'
The New York Times Book Review

'Maracotta, a Hollywood insider herself, uses her specialist knowledge of Tinsel City to pen a deviously mischievous account of the skulduggery that goes on there. Reminds me a little of the work of Janet Evanovich, and that's no bad thing'
The Irish Times

Lindsay Maracotta moved to Hollywood in 1985 and has been employed as a screenwriter, script-doctor and television producer. She writes for stars such as Goldie Hawn, Jessica Lange and Robert Redford, and for numerous magazines. Lindsay currently lives in Los Angeles with her husband, a feature film consultant.

Playing Dead

Lindsay Maracotta

CORONET BOOKS
Hodder & Stoughton

First published in United States of America in 1999
by William Morrow and Company, Inc.
First published in Great Britain in 1999
by Hodder and Stoughton
First published in paperback in 2000
by Hodder and Stoughton
A division of Hodder Headline

A Coronet Paperback

10 9 8 7 6 5 4 3 2 1

A CIP catalogue record for this title is available
from the British Library.

ISBN 0 340 74891 5

Printed and bound in Great Britain by
MacKays of Chatham PLC, Chatham, Kent

Hodder and Stoughton
A division of Hodder Headline
338 Euston Road
London NW1 3BH

To Virginia Maracotta Duame

And to the memory of Jerome Maracotta

Acknowledgements

My special thanks to Susan Wald, Paul Ventura, Teri Korbin Seide, and Detective Joseph Fabrizzio for being more than generous with their time and expertise. I'm also more than grateful to my editor, Doris Cooper, for her brilliance and enthusiasm and to my agent, Barbara Lowenstein, for her long and much-valued support.

PART
ONE

I suppose that when you are about to go downtown to identify your husband's body at the county morgue, you shouldn't be obsessing over what to wear.

Nevertheless, that was exactly what I was doing. For the past fifteen minutes I'd been hovering before the mostly vintage clothes in my closet, unable to decide whether the dusty plum-colored forties suit with fitted peplum jacket would be unsuitably snug over the seventeen-weeks-pregnant bulge of my midriff, or if the roomier canary yellow chemise à la Jackie Kennedy would look too Merry Widow, or whether I should just go with a librarianish tweed ensemble from the thirties. Meanwhile, the LAPD detective who had brought me the news that Kit had been shot and killed was waiting downstairs in the foyer, no doubt shuffling his sturdy crepe soles and peering at his Timex, wondering what in the name of creation I could possibly be up to.

Perhaps the reason I was in such a foggy dither was that until the arrival of Detective Langocetti, it had been a perfectly normal Tuesday. Normal for our household, that is. Kit, a movie producer whose recent success had reached considerable heights, had raced out the door some minutes before eight, grumbling about a sticky budget meeting for his latest project at Paramount. I had sat at the breakfast bar, munching Granola Crunch with my ten-year-old daughter, Chloe, listening to her complaints about the totally dorky uniforms her school had just imposed, until her car pool arrived and whisked her away. Then I'd propelled myself into my home studio to work on my latest assignment—to animate a song for *Sesame Street* on the Seven Basic Food Groups—and I'd spent several hours scanning my drawings of jitterbugging artichokes and vamping paper-pantied lambchops into the computer.

When I finally knocked off work, it was off to the veterinarian to pick up Rollins, the African red-bellied parrot who was the latest addition to Chloe's ever-expanding menagerie and who had come down with some languishing parrot disease. The bill was a cool nine hundred and eighty bucks, including X rays, medications and blood transfusions. On the drive back, Rollins had celebrated his recovery by squawking the snazzy new phrases he'd picked up at the vet's: "Sick puppy!" "You poor thing, you!" "No food, no water!"

At home, I stood luxuriating under the spray of a long, hot shower, mulling over the deeper questions of life: such as what sex would my newborn baby be? and where did they get parrot blood for Rollins's transfusion? and just what *was* the evolutionary purpose of cellulite? I looked up with a start when my housekeeper Graciela appeared in the bathroom. I felt a twinge of alarm—Graciela was not in the habit of intruding on my private functions.

"Mrs. Lucy?" she said diffidently. "The policeman is here."

"Policeman?" I echoed. "What does he want?"

"He say he want to talk to you." Through the water-sheeted glass of the shower stall, Graciela appeared as if painted by an Impressionist, one of the gauzier ones like Berthe Morisot. "He say is important," she elaborated.

Visions of Chloe's car pool hijacked by a gang of escaped sex offenders jolted my brain. "I'll be right down," I said, then shut off the taps and reached for a robe—Kit's triple-ply white terrycloth with the Hotel Georges V insignia. I turbaned a white towel over my sopping hair and padded barefoot downstairs.

A stocky, bristle-haired detective in an itchy-looking herringbone jacket glanced up. He had a stolid, full face with a protruding lower lip and pendulous earlobes, giving him a less than felicitous resemblance to Deputy Dawg.

"Mrs. Christopher Freers?" he intoned. His tone implied that a "yes" reply would be grounds for condolences.

Though the rest of my body was still damp, my mouth felt suddenly dry as Ritz crackers. I gave a curt nod.

"I'm Detective Roy Langocetti. I'd like to speak to you a moment." He paused, gazing a bit doubtfully at my turban and terrycloth robe ensemble: this being Los Angeles, it could well have been the costume of some let's-greet-the-millennium-with-a-dash-of-cyanide-in-our-Snapple cult.

"I was just taking a shower," I said quickly, pulling the robe tighter at my neck. "What's this all about? Has something happened to my daughter?"

"No, no, it's nothing about your daughter. Could we possibly sit down somewhere?" He looked like George Brent in *Dark Victory* when he has to confirm that his operation on Bette Davis's brain was not a success; my heart began to race like a revved-up Ferrari.

"We can go in here." I led the way into the adjoining family room and perched on the edge of the chenille-covered sofa. The detective chose an opposite armchair. His eyes inventoried some of the room's more unusual decor features: a garland of vividly colored cupids left over from Valentine's Day; a fake Al Capone–era machine gun, a prop from Kit's first feature film; Rollins preening in his elaborate cage.

"Would you please tell me what this is all about," I said shrilly.

Langocetti's eyes snapped back to me. "I'm afraid I have some unfortunate news. The driver of a green BMW registered to your husband has been shot and killed. It happened on a small street off Topanga Canyon."

"Kit's been shot?" I repeated wonderingly. The "killed" part hadn't registered yet. After all, someone who only hours before had bounced out of the house humming an off-key rendition of "Yellow Brick Road" couldn't just blink out of existence.

"We don't have a positive identification yet," Langocetti intoned. "There was no wallet or ID on the body and any watch or rings had been removed."

"They stole his watch?" I was still in an uncomprehending daze. All I could think of was how furious Kit would be at losing his beloved Rolex Oyster.

"It might have been robbery. Or the perpetrator might have just wanted it to look like a robbery to disguise other motives. We can't say just yet."

"You're a very sick puppy!" Rollins chose that unfortunate moment to squawk. Langocetti gave a start.

"Sorry, he's just come back from the vet," I muttered. With a sensation of sleepwalking, I went over to the parrot's cage and tented it.

"When was the last time you spoke to your husband?" the detective asked.

"When he left the house this morning. A couple of minutes before eight."

"Could you try contacting him now?"

"Yes, certainly." With an icy hand, I picked up the phone and punched up his number. "Where's Kit?" I quavered to his native-of-Malibu secretary Amber.

"Gee, I dunno," she replied. "He called at nine-thirty from his car phone and said the meeting at the studio had been cut short, but he wouldn't be back to the office till after lunch. Want me to . . ."

I cut her off, then dialed Kit's cell phone. Six rings, then an electronic voice informed me that the cellular customer I was trying to reach was out of range. I hung up, feeling clammy and disoriented, and gave a little shake of my head to the detective.

"Did your husband have a California driver's license?" Langocetti pursued. "Perhaps under another name?"

"Another name?" I repeated weakly.

"The victim's fingerprints don't appear to be on file in Sacramento."

I slumped back onto the sofa. "Kit liked to keep a Georgia license, where his parents live. It was just some quirk of his, something to do with hanging on to his roots."

Langocetti nodded, as if he'd suspected this all along. "Could you perhaps describe your husband? Height, weight, hair . . ."

A sudden surge of panic made me giddy-headed. I began to babble whatever came into my head. "He's about exactly six feet tall. Blond hair, sort of thinning on top, I always tease him about looking like a monk. I'm not sure about his weight, he never gets on the scale if I'm in the room, but he tends to get a kind of padding in the middle when he's not working out . . ." I realized I was starting to sound crazy even to myself. "Why don't I just get you a photo?" I finished weakly.

"That would be helpful, but not conclusive. You see, ah . . . the victim sustained a close-range gun shot to the face. The facial features are no longer identifiable."

I felt as if all the breath had been sucked from my body with a giant straw. Langocetti was saying something else but it was as if he were speaking some unfamiliar language, Swahili, perhaps, or Esperanto. "What?" I asked.

"Does your husband have any identifying marks or scars?"

I forced some air into my lungs. "Marks? Um, I know he has some moles . . ." For some reason, the only way I could picture Kit at all was in his daily uniform of soft cotton shirt and faded Big Star jeans. The Deputy Dawg eyes fixed rather dolefully on me. I could surmise his thoughts: *Lady can't describe her husband in the buff. Must've had one helluva sex life.*

I had the sudden loony desire to laugh. "Look, this doesn't make any sense at all. You're talking about something that happened in Topanga Canyon, that couldn't possibly be Kit. He had an extremely important meeting at Paramount, that's in Hollywood, way the hell over at the other side of town, and it was supposed to go on for hours. I mean, he couldn't have just flown over to Topanga, could he?" My voice was ascending into an interesting, cartoon-worthy falsetto.

"Is there somebody I could call to be here with you?" Langocetti crooned, obviously worried I was about to lose it all.

"Can I see the body?"

"It's not necessary. We can identify it through dental records . . ."

"I want to see him now!" I screeched.

"Well, if you're sure, then yes, I can take you down to the morgue." His glance flicked again over my medley of white terrycloth.

"I'll go change." I clambered up to my bedroom, threw open my closet and became engaged in the riveting existential confrontation with my wardrobe.

After a seeming eternity, I finally grabbed at random what appeared to be a suitably sober-colored jacket and pair of trousers and pulled them on. I crammed my feet into a pair of wooden-soled mules, then clattered rapidly back downstairs. Langocetti directed an even more perplexed squint at me, as if this outfit were no great improvement on the turban and robe ensemble. Must be my hair, I thought—left to dry on its own, it was probably beginning to resemble a maple-colored fright wig. I distractedly mashed it back behind my ears.

"I'm ready, let's go," I declared.

We hustled out to a Buick the color of ballpark mustard crouched at the curb outside. I slumped into the musty front seat beside the detective and we glided off, sans siren, but accompanied by the crackling and hiccuping of the radio. At the end of the block, my elderly neighbor Mr. Goldenstein glanced up from scooping the poop of his Cairn terrier and beetled his brows with interest at our passing. I checked my impulse to wave: this was hardly the occasion for breezy social conventions.

My thoughts were starting to collect themselves—kind of the

way Wile E. Coyote, after being flattened by a grand piano dropped on him by The Roadrunner, pops back into three dimensions. It was possible that Kit was dead! The man I'd been married to for fourteen years, the father of my daughter and unborn child, the person I knew most intimately in the world, might no longer exist.

I flashed on the problems there'd been between us over the past few years. Kit had always been attracted to the glitzier trappings of Hollywood life, and after his last movie had hit blockbuster heights, he'd begun to act as if he were the local franchisee of Luxuries "R" Us. Shopping sprees to boggle Imelda Marcos. Intimate relationships with facialists, hair stylists and body sculptors. At his instigation, our once cozy Pacific Palisades house acquired an echoing new addition, with sauna, screening room and a five-hundred-bottle humidity-controlled wine cellar. The husband whose idea of the perfect vacation had been a pup tent in the Grand Tetons now pored over catalogs of Relais et Châteaux, salivating over eight-hundred-bucks-a-night chambers in Scottish castles and converted Tuscan nunneries.

But three months ago, when I discovered I was pregnant, there had been a change. Kit had seemed even more excited about the baby than I was. He called about twelve times a day to check up on my morning sickness (which was more like a random-pattern nausea that could strike any moment of the night or day). He grasped my hand on the street, cuddled me in bed. And instead of trooping out every night to the Hot Restaurant of the Second, we were spending evenings at home whipping up comfort foods and playing marathon Monopoly with Chloe. Glimpses of the old Kit—the sweet-natured, slightly nerdy, nutty-about-movies guy I'd fallen in love with—were starting to emerge.

Could it really be possible that he was now lying lifeless in the morgue?

I stared blankly out the window, as the homes and gates and flowering shrubs of our neighborhood gave way to shops and umbrella-dotted cafés, then to the anonymous metallic flow of the freeway. As we veered off into industrial downtown canyons, I fought down a rising slick of queasiness and willed myself not to scream.

At last, Langocetti moored his car in the gloom of a subterranean parking structure. I clip-clopped in my mules numbly behind him as he led the way up a ramp into a grimly functional building. He signed us in at a counter and we were buzzed through a heavy door.

A young man in shirtsleeves and diamond-patterned tie hurried up to meet us: his slight build and delicate Asian features made him look scarcely out of high school. "I'm Leonard Yi, coroner's investigator . . ." he began. Then he faltered, treating me to much the same startled squint as Langocetti had when I'd reappeared downstairs.

"Could Mrs. Freers see the body now?" Langocetti said crisply.

Yi recovered his poise. "Certainly. Please follow me."

He forged the way to an elevator and we whooshed up to a second floor. We entered a carpeted room that might have been the reception room of any ordinary business, a maritime insurance firm, say, or a button wholesaler, if it hadn't been for the smell. A faint but impossible to ignore stench, one that conjured up images of fast food restaurant Dumpsters on a sweltering day. I put my sleeve to my nose as we trudged through another door, into an antiseptically tiled room lined with large stainless steel lockers: it seemed to cry out for large slabs of beef suspended from hooks, with perhaps the odd Mafia informant dangling upside down among them. The stench was stronger here, asserting itself like a schoolyard bully. I took a gagging breath.

Langocetti gripped my arm. "Okay?" he asked. "Remember, you don't have to go through with this."

"I'm okay," I insisted. "I'll make it."

Then I caught a sudden glimpse of myself mirrored in the polished surface of one of the steel lockers. I gave a start. The jacket I had finally yanked out of my closet had a pin fastened to the lapel—a salsa red-and-orange Bakelite novelty pin from the forties

in the shape of a guffawing horse's head. No wonder both Langocetti and Yi had looked at me as if I were not quite compos
mentis . . . It would make a nifty tabloid item, I thought, with a
lunatic silent giggle:

Producer's Wife Wears Wacky Pin to View Hubby's Corpse.
"I've got a lovely clown's suit picked out for the funeral," Lucy
Freers told reporters. "With baggy pants and a squirting
boutonniere . . ."

"Are you ready, Mrs. Freers?"
Yi's rather prissy voice caused my thoughts to snap back like a
released rubber band. This was one confrontation I wouldn't be
able to joke my way out of.
"Yes," I whispered and braced myself for the ordeal. Langocetti's
meaty hand clutched my arm again as Yi opened one of the meat
lockers.
"Remember, the wound to the face is going to be quite disturbing," Yi continued. "Are you certain you want to proceed
with this?"
What I was certain I wanted to proceed with was to swivel
smartly on the wooden heels of my mules and make fast tracks
out of this Frankenstein's pantry. But I nodded and croaked out
a "Yes."
Yi rolled out a slab from one of several tiers in the locker. The
body, in the best horror movie cliché, was covered with a white
sheet. I began to shiver uncontrollably as Yi removed it and then
began unzipping the plastic body bag.
Langocetti steered me forward. With my vision suddenly become blurred, I looked down at the exposed head.
And then I let out a sharp shriek. I saw a familiar head, with
fine blond hair and small, neat ears . . . But where once there had
been a face was now a ragged crater; and inside the crater was a
ghastly muck of gristle, gray wormlike tubes, blackened shards of
bone and congealed blood. My chest contracted violently, my heart

thudded like a pounding ball, and my knees liquefied; I could hardly stand.

"Is this your husband, Mrs. Freers?" said the coroner's investigator.

I tried to speak, but my throat was too constricted. I closed my eyes, drew several breaths, then located what could pass for a voice.

"No," I got out. "It's not."

Langocetti didn't change expression. I had the feeling that even if the corpse should suddenly leap up and perform an energetic Hully Gully, it still wouldn't alter his stolid Deputy Dawg deadpan.

Yi had a somewhat different reaction. He opened and closed his mouth several times, as if in search of a suitable exclamation, something in the nature of "Caramba!" or "Egad!" Finally he sputtered, "Do you know who it *is*?"

I was still finding it hard to form words. My world which had flip-flopped to adjust to Kit's death was now having to flip-flop again in an entirely different direction.

"His name is Brandon McKenna," I managed.

"A friend?" Langocetti inquired.

"Yeah, a friend. And, um, he worked for us as well."

"In what capacity?" demanded Yi.

"As a live-in. I mean, mostly to help out with our daughter. He took her to her activities and drove car pool, and when we went out, he stayed with her. That kind of thing."

"You mean, he was like your nanny?" Yi piped up in an incredulous voice.

"I guess you could say that. Brandon was our nanny."

I forced another look down at his destroyed face, and at the naked neck and shoulders below it, which were now turned the color of frosted pewter.

I saw no reason to add that he had also once been my lover.

My very first lover, to be exact.

I had been a freshman at Barnard, making an exceptionally slow adjustment from my semirural hometown in Minnesota, where the all-night Frostee Freeze was the wildest attraction, to the complete sensory overload of uptown Manhattan. Brandon was a senior at Columbia and the star of the art department, a glamorous figure in faded work shirt and paint-splotched jeans, with a Nikon draped perpetually around his neck. Everything about him seemed unutterably romantic: that he was one-quarter Oglala Sioux; that he could quote both William Blake and David Bowie, as well as entire passages of the Bhagavad Gita; that he had been orphaned as a baby and raised by a gangster uncle who was now also deceased, rubbed out by a rival faction of the mob. Second semester, we both took a class in Nouvelle Vague cinema: In the darkened screening room, while the rest of my classmates focused on *Last Year at Marienbad*, I concentrated on Brandon McKenna's sinewy shoulders.

When he asked me out, I was stunned. We ate Vietnamese, and

talked of Truffaut and reggae rock and the future of art, if any, after Minimalism, and by the end of the evening I was wiltingly in love. On our third date, in his cockroach-ruled Morningside Heights apartment, after consuming half a jug of Gallo Hearty Burgundy and a few tokes of Rio Bravo gold, I said so long to my virginity.

As deflowerings go, mine was not exactly in the Earth Moves category. There was a lengthy prologue of fumbling with buttons, zippers and hooks, some frantic groping and hit-or-miss rubbing of erogenous zones, followed by poking, a brief, sharp pain and then That's all, folks! That pretty much set the pattern for sex over the course of our six-week affair: heavy on the boozy passion, a bit short in the physical fulfillment department. It seemed natural when it simmered down into a platonic friendship.

Brandon graduated and added to his romantic aura by becoming a war photographer. For some years afterward, I'd get postcards from whatever part of the globe was currently in turmoil: "Greetings from Granada. Shot the invasion for *Time*. Cheers, B." The postcards tapered off, then stopped altogether. I heard he had segued into documentaries; I once caught the tail end of one on PBS. I hadn't thought of him for some time when, several years ago, he was nominated for an Academy Award for Best Documentary for an exposé of ivory poaching in Zimbabwe. He didn't win. The year before, I'd scored a nomination for one of my short animations and also lost, making us both Oscar also-rans: I whipped out a breezy note of solidarity, sent it care of the Columbia alumni association, received no reply, and Brandon McKenna vanished again from my thoughts.

Until two months ago.

I had made a morning run to Hollywood to buy drawing supplies and browse the vintage fountain pens at Michael's. As I slogged my way home, I realized I was starving. One thing about pregnancy, it makes me perpetually ravenous, craving in the traditional manner all sorts of nutty food combos—peanut butter and blueberry chutney, eggs scrambled with tuna, Tabasco and tiny cocktail onions; and now it was the Cajun shrimp gumbo at the Farmers' Market, with maybe a side of okra and sesame salad, that called to me.

As I carried my heaped-up tray from the takeout counter to an outdoor table, a man polishing off a bowl of Spanish rice glanced up.

"Lucy Kellenborg!" he exclaimed. "Is that really you?"

"Brandon?" I said with equal astonishment.

He was, if possible, even more gorgeous than ever. Still rock-star lean, his golden hair, if a whit thinner, now glamorously threaded with silver. We hugged vigorously, I plunked myself into the chair at the table beside him, and we began talking as easily as if it had been only months and not going on two decades since we'd last been together. I gave him a recap of my life in the interval. It suddenly seemed dull and ordinary compared with Brandon's globe-trotting adventures.

"Yeah, well my globe-trotting is a thing of the past," he said with a slow smile. "I picked up some shrapnel in Iraq, there's a few shards left in my ankle and it flares up more and more these days. I think I'll stay put for a while. Write a memoir of my days in war-torn Africa. I just need a gig to support me while I'm cranking it out."

"What kind of gig?" I asked.

"I'm not fussy. I'll take anything that'll pay me enough to live and leave enough time off to write. Do you know of anything?"

I was about to give the conventional "I'll ask around" response, when I'd been struck by an idea. The night before, Kit had ceased flipping between a half dozen movie channels to announce that, what with the coming baby and all, we needed more help. "Do you realize we're the only people we know who don't have a live-in?" he elaborated. "We've got the room and god knows we can afford it, so what's the problem?"

I had been able to think of many problems. In fact the Problem of Good Live-in Help was Topic A among the moms of Winder-mere Academy. You could get a Latina, Nicaraguan or El Salvadoran, very good with children, but then you'd have to cope with their understandable depression at being isolated from family and culture; even though you'd fixed up the little room behind the kitchen so fetchingly with sunny curtains and fluffy aqua comforter and twenty-four-inch cable TV, you'd still hear them weeping at night over the inexhaustible mutter of the Spanish-language channel. You could opt instead for a young European, one of the legions of Irish, German or Scandinavian girls always gung ho for the bright lights and easy money of America, but better make sure they weren't too good-looking, prancing around in front of your husband in their cropped tops and butt-tight trousers; though even the plain ones, after four or five months, would generally up and quit for a sales job at Retail Slut or to shack up with a bass guitarist. And no matter what, nannycams were a must—hidden video cameras to spy on the live-ins when you weren't around, to make sure nanny wasn't stuffing your kids with Twinkies and Mallomars, or plunking them for hours at a time in front of her favorite soap operas or even, god forbid, *hitting* them . . . And even if you found a treasure, the Perfect Live-in who spoke English and had a valid driver's license and didn't pilfer your jewelry and knickknacks, along would come Mrs. Big Time Director or Mrs. International Superstar, who'd offer your treasure three times the salary, plus a Jacuzzi in their bathroom and use of the Jaguar on their days off; and there you'd be, back on the phone with some snot at Beverly Hills Domestics, pleading with them to send somebody, *any*body they had available . . .

I had been too exhausted to go into any of this with Kit, figuring I'd have ample time in the weeks to come. But now, in the cool shade of the Farmers' Market, staring into Brandon's pale green eyes, it occurred to me that I could offer Brandon the job. Male nannies were not unheard-of in our circles—in fact they even carried a certain cachet. It was the perfect solution: Kit would get a live-in, Brandon would have the means to write, and by hiring an old friend, I could safely dispense with a nannycam.

I tentatively made the proposal to Brandon. He accepted on the spot and three days later moved into what our contractor had rather grandly called a "chauffeur's unit" that we'd recently added over the garage.

He was an immediate hit in our household. He and Kit clicked instantly, swapping scenes from an eclectic array of movies, from *Contempt* to *Surf Nazis Must Die*. Chloe, whose first reaction had been, "An old guy? Ew!" was within a day or two babbling his praises: "Brandon knows magic tricks and all the words to 'Stairway to Heaven' and when it gets hotter outside he's going to help me with my double gainers!" He even seemed to bond with Chloe's animals. The cats curled in contented blobs on his bed, the chinchilla raced ecstatically on its wheel when he peered into its cage. Even Gordon the gecko, who rarely emerged from under the furniture, had been known to poke his prehistoric head out when Brandon was around.

In fact, the only one not thrilled with the arrangement was me. For one simple reason: I discovered I was still attracted to him. Hugely, toss-and-turn-at-night attracted. I caught myself using a huskier, *Garbo Speaks!* voice and leaving a second, then third, button open on my shirts to reveal what I hoped was a tantalizing froth of bra. I found excuses to knock on his door—would he like one of the nectarines I'd just bought, had he seen my suede windbreaker anywhere? So what if the ground hadn't shaken the first time we'd been lovers? Now I was running blue movies in my head starring the two of us entwined in positions that would have made Masters and Johnson blush.

Cut it out! I'd tell myself abruptly. You're a happily married mother with a second kid well on the way. Stop fantasizing like a hormone-crazed eighteen-year-old. You're pregnant, for godsake!

Yet no matter how many sensible sermons I preached to myself, I couldn't help feeling a hot shiver of lust whenever he came into the room. It seemed to me that he felt it too—and it was only by exercising tremendous restraint that he didn't sweep me Rhett Butler–style up to the room above the garage and ravish me on the double bed.

*   *   *

These were the thoughts that were roiling through my mind as Langocetti and Yi shepherded me back to the carpeted reception room. A tumbler of lukewarm water materialized in my hand. Then the two, in custard-smooth voices, began questioning me. How long had Brandon lived with us? Had he ever exhibited any unusual behavior? Received any phone calls or mail that seemed out of the ordinary?

"Not that I know of," I replied glumly to this last.

"What about visitors?" Langocetti asked.

"He didn't have any."

"None at all?" Yi's teenaged-looking features squinched with suspicion.

"He was new to Los Angeles," I pointed out. "You could hardly expect him to have a wide acquaintance."

"So he wasn't one to make friends easily?"

"No, he was actually pretty gregarious. Look, he'd sometimes head out on his days off, but I don't know where. He was very respectful of our private lives, and I didn't go snooping into his."

"Did he have permission to use your husband's car today?" Langocetti inquired.

"I guess so. I mean, I doubt very much if he was stealing it. Look, I really want to go home now," I said plaintively. "Can't we do this later? I'm kind of upset." This was a significant understatement. It was in fact only by the sheerest act of will that I was neither shrieking nor gibbering senselessly.

"I understand," Langocetti intoned. To Yi's evident disappointment, he escorted me back down to the car. I sat huddled into myself for the trip back, grateful that the detective made no attempt at conversation but merely engaged himself with his crackling radio. He dropped me at my driveway with merely a Gary Cooperish "Thanks for your help, ma'am" and drove away.

My first instinct was to hustle to the wet bar in the den and pour myself a double shot of Cuervo Gold; then I reminded myself I was With Child and settled instead for a bracing swallow of V-8 juice fortified with a liberal dash of Tabasco sauce. As I was swallowing the dregs, I had a sudden and almost insupportable memory from the week before. I'd been having the kind of day that wallops every pregnant woman eventually: I was bloated and blotched and sapped of energy, so tired I could almost sleep standing up. Then Chloe bounced in from her car pool, moaning that her best friend Miri wasn't speaking to her because another girl had told her that Chloe had called Miri's hair geeky. "And it's not true, Caitlin was lying!" Chloe continued, close to tears. I felt utterly incapable of coping with fifth-grade feuds and muttered something about how Miri would get over it.

But then Brandon had come in and listened intently to Chloe's lament. "Let's go call Miri," he suggested. "We'll tell her how much you miss her."

"I can't call her because she's not speaking to me," Chloe wailed.

He took her hand. "I'll bet she will. Because I bet she misses you too. There's nothing lousier than not being able to talk to your friends."

Chloe had let him coax her here into the den, where the call was placed and the best friends reconciled. Thinking of this, I allowed myself a short but violent cry, then blotted my eyes with a cocktail napkin and poured myself another stiff shot of V-8.

The phone rang. I snatched it up with some deep-in-denial hope that it could be Brandon calling, that maybe the whole morgue thing had been one colossal mistake.

"It's me," said Kit. "What's going on? Amber said you called sounding absolutely hysterical."

"Where the hell are you?" I shouted, thereby corroborating the "hysterical" diagnosis.

"Back at the office. The Paramount meeting was canceled, so I ran out to the desert with Bob Petroski to check on some possible locations for the Nick Cage film. Would you please just tell me . . ."

"It's Brandon. He's been killed. I've just been down to the morgue to identify his body."

"Jeez!" Kit breathed. "How did it happen?"

"He was shot. Right in the face at close range. It was out in Topanga, in some deserted little side street. The cops had the idea it was you, which was why I went down to see the body." I pictured again that head with its ghoulish cavity. "Oh god, you should've seen him, it was hideous. He had no face, just this terrible muck with bits of bone and tubes . . . I can't even describe it!" My legs gave way. I collapsed into a chair, clutching the phone as if it were a means of life support.

"Jesus Christ!" Kit breathed again. "Do they know who did it?"

"No. His wallet and watch were gone, and that silver Navajo bracelet he always wore. But the cops said that the killers could have taken them just to make it look like a random robbery. Except they didn't take the car. *Your* car," I added, remembering this puzzling detail. "That's why the police thought it might have been you. What was he doing with it?"

"I asked him this morning if he'd take it in for a smog check. I've got the Stingray."

This gave me a moment's pause. In the shock of hearing the news, I hadn't thought to check to see if both the BMW and Kit's other car, a midlife-compensation red Corvette, were in the garage. "Did you give him any other errands to do?" I asked.

"No, why?" In the background, I heard the clink of bottles, then the sound of liquid gurgling into a glass. Kit was no doubt helping himself to the stiff drink from which I had virtuously abstained.

"He was killed in a remote part of Topanga Canyon. Not exactly a hotbed of smog check stations."

"Maybe he just got a kick out of driving the Beemer and was taking it for a little spin in the country." Kit paused a second to gulp down his drink, then said in an agitated voice, "Was he in the car when he was shot?"

"Don't tell me you're worried about your damned leather upholstery!"

"Of course not," he returned briskly. "For godsake, how callous do you think I am? I meant that if the *cops* thought it was me, then maybe whoever shot him did too."

"Why would anyone want to kill you? You're a movie producer, not a bag man for the mob or anything."

"I work in an extremely high-stakes industry. I make a lot of enemies. It's not so far-fetched to think there are nut cases out there who'd want to get me. And besides, Brandon was just a nanny. Who the hell would want to murder him?"

"He used to make documentaries, don't forget. He must've made a few enemies himself." For a moment I had the feeling we were about to get into some surreal argument over Who Was the More Worthy to Be Bumped Off, Kit or Brandon McKenna? "We'll know a lot more when the cops finish their investigation," I said quickly. "Right now we have a more immediate problem. We've got to go break the news to Chloe."

I could hear Kit refreshing his drink and felt a deep surge of envy. "I suppose we both should be there," he said.

"You're damned right we should," I said. "I'll call The School and tell them we're coming."

The approach to the Windermere Academy for Progressive Education, known informally as simply The School, is down an inconspicuous dusty lane off the Bel Air side of Mulholland Drive. The lane abruptly turns into a eucalyptus-shaded drive which meanders to the gates of a massive stone wall of the sort which, in another time and on another continent, would have been defended by vats of boiling oil. Behind this wall rises an edifice of equally massive proportion which—except for a certain sheen of newness on the gray stone and slate—could pass for the eighteenth-century country seat of, say, the Duke of Bolingbroke. Since Windermere was the learning institution of choice for the aristocracy of Hollywood, the fact that its campus was a knock-off of a ducal manor had a certain semiotic appropriateness.

Less than an hour after hanging up with Kit, I drove up to the guard station in front of the gates. A sticker on the windshield of my new Volvo station wagon identified me as a parent whose child was privileged to be among the student body. One of the two resident guards squinted at the sticker, gave me the kind of steely-eyed scrutiny once so effectively employed by petty border officials of Iron Curtain countries, jotted my license number on a clipboard pad, and at last, and rather grudgingly, allowed me to pass through the portals: Windermere security would have made Alcatraz look as if it operated on the honor system.

I headed on to the visitors' lot where Kit's Stingray was already parked, looking like a toy between two immense Range Rovers. I pulled in beside an XKE and hurried in to what The School's principal, Connie Baljur, dubbed her "study." It was a richly appointed chamber, with a Turkish carpet on the floor and an authentic Mary Cassatt gilt-framed on the wall. Kit sat slumped rather dejectedly in a brocaded chair. He jumped to his feet at my appearance and hugged me tight.

"You doing okay?" he murmured.

Suddenly I wasn't. I nestled into his chest, fat tears glistening at my eyes, my shoulders heaving. "It was the worst thing I've ever seen," I choked out. "Poor Brandon, it was awful, hideous . . ."

"Try not to think about it," Kit muttered.

"I can't help it. And I keep thinking about that old superstition that if a pregnant woman sees something that scares her, it'll affect the baby. Like if she's startled by a guy with no arms, the baby might be born with its arms withered or something."

"So what are you saying? You're afraid the baby might have no face?"

"It's just crazy, I know," I said with a hollow little laugh. "I guess I'm still in shock."

Before Kit could reply, the door opened and a woman walked in—not the principal, Ms. Baljur, but a trim, pageboyed blonde in her early fifties. "Hello, I'm Dr. Minna Luchstein," she announced. "I'm the consulting psychologist for Windermere."

That The School had a shrink on its payroll was news to me, but hardly a surprise: this was an institution after all that also employed a fencing master, a dramatic coach and a certified holistic nutritionist.

Dr. Luchstein clicked forward on navy pumps and briskly shook our hands. A cloying burst of her perfume hit my nostrils—fittingly, it was Eternity by Calvin Klein. I wondered if she always matched her scent to the counseling occasion, i.e., My Sin for a cheating marriage partner, or Obsession for a patient given to stalking.

"Connie Baljur filled me in on the situation," she said in a tone as professionally brisk as her handshake. "Chloe will be here in a few moments."

"Are you going to tell her what happened?" Kit asked with a rather hopeful expression.

Both Dr. Luchstein and I stared at him, myself with surprise, Dr. L. with a shade of disdain. "Absolutely not," she said. "That has to be your responsibility. My function here will be simply to guide the encounter." Her rather pillowy lips curved in a smile. "I'd like to get a little background first. Your daughter is nine?"

"Ten last October," I corrected.

"Mmm-hm. And has she had any previous experience with confronting death?"

Kit and I exchanged uneasy glances. "There was one time about a year and a half ago . . ." he began, then faltered.

"It was our neighbor," I filled in. "A former actress named Julia Prentice who lived across the street. She was . . . um, murdered in our swimming pool."

Dr. Luchstein clutched her throat, a gesture I'd heretofore seen enacted only by dowagers in thirties movies.

"It was a pretty famous case," Kit said, somewhat superfluously. "Followed by all the media."

"But Chloe never saw the body," I added hastily. "And she hardly knew Julia; our families weren't really close or anything . . ."

Dr. Luchstein peered at us with somewhat more interest, the way I imagined a laboratory scientist would examine a pair of freshly hatched fruit flies that were exhibiting an unpredicted mutation. "Has Chloe lost anyone more closely connected to her?" she pressed on. "A grandparent or near relative, for instance?"

Kit shook his head. "Both my folks are alive and well. So is the rest of my close family."

"My mother died but way before Chloe was born," I said.

"So she's actually had no personal encounter with death at all," Dr. Luchstein summed up.

"Except for Cookie Dough," I said.

The psychologist's eyes took on a wary glaze, as if her fruit fly specimens were now threatening to evolve into something altogether out of hand. "Cookie dough?"

"That was the name of her pet rabbit," I elucidated. "She woke up a couple of weeks ago and found him dead in his cage. Chloe's crazy about all animals, especially her own pets, so it was extremely traumatic for her."

"I see," murmured the shrink. "And how did you explain this animal's death? Did you say it was only sleeping, or that it had gone to heaven? Or were you straightforward about it?"

The answer to this multiple choice quiz was actually D: none of the above. Chloe, upon discovering the stiff rabbit, had bounded into our room, announced, "Cookie Dough is *dead!*" and burst into torrential tears. She wouldn't stop crying until I hustled her off to Fabulous Fauna, which had happened to be out of bunnies at the moment, but had just gotten in an African red-bellied parrot. In the meantime, Kit entombed Cookie Dough's corpse in an empty Tide detergent box and buried it in the thick of the rose garden.

I was spared from detailing the particulars of this little saga by the entrance of Chloe herself. Her vivid red ringlets looked ratted and blown as if she'd just come from a game of outdoor tag. The teacher who had escorted her slipped back into the hall. Clutching the hem of her plaid uniform jacket, Chloe stared wide-eyed at our little assemblage.

"I messed up, didn't I?" she said.

Kit and I both shouted a hasty "No, no!" and scrambled to her side, sandwiching her in a four-armed hug. This unsolicited display of affection seemed to alarm her even more. She wriggled free of our clutches. "So why are you guys here?" she demanded.

Dr. Luchstein took an assertive step forward and squatted down to Chloe's height. An equally assertive pouf of Eternity burst in the air. "Your mom and dad have some very sad news for you, Chloe," she said unctuously. "I know you can be a brave girl, can't you?"

Chloe looked dubious. Kit and I exchanged "After you" glances, then I took the plunge. "Sweetie, a bad thing has happened to Brandon. He was hurt by some really bad people . . ." I hesitated, and Kit chipped in, "And now he's dead and gone to heaven." I sensed a wave of disapproval waft up with Dr. Luchstein's perfume.

Chloe's face acquired a hard, almost iridescent shell. "That's not true," she pronounced. "You're lying."

"No, we're not, sweetheart," I said softly. "I'm really sorry."

I reached for her. She shrank away. "It's not true!" she insisted. "You fired him, and you just don't want me to know!"

The encounter had evidently become ripe for guidance: Minna Luchstein spoke up with a tone of creamy authority. "Your parents would never lie to you about something like this, Chloe. We know it's very hard for you to accept . . ."

Any further remarks were cut short by Chloe bursting into tumultuous tears. I cradled her tightly and crooned, "It's okay, baby, it's okay."

Dr. Luchstein, who had so far remained in a semisquat position, now lifted herself to her feet. "I want you to understand, Chloe, that this is not your fault. Nothing you did or said could have made this happen or stopped it from happening."

"I know that," Chloe shrilled. "It was because he wasn't wearing his disguise."

"Disguise?" I repeated blankly.

"Children sometimes invest articles of clothing with magical properties that they think can keep them from harm," Dr. Luchstein pronounced. "The item can even be imaginary, such as an invisible cape or a magic pair of shoes . . ."

Chloe vigorously shook her head. "It was his New York *Yankees* hat! And these big sunglasses that made him look like a *grass*hopper. And he stuck the collar of his shirt up so nobody could recognize him."

Kit and I engaged in another silent powwow. "Are you sure about this, honey?" he said to Chloe.

She nodded just as vigorously. "When he picked me up from school yesterday, he said it was his disguise so these bad guys wouldn't get him."

A spidery chill crept up the back of my neck. "I'm sure he was just fooling around," I said soothingly. "You know how he always liked to make you laugh."

"But you *said* the bad guys got him, so he wasn't just fooling around," Chloe wailed with irrefutable logic. She dissolved into heavy sobbing again. I could do nothing but stroke her hair and continue to murmur, "It's okay."

Kit retreated to an opposite corner of the room for a sotto voce sidebar with Dr. Luchstein. After several minutes, he came back over. "I was telling Luchstein I was planning on taking Chloe skiing on spring break," he said to me. "She thinks it would be a good idea if I moved it up and took her now instead. We could leave Thursday, make it a five-day weekend." In a tone of forced jollity, he said to Chloe, "We're going skiing, honey, isn't that great? Day after tomorrow!"

So this is the way we treat death nowadays was my sudden thought. Substitute something in kind: a parrot for a bunny, a ski trip for a nanny.

How about for a mom? If I were to turn up on a slab in the morgue, what would Kit dangle as a substitution for me?

The thought hit me with a wallop, as if it were some kind of hideous premonition. "Let's go home, sweetheart," I said to Chloe, who was still crying without restraint. I grasped her delicate hand in mine and led her out the door.

3

At home, Chloe ran a frantic check of her entire menagerie to make sure all her pets were okay, dissolving into tears every time she came across something in the house that reminded her of Brandon: his Miles Davis anthology CD, the fuchsia cat's-eye sunglasses he had bought her on Montana Avenue. Kit and I worked rigorously through the evening Maintaining a Cheerful Face, chattering with manic enthusiasm about what barrels of fun the Aspen trip was going to be. Finally Chloe fell asleep, both cats commaed at her feet; and then Kit and I turned in, too emotionally wrung out to discuss the day's events further.

A late evening call from Minna Luchstein advised us to send Chloe to school in the morning. "At this stage, she will be feeling that her entire world is threatened," the psychologist intoned. "She needs the reassurance of finding that her normal routine has not been substantially disrupted." She added that Chloe's class had been filled in on "this shocking tragedy" and had participated in an "encounter session" (led of course by the indefatigable Dr. L.) to sensitize them to Chloe's feelings of "loss, anger and bewilderment." In the morning, Kit and I decided to follow her advice. It was our car pool day, and I took the precaution of calling each parent in the pool and relaying the grim news, so that their kids didn't bounce into the car and squeal, "Where's Brandon?" I took the further precaution of blasting a Spice Girls CD en route to squelch any talking at all and managed to deliver Chloe to the gates of The School without a further crying jag.

When I returned, I decided the best thing for *me* would be to get back to my *Sesame Street* animation. Singing carrots and fox-trotting hunks of cheddar cheese were exactly what I needed to dispel the horrors of the day before. I had just begun scanning my drawings of a pork chop skipping rope into the computer when the buzzer of our front gate sounded. From my studio window, I glimpsed a familiar car—a tan Chevy Caprice of hardy wear and tear—idling in front. "Shit," I muttered to myself. I buzzed the car through and trotted downstairs to let in my old pal Detective Teresa Shoe of the LAPD.

We gave each other the mutual once-over. She looked somewhat dumpier than the last time I'd seen her, which meant either her cranberry polyester pantsuit was exceptionally unflattering or she'd been caving in to her weakness for dinner plate–sized blueberry muffins. Her amber eyes lingered on the bulge of my midriff under my forties vintage middy blouse.

"What are you doing here?" I blurted.

"Yeah, it's really great to see you again, too," she replied dryly.

"Sorry," I conceded. "I didn't mean it like that. I've been kind of on edge since yesterday."

"Yeah, I heard you got quite a shock. Hell, a face wound from a close-range firing of a .44 would give anybody a shock. I wouldn't have recommended it in your present condition."

"Detective Langocetti advised me not to go."

"And you didn't take his advice? Now *there's* a real surprise." She produced a soft but eloquent snort.

I shot her back an equally eloquent dirty look. It seemed that the dynamics of our interpersonal relationship were going to remain pretty much the same: I respected her as a top investigator, was supremely grateful that she'd once saved me from being strangled to death by a homicidal celebrity, and that she didn't seem to hold it against *me* that I'd once unwittingly almost caused her to drop dead from consuming a particularly virulent poison—but I also thought a stint in a top-notch charm school would do her no harm. As for Terry, I knew that she had a grudging appreciation of my "pluck," but generally considered me an annoyingly impulsive Nosy Parker and all in all—given my taste in wardrobe and collectibles—a somewhat sorry excuse for a grown woman.

"So can I come in, or what?" she demanded.

"Yeah, of course, come on in." I opened the door wider, noting her familiar duckwalk as she entered the foyer.

She peered around unabashedly. "I see you've added quite a lot on to the house," she remarked.

"Yeah, well, what with the new baby and all, we thought we could use more room," I mumbled. The uncomfortable fact that the house was now roomy enough to accommodate an entire orphanage remained unspoken.

"So what are you now, five, five and a half months?" Terry asked.

"A little over four." I placed a hand on my stomach. "I'm showing early."

"Are you planning to do Lamaze? They talked me into it with my last one, Sunny. All that breathing rigmarole, it's a lot of hooey no matter what they say. You can pant till you're purple and it's still gonna hurt like a son of a bitch."

"I presume you didn't just come here to kibitz about the joys of childbirth," I cut in.

"You presume right."

"Are you taking over the investigation of Brandon's murder?"

"Absolutely not!" Terry bristled at the presumption that she would muscle a fellow detective out of his rightful investigatory claims. "It's still Langocetti's case. I'm just doing him a favor. Seeing as how you and I have a personal connection, I thought you might allow me to look around a bit. Save him the headache of scrounging up a warrant." She flashed me a suspiciously chummy smile. "I'm sure you've got nothing you need to conceal."

"You want to search the house?" I gave a nervous chuckle. The first time I'd met Terry Shoe, she'd had on white gloves and was rummaging through my dresser drawers; I wasn't sure I was quite ready for this bit of history repeating itself.

"There's no need for that at this point. I'd just like to take a look around McKenna's room, if you don't mind. To see if anything stands up and shouts at me."

"I guess that wouldn't hurt," I conceded. "He had the room over the garage. There's a stairway off the back of the kitchen, I'll show you."

"So now you have a servants' quarters?"

I responded with a second dirty look and led her to the stairs, studying her sturdy legs and sensible low-heeled shoes as I trooped up behind her. The door at the top of the stairs was shut.

"Is this locked?" Terry asked.

"No, never," I said.

She turned the knob and let herself in. I hesitated on the threshold, recalling with a cringe of shame those many times I'd contrived excuses to appear at this door. Hoping . . . what? That he'd be stark naked? That he'd attempt to rip *my* clothing off? And if he had, how would I have responded?

This was not the time for making a clean sweep of my conscience. I followed Terry into the room and helpfully pulled back the natural-weave curtains. A flood of sunlight washed out the biscuit-colored walls and muted the vivid clarets and blues of the Turkish kilim. The bed, with its antique brass bedboard and Depression-era quilt, had been freshly made by Graciela the day before—probably, I thought blackly, just about the same time that Brandon was being summoned by his own maker.

"Pretty fancy digs for a nanny's room," Terry said.

"What did you expect?" I flashed back. "Broken sticks of furniture and a straw pallet on the floor?"

"Hey, I've been in the homes of some of the richest folks in this city. You ought to see some of the dumps they park their help in. Rooms without windows, dark as a dungeon. Crapholes you wouldn't shut a dog in." Her mouth buckled in disgust at the manifest inhumanity of the rich toward their household help. Then she swiveled to the Danish pine dresser and began opening and shutting drawers, not disturbing any of the neatly stored socks and shorts inside.

"Still, this room's kind of spartan, wouldn't you say?" she remarked after a moment. "I mean in terms of personal effects."

"Brandon wasn't very acquisitive," I said. "He was what you'd call a free spirit. He didn't need a lot of possessions in his life."

Terry didn't seem to hear me. "No photos, no mementos, nothing in the way of knickknacks . . ." she mused. "It looks like somebody just passing through, not a guy settled in for the long haul."

"I never expected him to stay for the long haul. We both knew this was just a temporary gig, something to let him get a start on writing. He was working on a memoir of his years as a war photographer."

Terry moved to a Toshiba laptop which sat in isolation on the bedside table. She turned it on. "You wouldn't know his password, would you?"

"Of course not. Why would I?"

She switched the machine off. "I wondered just how chummy you really were."

I felt a jolt of guilt. "And what's that supposed to mean?"

Terry opened the closet and began efficiently flicking through the racks. "Langocetti said you seemed pretty broken up when you realized the identity of the corpse."

"What was I supposed to do?" I flared. "Click my heels and shout whoopee?"

"Maybe he thought that some wives, when they saw it wasn't their husband on the slab, but just some guy who worked for them, might have acted a little more relieved."

"Of course I was relieved it wasn't Kit. But it was still devastating to realize it was Brandon."

Terry took down a denim shirt, shook it lightly, then returned it to the hanger. With studied casualness she said, "Langocetti was cooking up a little theory. You're a bored rich housewife who starts up an affair with her good-looking live-in. He calls it off, or maybe he two-times you with the lady down the street. You go into a jealous fit and send him off on some wild goose errand. Then you wait in ambush and blow the cheating SOB away. And put on a big surprised-and-devastated act when they show you the body.

"That's ridiculous," I said—though, remembering my triple-X fantasies, with somewhat less force than I might have.

"That's what I told him," Terry giggled. "You're not the type for afternoon delights. You'd of been more interested in straightening out his life for him, than of getting into his pants."

I wasn't exactly thrilled by this picture of myself as a buttinski Donna Reed. I was about to crisply inform Terry Shoe that, for her information, less than a year ago I came within one drop of a bra to indulging in a hot and heavy extramarital affair with a blue-eyed, five-years-younger-than-myself screenwriter.

But then I realized she was fixing me with an intense stare. In an otherwise plain face, Terry's eyes were almost alarmingly lovely, enormous, deep-lidded and with irises that shifted shades, from the palest golden brown to a stalking cat's-eyes yellow. Now they were the amber of a traffic light and signaling the same message of warning.

"There's one thing I don't get," she said.

"Yeah? What?"

"You've got some far-out ideas, especially when it comes to clothes and cluttering up your life with old stuff. And sometimes you're inclined to leap without looking. But I've always thought of you as a pretty good mother."

"Thanks," I said coldly, "but I happen to think I'm a damned good mother."

"So then how is it you go ahead and give some total stranger charge of your kid? Not to mention the complete run of your house."

I bristled. "Brandon was hardly a total stranger. In case you weren't filled in, he was an old friend. I've known him for almost twenty years."

"Excuse me, but according to my info, you knew him twenty years ago but had pretty much no contact since. For all you know, he could've been up to anything in between. He could've been the king of kiddy porn."

"He happened to be an extremely well-regarded photographer and documentary maker."

"So what do you think, no well-regarded photographer has ever dabbled in a little kiddy porn?"

That infuriating way she had of batting my words back with a twisted spin . . . "Brandon was one of the kindest people on earth," I declared. "He had a hell of a lot more integrity than almost anyone else I know. Look, he lived with us for over two months. I think I'd have noticed if he'd changed." In agitation, I picked up a comb from the bureau and began running a thumb over the teeth.

"Did you know the Social Security number he gave you was fake?"

I abruptly stopped strumming the comb. "What?"

Somewhat smugly, Terry removed a small pad from her suit pocket and consulted it. "The number you reported for him belonged to one Edwin Lewis Brownsley of Middlebury, Vermont, now deceased."

"Maybe that was just a mistake. Maybe when Brandon filled out the form, he accidentally transposed one of the numbers. Or maybe his sevens looked like nines, that can easily happen . . ."

"Did you also know he had no valid driver's license?"

I began to feel a tingle of alarm. "No, I didn't."

"Last one he had was from New York, expired four and a half years ago. Never bothered to renew it all the time he was driving around in California."

And the Damned Good Mother never bothered to ask to see a license before blithely letting him chauffeur her daughter around town.

"He also had no bank account, no credit cards or charge accounts," Terry went on. "He left no tracks—nothing to show he ever existed, at least in the state of California."

I sank into a chair, my brain suddenly swirling with details of Brandon's behavior that I'd previously chosen to ignore. How he'd winsomely explained that he was inept at balancing a checkbook, always ended up accidentally bouncing a lot of checks, but if we'd pay him in cash, he'd know exactly how much he had to spend. How, when we'd offered to give him a phone line in his own name, he had said he didn't even want an extension in his room since it would just distract him from concentrating on his writing . . .

How he'd never received one piece of mail the entire time he'd lived here . . .

Terry had pulled Brandon's battered old brown aviator's jacket from out of the closet. Now she oddly began to knead the leather.

"He was wearing that jacket the day we ran into each other again," I offered, adding rather extraneously, "It was at the Farmers' Market."

"Ever see him wear it recently?"

It occurred to me I hadn't—even though the nights had been cool enough to call for it. "Actually no. Why?"

"There's something in the lining." I watched her grope along the interior seam of the left sleeve; then, using two fingers as pincers, she fished out something from a small slit in the seam. It was a twenty-dollar bill. "This'll keep you warm," she chortled. "Terrific insulation." She tweezed out several more bills.

"Good lord!" I gasped. "Is that jacket totally stuffed with money?"

She pried the seam open further. "Yep. Looks like this is where he did his banking."

"So he *was* a crook!" I blurted.

"Why? As far as I know, it's not yet a crime to keep your dough stashed in your jacket."

"But it's got to be stolen money, doesn't it? He probably robbed a store or a bank or embezzled it from some company. And that's what he was doing here," I jabbered on. "He was hiding out until the heat was off. Except that they caught up with him and rubbed him out!"

Terry giggled.

"What's so funny?" I asked sourly.

"You sound like something out of some old-time movie. I feel like any minute Humphrey Bogart is gonna come shooting his way through the door."

"I see nothing amusing about the fact that I might have been harboring a criminal in my own home," I said icily.

"There you go, taking your usual giant steps into totally wrong conclusions."

"Oh yeah?"

She poked gingerly through the wadded currency. "In the first place, this looks like it's all small bills, mostly twenties, a few tens and hundreds. There can't be more than a couple of grand in here. Which wouldn't exactly add up to the heist of the century." She giggled again. "Did you pay him in cash?"

I nodded sheepishly. "And mostly in twenties."

"Then I'd say it's probably what he saved up working for you people."

"Oh."

"In the second place, we're ninety percent sure he was killed in the course of a robbery. It fits a pattern. In the past month, there've been two similar cases, one down in La Jolla, one in Long Beach, on an off-ramp of the 405. Both victims were in their cars, both shot at close range with a .44. Both were stripped of all valuables. We've got a lead on suspects, two Hispanic males in their early twenties, driving a beat-up green Nova. Looks like they're making their way up the coast."

"Why the hell didn't you say that to begin with?" I grumbled.

Terry hooked the money-stuffed jacket on the closet doorknob. "I knew it would be fascinating to get your take on it all. Besides, I said ninety, not a hundred, percent sure."

"So what's the missing ten?" I cocked my head with renewed interest.

"For starters, all three victims were shot with .44 Magnums, but the first two were with the same weapon, a Super Blackhawk. McKenna was killed with a Smith and Wesson."

"But you said there might be two suspects. So they each might have had their own gun."

"Correct. And even if it's just one perpetrator, there's nothing that says he can't have two guns, or even an entire arsenal." Terry furrowed her brow at the thought of such a homicidal Rambo.

"And there are other differences?" I prompted.

"Well, mainly that in the first two cases, a lot more was stolen. Radios and tape and CD players were jimmied out of the dash, and the trunks were totally cleaned out. McKenna was only robbed of items on his person."

"So you don't think it *was* part of the same pattern."

Terry ran a hand through her mousy brown hair, making it rise in a brief Mohawk before collapsing back to its usual limp bob. "What I think is that I'm done here," she said abruptly.

"What about the computer? Don't you want to get someone to try to break the password?"

"That's up to Langocetti. My bet is he's gonna stick to the robbery motive, unless some pretty strong evidence turns up to the contrary." She turned and began heading to the door.

I took one last look around the room. Terry was right, it was eerily barren of any personal touches. I'd been far too busy ogling Brandon's rangy bod and staring moonily into his green eyes to notice.

And Terry was also right about another thing—I really knew precious little about this man I'd so casually let into my home.

4

"**M**aybe I should come to Colorado with you," I said to Kit that evening.

We were down in the cellar, fishing his and Chloe's snow clothes from the cedar trunks in which they were stored. He pulled out an aquamarine Patagonia parka and scowled at a rip at the shoulder. "Why would you want to come?" he said. "We're going to be on the slopes all day and too exhausted to do anything but flop into bed at night. And you're obviously not going to want to go skiing in your condition."

Obviously not, which didn't distress me. Athletically, I fall firmly in the klutz category. The few times I've been coaxed onto a pair of skis, I've spent dangerous and unpleasant hours wobbling down a bunny slope, while six-year-olds gaily swooshed and stem-christied around me.

"I just thought it might be better for Chloe's sake," I pursued. "She might feel anxious if I wasn't along."

Kit flicked a daddy longlegs spider off a pair of yellow-and-black gloves. "I asked Minna Luchstein that, as a matter of fact," he said. "I gave her a call this morning. She seems to feel it's good that it's going to be just Chloe and me. As she pointed out, Brandon was a male, not a female, caretaker. She feels it's important that Chloe knows that even though Brandon has deserted her, her *primary* male caretaker is still there for her." He placed the gloves on the "take" pile. "It's mostly psychological gobbledygook, but I think there's something to it."

I was less than thrilled at having the odoriferous Dr. Luchstein decreeing what I should or shouldn't be doing with my daughter. "The woman spent ten minutes with Chloe," I flared. "How the hell can she be an expert on her 'needs'?"

Kit glanced at me with some surprise. "Hey, it's just her professional opinion, not any kind of official order. Anyway, what about that meeting you've got with Excelsior? It's tomorrow, isn't it? Something like that could make your entire career."

I looked up, startled. I'd completely forgotten. The meeting he was referring to was with an agent named Donny Geller. Excelsior was the less than modest name of the hottest new talent agency in town, formed by a cadre of under-thirty-year-olds who had defected from the powerful, and previously hottest, agency in town—International Talent. I had recently acquired some minor fame as an animator with a regular segment on a Saturday morning kid's show called *Excellent Science*. My segment starred a flying blue hedgehog named Amerinda, whose antics, along with those of a motley assortment of barnyard pals, had each week illustrated a different scientific principle. The call from Donny Geller had come about a week ago—a voice that sounded as if it had not quite changed yet calling me "Babe," motoring on about how his five-year-old niece had turned him on to Amerinda and that what with these new rating systems and V-chips and the whole *schmear*, the networks were selling their grandmothers to bring in more family programming . . . "I want you to come in and meet some network folks," the prepube voice had piped. "Pitch your stuff, show 'em some clips, and I betcha we can get this hedgehog her own series."

The Amerinda Show! Animated by Lucy Freers! I'd been so excited, that last week I'd been practically walking into walls.

But a week ago I was also positive I was a Damned Good Mother. Now I was wondering if I was even a competent one.

"I'll reschedule the meeting," I said staunchly. "Chloe's more important than my career."

"Why don't you just ask her if she wants you to come?" Kit said.

A sensible idea. A Damned Good Mother should have thought of it herself.

My Guilt Fest was added to by the fact that I had not yet gotten around to telling Kit what I'd learned about Brandon. The evening had been occupied in a bustle of packing, limiting Chloe to what she could bring (yes to her amber teardrop necklace and three *Baby-Sitters Club* books, no to her seashell collection, the Sugar Plum Fairy costume from her last ballet recital and Hamlet the hamster), and locating sweaters, knit hats and long underwear that hadn't been worn in a year. There just hadn't seemed to be an optimum time for me to say, "Oh by the way, honey, I found out some interesting tidbits about Brandon. Turns out he had no driver's license or any kind of identification, and he was stashing his cash in an old bomber jacket."

Perhaps now was the time to fill Kit in. But he was already trudging toward the stairs, his arms filled with hummingbird-colored clothing. "I'm too beat to make any more decisions tonight," he muttered. "I think I'll turn in."

I decided to wait to give him the glad tidings; grabbing my quota of thermal socks and ski boots, I followed him upstairs. I dumped the stuff beside the half-packed suitcases and headed to Chloe's room.

She was in bed, snuggled in candy-cane-striped pajamas, her TV burbling a Miller beer commercial. I had always cherished the notion that she looked just like me—she had exactly the same Orphan Annie mop of hair I'd had at her age; but now in the lamplight it struck me how much she was growing to resemble

Kit—the identical here-comes-the-sun-blond face with china-blue saucers for eyes.

I perched on the edge of the bed, smoothed the bright curls back from her forehead. "Listen, honeybun," I said. "Would you like it if I came with you and Daddy to Aspen?"

She directed a worried squint at me. "Somebody's got to stay here and take care of the animals."

"Graciela will. Like she always does."

"But she's not here at night. What happens if Rollins gets sick again?"

He could die, she didn't have to add. Like Cookie Dough.

And like Brandon.

"So you'd feel better if I stayed here with them?" I asked.

She gave a little shrug. It seemed that my first step to reestablishing my Damned Good Mother credentials would have to be as Primary Caretaker to a parrot, a chinchilla, a couple of cats, et al. "Okay, then that's what I'll do," I assured her. She awarded me a tremulous smile.

Then I noticed she had a piece of green cloth crooked in her arm. "What's that?"

"Brandon's T-shirt. I got it from out of his bureau drawer. Is that okay?"

I recognized it now, a faded gray T with a boxing kangaroo and the legend "Thunder from Down Under"—a souvenir of his globetrotting days. I had a sudden, vivid picture of him wearing it, his lean body slouched sexily in a doorway. Then up flashed another, equally vivid, picture of that same body stiff and cold on a slab, and the hideous congealed pit for a face.

I bent down and kissed Chloe. "It's okay," I told her. Hoping I sounded more convinced than I felt.

At seven-thirty the next morning, still blinking sleep from my eyes, I ferried Kit and Chloe to the Santa Monica airport where they were catching their ride to Colorado. This happened to be a private Gulfstream V jet belonging to one of Kit's new tycoon pals, Bernie

Reisler, who'd made zillions in exactly the kind of blood-spurting, head-hacking-off video games I was forever trying to keep Chloe away from. Bernie himself would not be onboard; he and his family had popped out to Colorado the night before, but he'd thoughtfully ordered the plane back to give a lift to a few friends.

"This jet cost over thirty million stripped," Kit informed me as we tooled up to the hangar. "And then Bernie put in another two or three million for decor. The master suite's got a sitting room and a sauna. There are bidets in all the johns and the seats all convert to full-size beds. And Bernie says it can go from here to Tokyo without refueling." He shook his head wistfully. "Imagine never having to deal with commercial airlines again. It's the only way to go."

I glanced at him. He had that Keeping Up with the Moguls glint in his eye, which gave me a twinge of alarm. We already had a home that my Midwestern relatives referred to as a mansion, plus a three-car luxury fleet and enough electronics and armoires and sporting goods and gourmet gadgets to stock a suburban Bloomingdale's. Did we now have to strive for our own jet propulsion as well?

He hopped out to greet his milling fellow passengers who included a daytime soap star, a stock car racer and a rapper who went by the sobriquet of Kool 2 Kill. A gorgeous young woman in a snug violet uniform was asking Chloe whether she'd like waffles or French toast for breakfast, another violet-clad crewman was grabbing the bags. I tearfully hugged Chloe and then suddenly I was watching the gleaming silver plane taxiing down the runway and leaping into the mist. And I realized that in all the hubbub of the departure, I still hadn't enlightened Kit about Brandon.

But I had no time for self-recriminations. I had my career-making meeting to prepare for. Once again I found myself hovering with indecision in front of my closet. This time I chose a vintage Hawaiian shirt printed with hula girls strumming ukuleles, hoping it would indicate creativity. I paired it with Kate Hepburnish pleated trousers to suggest down-to-earth efficiency. And, I noticed with approval, in this outfit, my pregnancy hardly showed at all. Then into an oversized knapsack, I stuffed my résumé listing all my awards and accolades and a cassette of my clips, and I set off.

The Excelsior offices were on the third floor of a newly built edifice on Wilshire constructed of the kind of roseate marble that, a century earlier, the robber barons had favored for the ballroom floors of their Newport "cottages." The agency's reception was dominated by an enormous Wesselman painting of a hot pink nude; the significance of having to pass beneath a three-foot-long pubic triangle on your way into the inner chambers was something that at the moment I didn't care to ponder.

I sat waiting for some ten minutes in an antechamber of Donny's office, sipping the Calistoga water his secretary had proffered, trying to keep a look of coolly amused nonchalance plastered on my face. Finally a girl with intimidating Wonder Bra cleavage sashayed in. "I'm Margo!" she announced vivaciously, as if that explained everything. "We're meeting in the conference room, so come with me."

I traipsed behind her to a door down the hall. Inside, four people sat around a long blond wood table in a room as sleekly surfaced as an operating theater. The table, by contrast, was littered with the remains of a takeout Chinese meal: a dozen white cardboard containers from an eatery called Wok 'N Roll; plastic chopsticks scattered like Pick-Up Sticks; tiny packets of hot mustard and plum sauce. The homey odors of Kung Pao chicken and Hunan smoked duck clashed with the waxy pristineness of the decorating scheme.

Donny Geller sat at the far head of the table, expertly chopsticking fried rice directly from container to mouth; he was wiry-haired and gangly thin and wearing precisely the kind of pastel Ban-Lon sports shirt my great-uncle Walter had favored just before his death from emphysema at the age of eighty-two. The three network execs were arrayed on his left: a silvery-haired man of about fifty, a chubby, baby-faced guy twenty years his junior, and a splendidly made-up woman whose age was anybody's guess. All three wore snappy suits in luxe Italian fabrics.

By way of greeting, Donny waved a chopstick in my direction. "Lucy, terrif of you to come in," his high voice piped. The chopstick pointed to an empty chair on his right. I slid into it, placed my knapsack on the floor. Through a mouthful of rice, Donny mumbled the names of the network folks, none of which I quite caught. There was a flurry of handshakes and "delighted to meet you" grins, followed by a moment of strained silence.

"How about some Hunan?" Donny offered.

The female exec peered into a container. "There's some of the eggplant left . . ."

"No thanks, I'm fine," I said quickly. I was nervous enough already without having to worry about manipulating chopsticks.

"Excellent. Terrific. Then what say we get down to business?" Donny jabbed his utensils into the fried rice container and swiped his mouth with a yellow paper napkin. "As I'm sure you know, Lucy, Garren has just been made president of daytime programming. His mandate is family, family, family!"

I turned attentively to the silver-haired man. Everyone else in the room swiveled toward the chubby twenty-something.

That the new president of daytime programming for a major network should be scarcely hatched from college was something I should have figured—after all, television was not an industry given to rewarding such attributes as age, wisdom and maturity. I redirected my attention.

"I intend for us to be known as the family-friendly network," pronounced Young President Garren. "The feedback I'm getting from parents right now is that they don't feel comfortable with the present state of early morning animation. They feel it's a bit too violent. Too much karate chopping, too many superheros zapping aliens with ray guns, and so on and so forth."

"My Amerinda series is totally nonviolent," I remarked virtuously. "My characters have never even engaged in a fist fight."

"Of course you need a certain amount of confrontation to make a good story," put in the female suit. "And good sometimes needs to use force to overcome evil." Her eyes had the glitter of someone who quite relished the spectacle of superheros zapping vast numbers of aliens to smithereens.

"The FCC now requires us to air three hours a week of children's educational programming," stated her silver-haired colleague, fairly gnashing his teeth at such an onerous concept. "We believe all our programming is to a certain extent educational. Each of our shows provides kids with valuable life lessons."

Yeah, right, I thought. Truly valuable instruction on how to choose brand-name products over cheaper imitations.

"What we don't want is what we call broccoli TV," the woman went on. "Stuff that's good for kids, but you have to force feed it to them."

"We've got our ratings to consider," declared her boss, Garren. "Bottom line is, we're still in the entertainment business."

"That's where Amerinda delivers in spades!" Donny yelped. "You get your educational content, but also a fabuloso cartoon that keeps kids glued to the screen."

Garren treated himself to a decorous swig of Dr Pepper from a sweating can. "Why don't you tell us a little about yourself, Lucy?" he suggested. He leaned forward and placed his Italian-tailored forearms in an anticipatory position on the table.

"Lucy's husband is Kit Freers," Donny said. "He produced the last Jim Carrey film. You know, *Willigher*."

At the mention of a two-hundred-million-grossing blockbuster, everyone perked up. My stock as Mrs. Big Time Producer shot up perceptibly.

"That movie had spectacular special effects," remarked Silver Hair. "Did you by chance have anything to do with that, Lucy?"

"Well, no, I wasn't involved in *Willigher*," I said. "I work on a somewhat smaller scale."

My stock plummeted back to its preinflationary level.

"Tell you what, why don't we take a look at your material, and then we'll take it from there," Donny said. "You brought a tape, didn't you?"

"Yes, I did," I said quickly and dug into my knapsack for the cassette. "This has got several Amerinda episodes and clips from a few of my short films."

"Okay then. Let's go to the videotape." Donny selected one of several remote controls that were arrayed in a glass bowl on a shelf behind him. He aimed it at the opposite wall and clicked: two blond cabinet doors parted like the Red Sea, revealing the majestic breadth of a fifty-five-inch Sony. Margo, the Wonder Braed aide-de-camp, snapped my cassette into a built-in VCR and dimmed the lights to a rather romantic level. Donny clicked another remote: the Frugal Gourmet chopping garlic swam into view. "Oh shit, that's not the VCR," muttered Donny. He had a quick confab with Margo, clicked yet another remote and finally the lilting notes of Amerinda's theme song announced the start of my tape.

"Now we're cooking," Donny chortled. The network execs settled back to watch.

The first episode was "Gravity." When Amerinda plummeted out of the sky and landed plop in a mushy pigpen, it drew a chuckle from the audience, and there were hearty guffaws during her dream sequence in which she was chased around the farmyard by an assortment of cheery ghosts and skeletons. With the next episode, "Solar Energy," I sensed a restlessness in the crowd: the lady executive stifled a yawn; Silver Hair's eyes flicked to his watch— admittedly it was not one of my most inspired efforts. But with "Magnetism," things picked back up. Young Garren beamed broadly at the romance between Sally the North Pole seal and Porter the South Pole penguin; and when the entire animal cast swung into a show-stopping "Opposites Attract" jitterbug number, all three network execs were rocking to the beat.

It was working! I thought with a thrill. I could picture the show already, *Amerinda and Her Pals,* brought to you each week by Jell-O, or maybe Mattel, a nine A.M. time slot . . . Or hell, maybe even prime time! Amerinda would take her rightful place in TV animation history, right up there with Fred Flintstone, Bart Simpson and Butt-head.

Then suddenly, on the Sony screen, my cartoon characters blinked off. To my astonishment, live footage blinked on: a small boy with floppy blond hair and apple cheeks, dressed in a country bumpkin's loose denim overalls, was performing a fairly professional soft-shoe on a wooden floor. He was accompanied by music, Barbra Streisand belting the title song to Cats. I stared at it, mesmerized: I'd never seen the footage before, had no idea where it came from.

"I didn't know you did live action as well," Donny remarked, with why-wasn't-I-informed irritation.

I was too astonished to even stammer out a reply. The scene had now cut to a woman standing on top of a flight of stairs. It had been filmed in low light, so her image was grainy and indistinct; but she appeared to be about thirty, in an apricot-colored power suit and the kind of slick, short haircut that practically bellowed the message "I'm in charge here!" She was crisply flipping through pages on a clipboard, while Streisand continued to blare away.

Then a child appeared directly behind her. Because of the low light and the way the kid was dressed—a big straw hat and ur-chinlike ragged shirt—it was impossible to tell whether it was a boy or a girl. The woman was startled by the kid's appearance; she turned her head with a slight jerk. As she did, the child suddenly darted forward and shoved her with two hands at the small of her back. The woman dropped the clipboard and went tumbling down the steep flight of stairs, the camera staying efficiently on her as her skull cracked against the sharp metal edge of the last step. Her body crumpled in a rag doll heap at the bottom.

The camera zoomed in for a close-up. Her eyes were wide open, staring with a lifeless glaze. Her smashed skull oozed a slow, black cherry pool of blood.

And then the tape abruptly ended.

There was utter silence in the room. I pried my eyes from the black screen to glance at my companions.

Five jaws hung wide open. And five pairs of eyes were fixed on me in utter stupefaction.

5

Another thirty seconds elapsed before anybody uttered a word. "Well," the silver-haired gent finally remarked. "That was certainly very vivid. But I'm afraid it's got rather more of an edge than we're looking for." He glanced at Garren for corroboration.

"But that last footage wasn't mine," I blurted. "That wasn't from any movie. I think it was something that really happened."

"You mean that was actually somebody getting killed?" breathed the female suit.

The idea that we'd just been viewing a snuff film made us all shift a bit queasily in our seats. The further fact that the snuffing appeared to have been done by a grade-schooler in a Huck Finn straw hat acutely added to our discomfort.

"I'm at a loss for words!" Donny finally exclaimed. His complexion had acquired an interesting shade of blotched purple; his Adam's apple moved compulsively up and down like an elevator on overdrive. "I don't know what to say."

A speechless agent was something so unprecedented that for a moment it kept the rest of us mute as well. Then Garren, as befitting his presidential title, decided to take charge. "Now, Lucy, this *is* your tape, so surely you have some explanation of what we've just seen."

"I don't," I insisted. "I've never seen that last footage before. I've got no idea where it came from. I certainly didn't put it there."

"So who did?" put in Margo.

"I haven't a clue. But I think I ought to take it to the police."

"The police?" Donny repeated, as incredulously as if I'd proposed the KGB or the Spanish Inquisition.

The two junior network execs were examining their watches as intently as if the faces were revealing some precious and heretofore hidden meaning of life. But Garren was leaning forward with shining eyes. "This is incredible! We could all be in on something big here." Visions of leaping out of children's programming and into prime-time specials were no doubt dancing in his head.

"If I might inject a word of caution," Donny said. "Before any of us get further involved with police or anything else, I think we should check with our respective legal departments. No reflection on you, of course, Lucy," he added smarmily.

"I totally agree," piped the female exec. "We could be exposing the network to some kind of hornet's nest."

"Second that." Silver Hair smiled grimly. "Something like this hardly comes under the category of family friendly."

Garren bit his lip, then, reluctantly, nodded. "Agreed. Sorry, Lucy, but under the circumstances we'd better cut this meeting short."

He rose and his two confederates popped up with him.

"I'll walk you out, Garren," Donny said.

The three execs moved in a swift phalanx to the door, Donny hard on their heels, the Wonder Braed Margo bringing up the rear, her red tank top giving the impression of a caboose on a fast-moving freight train. I was left alone with plates of congealing stir-fried shrimp and half-consumed cans of Sprite and Dr Pepper.

I stood for a moment, as if waiting for further instructions. Then I went to the Sony and ejected the Cartridge That Had Ruined My Career from the VCR. As I was stuffing it back in my knapsack, I heard a whrrrr . . .

It was the sound of the big cabinet doors automatically sliding shut.

Within thirty minutes, I was threading my way through the jammed detectives' room of the LAPD's West Los Angeles station. Terry Shoe's table was located almost directly under a floating white sign marked "Homicide." It was as impressively and eclectically cluttered as the last time I'd had occasion to drop by her place of business: buried among the listing towers of files, papers and notebooks, dog-eared Hallmark cards and framed snapshots were such puzzling items as a Lucite yo-yo, a Turkish-English phrase book and a little plastic Christmas tree which, three weeks after Valentine's Day, lent the whole mélange an almost dotty eccentricity.

She greeted my approach with a sardonic smile. "This better be good," she said. "I'm late for a deposition. Guy we apprehended last month is coming up for trial. Got fired from some packing job in one of those box-and-ship stores, came back with a seven-gage and blew away the manager and two customers. One of them was in a wheelchair. I'd be sincerely happy to see this creep put away." She motioned me to have a seat in one of the torturous metal chairs opposite her. "So what have you got?"

I pulled the cassette out of my knapsack.

"That's it?" Terry remarked. "From the way you were carrying on over the phone, I expected at the least a severed head."

"Before laughing yourself sick, why don't you take a look at it?" I said coolly.

Terry leaned toward a long-chinned detective who was muttering into a phone at a neighboring table. "Hey, Coleman, is the VCR still jammed?"

The detective slapped a palm over the mouthpiece. "No, it's back on line, if you don't mind lousy sound."

"Sound's not important," I said.

"So I guess we won't be hearing the confession of a serial killer," Terry chortled. "We can check it out in the coffee room." She got up and led the way through the maze of tables to a small adjoining room. A Reagan-era Hitachi TV with an equally venerable VCR shared a counter with a microwave and a Mr. Coffee. I clapped the cassette into the VCR and rewound it to roughly where I judged the live action began. Amerinda appeared, acrobatting through a burnt orange sky.

"Are we gonna watch cartoons?" Terry asked querulously.

"Hold on a second. It's going to change."

Amerinda flickered off. Then on came the dimpled blond boy, soft-shoeing madly away.

"What the hell's this?" Terry demanded.

"Just keep watching."

Then here was the slick-haired woman, still dressed for success at the top of the stairs. Once again she flinched in surprise at the appearance of the urchin behind her. Once again, the kid shoved her from behind. Then here came her flailing tumble down the grimy metal staircase, the crack of her head, and the zoom-in on the dead, staring eyes and gory muck of broken skull. And again the picture abruptly snapped to black.

I glanced at Terry. With grim satisfaction I noted that the smirk had vanished from her face. She was gaping with the same slack-jawed astonishment recently featured by both Donny Geller and the network folks.

"I was speechless too," I said. "Seeing a child push a woman to her death is too staggering for words."

"Who are they?" Terry snapped.

"I don't know. I just saw this for the first time myself right before I called you." I gave her a quick encapsulation of my aborted meeting with Donny and the network folks.

"I don't get it," Terry cut in. "How could this just appear at the end of your cartoons?"

"Obviously, it didn't just appear. Somebody deliberately crashed it into my tape."

"Huh?"

"They recorded this footage over mine. Anyone can do it, all you need are two VCRs." I paused to give dramatic éclat to my next statement. "And I'm positive that the one who did it was Brandon McKenna."

From experience, I knew that little short of a thermo-nuclear detonation could get a rise out of Terry Shoe; this seemed to be a trait she shared with her comrade in crime-stopping, Detective Langocetti. Now she fixed her eyes on me, her expression implying she was prepared to hold out well into the next millennium if need be to hear out the extent of my ravings.

"It all makes perfect sense," I began. "Brandon was a documentary maker, remember? He always worked in 16mm film, not video—and I'm pretty sure this was originally shot in 16mm. If it had been originally video, in that kind of dim light, the whole scene would have been so cloudy we wouldn't be able to make out anything at all. And of course, since Brandon lived with us, he had easy access to my cartridges. I've got stacks of them on the shelves of my studio at home. He must have taken one of my tapes at random and recorded his footage on the end, then returned it back to the shelf. He probably didn't intend to park it there too long."

I paused and drummed my foot impatiently on the sticky linoleum, waiting for a response. At last Terry said, "How do you know this is real? Maybe it's a scene from some movie."

It was my turn to pause. "No, it wouldn't make sense," I said. "To do a scene of somebody getting killed like that would take very expensive and sophisticated special effects. I mean, to make it look so incredibly real. So then why would the lighting be so bad? And the sound quality as well?"

"So let's say it is real. And that it was shot by McKenna. Why did he stick it on the end of your tape?"

"It's obvious, isn't it? Because he witnessed a murder and this was the recorded evidence of it."

"Generally speaking, when people have evidence of a homicide, they bring it to the police."

"Not if he'd been threatened. He'd be too afraid to. It all adds up to why he had no ID or driver's license. He was on the run from whoever it was who was threatening him, and he was afraid of being traced."

"So you're saying McKenna was living in terror of a seven-year-old kid?"

"Of course not," I spluttered. It seemed to me she was being deliberately obtuse. "But seven-year-old kids have parents, some of whom will go to pretty great lengths to keep their precious darlings out of trouble. Don't you see?" I went on. "Brandon obviously thought that if anyone came hunting for the tape, the chances of their deciding to check out all my cassettes all the way till the end would have been pretty slim."

"Just like the chances of your selecting that particular cassette to play?"

I hesitated. Then I had a sudden realization. "He knew that was my demo tape, I had played it for him just after he moved in. So he knew that if anything happened to him, I'd find the footage eventually."

"Meaning he was thereby throwing you into the same kind of danger he was in."

I was about to protest that that couldn't be true, that Brandon would never have consciously done anything to put me in danger. But that was only the Brandon I thought I knew—not the mystery man who had actually occupied the room over the garage.

"I think you ought to know that Langocetti's closed the case," Terry said.

I stared at her in astonishment. "The investigation's over?"

"Two suspects were apprehended this morning up in Thousand Oaks. We were right in thinking they were making their way up the coast. They used the same MO—forced a car off the road in an isolated area and approached the motorist with drawn weapons. But this time the motorist had the presence of mind to yell and honk his horn. It got the attention of some dog walkers nearby. The dogs started barking, adding to the ruckus. The suspects panicked, jumped back in their own car and while trying to speed off, they crashed into a eucalyptus." Terry chortled. "Not what you'd call your master criminal mind."

"So it's positive that they were the ones who shot Brandon?"

"Like I said, it was the same MO. Also, there was a pretty sweet little arsenal of handguns stashed in their trunk. Unfortunately, we didn't retrieve either the one that killed McKenna or the .44 used in the first two hits. But it's safe to assume that this scum began jettisoning the incriminating weapons as they went along. Starting with McKenna, they used fresh guns for a fresh kill."

I sat glumly for a moment, turning things over in my mind. "So I guess what you have to do now," I said, "is find out who the dead woman is on the tape."

Terry gave one of her infuriating giggles. "I suppose you think it's like the movies, we're gonna launch an intensive investigation. Maybe assign a couple of top detectives to work on it exclusively."

"It doesn't have to be exclusive," I said.

"Look, we've got absolutely nothing to go on here. No clues to the identities of any of these people, or even where this is located. We don't even know when this was taken, it could've been six days ago, it could've been six years."

"The woman who fell was wearing Manolo Blahnik platform pumps."

Terry eyed me narrowly, obviously disconcerted by my sudden segue into fashion chitchat.

"Blahnik came out with that style about four years ago," I explained—a fact I happened to know because all my vintage platform shoes had suddenly popped back into fashion. "Which means this couldn't have been earlier than that. Also, the woman strikes me as having been a pretty chic dresser, so I doubt if she'd have worn a style for more than a couple of years in a row. So my guess is this happened anywhere from two to four years ago."

My sudden talent for Sherlock Holmes–worthy observation of detail seemed to catch Terry off guard. She puckered her lips, then made a sort of smacking sound while processing the new information. "Okay, but that still doesn't do us a fat lot of good," she finally declared. "We'd have to search accident reports and missing persons files throughout the whole country, going back four years. You know what something like that would cost? This department can't even come up with the resources to spring for a reliable video machine. Besides," she added, "I'm still not totally convinced this isn't fake."

"You think I'm faking this?" I said indignantly.

"Not you necessarily. But you've got a lot of pals who could do the dirty, don't you? Maybe somebody came over for dinner, swiped the cassette and next time around returned it with a new ending."

"Why the hell would anybody want to do that?" I snapped.

"Beats me. Maybe for a practical joke."

Ridiculous, I was about to protest. Then I checked myself. One friend of Kit's, an assistant director named Harvey Gleason, was infamous for pulling off stunts like this. Once when Kit had just returned from a film festival in Rio, Harvey had sent an actor to knock on our door, flash a phony Department of Health badge and claim there had been an outbreak of cholera among passengers on Kit's return flight. We had actually rung up our internist in a panic before a grinning Harvey showed up and revealed the hoax.

As I hesitated, Terry's eyes darted to a wall clock. "If I don't make this deposition, there's gonna be one homicidal packing clerk back walking the streets."

"So what am I supposed to do, then?" I said plaintively.

"Tell you what. Leave the tape here. I'll have the rest of the department take a look at it, see if it rings any bells. Maybe someone remembers hearing about a gal who tumbled downstairs and bashed out her brains. If we get a handle on a victim, then we can proceed from there."

"Yeah, swell," I said. I had, after all, zilch in the way of alternative options.

6

The day following my Videotape Surprise, I headed back to Windermere, this time to fill my required hours as a volunteer.

It was a hard and fast rule of The School that every mom and dad log in volunteer time. Absolutely no exceptions. And so, should you be meandering through the campus, it would not be unusual for you to stumble upon a movie star in leopard skin leggings reading *The Cat in the Hat* to a gaggle of six-year-olds or the current Heisman Trophy winner coaching a dozen adolescents in warm-up jumping jacks.

I had signed up, rather predictably, to lead an after-school animation workshop. I had considered putting it off, since at the moment I was hardly at my most sparkling. But I needed to get out of the house, steeped as it was in memories of Brandon; and I needed to divert my mind from the tenacious and gruesome image of his obliterated face. The workshop, I decided, was just the ticket.

Now, as I often did when I cruised through the Baroque ironwork gates of The School, I began to calculate the staggering sum we were shelling out to keep Chloe in attendance. The officially quoted tuition is a heart-stopping thirteen grand a year, but the actual cost is substantially higher than that. A, there's the constant barrage of extra fees you'll be hit with throughout the school year—these range from as little as the cost of a box of De Cecco ziti as a donation to the third grade's Feed the Hungry day, to the forty-five-hundred-smackers-a-kid for the middle school's field trip to the Seychelles.

Then B, there's the annual "tithing drive." This is when each of us Primary Caregivers is asked to pledge a sum in addition to the listed tuition. The unspoken rule is that you cough up at least five grand if you're just among the rank and file of parents, fifteen to twenty if you're someone whose credit appears in a movie's opening sequence, and a walloping six figures if you're a bona fide household name.

And C, there's whatever value you want to place on your volunteer time.

As always I tried to justify the decision to send Chloe here by reflecting on the fact that at ten, she could already converse in French and had a working acquaintance with the major principles of astronomy, the new math and human biology. Still I never felt entirely at ease walking across these manicured grounds or navigating the spotless halls that had never seen a hint of graffiti.

An art studies classroom had been designated as the scene of my workshop. It was a large, airy room with round pearwood tables and floor-to-ceiling shelves crammed with the sort of richness of paints, brushes and quality drawing paper for which Vincent van Gogh would gladly have sliced off his other ear. The walls were adorned with reproductions of the great works of art history; they were multiculturally chosen but haphazardly arranged, so that a jutting-breasted Samoan fertility goddess hung haunch to haunch with a chaste Raphael Madonna, and the Degas *Absinthe Drinkers* bleakly contemplated Hieronymus Bosch's far more entertaining hell directly opposite them.

"Here comes our illustrious leader," trilled the art studies teacher as I entered the room. "People, this is Lucy. Let's give her an enthusiastic welcome."

An anemic chorus of "Hi Lucy" rose from the fifth- and sixth-graders grouped around two tables. It was one of the less endearing traits of The School that students were encouraged to address all adults by their first names: should the Pope ever drop by, they'd be "Hiya, John Paul"ing him within seconds.

The art teacher snapped a satchel shut, mumbled that she was sure it would be a super workshop, and to my dismay, slipped hurriedly out the door. With some trepidation, I turned to my new charges. A dozen kids with salon-cut hair, their maroon plaid uniforms gorgeously tailored. Here a flash of a diamond stud earring. There the gleam of a rich leather shoe. The thought nagged at me that I could spend my time more worthily, say, in tutoring a South Central child in his ABC's, than in trying to enrich the lives of kids whose typical family outing was a safari in Kenya.

The feeling was reinforced by two new arrivals. One was Jamie Alston—*the* Jamie Alston, currently the top child actor in the world, star of four megahits and only one dud. His chronological age was eleven; his flaxen bangs, ruddy cheeks and cherubically pursed lips kept him a perpetual nine years old on screen; and in person, his sardonic leer and swaggering gait gave him the air of a growth-stunted thirty-five. The scuttlebutt was he'd been kicked out of at least three boarding schools back East. And since his enrollment at Windermere last month, the faculty had already given him the off-the-record nickname of The Dreaded Spawn of Satan.

He was accompanied by his bodyguard, a scowling baldy with a squat wrestler's build who was never known to have uttered a word, not even to return a pleasant "Good afternoon."

Scurrying in lockstep right behind them was Kerrin Granger. He was ten and also an actor, one of a family of five kids relentlessly pushed by a father who had flopped in his own attempt at a Broadway career. Kerrin had so far had little success, no doubt hampered by having eyes the size and shade of chickpeas and a down-turned, perpetually disgruntled-looking mouth. I had recently caught him in a TV spot for a local Italian restaurant chain: he was one of a gang of kids who were supposed to be ecstatically chowing down deep-dish pizza, but Kerrin looked as if he were being force-fed liver and onions. Since Jamie's first day at Windermere, Kerrin had attached himself to him like a barnacle, perhaps hoping a little of Jamie's stardust would sprinkle off on himself.

The bodyguard assumed a rigid lookout's position at the door. Jamie flopped into a chair and sat sprawled, knees splayed insolently apart. Kerrin grabbed the place beside him, dutifully aping his mentor's body language.

"Something stinks in here," Jamie remarked.

"Yeah," sniggered his second banana, "maybe somebody took a dump."

"Was it you, Barnes?" Jamie leered at the boy beside him.

This was Marcus Barnes who was in Chloe's class. He was half-black, one of only a sprinkling of non-lily-white faces at The School. He had delicate, high-boned features and a near-genius I.Q.—I had once heard him use the word "ineluctable" in a sentence. This time he employed a more succinct vocabulary. "Drop dead," he declared emphatically.

"Who's gonna make me?" taunted Jamie.

An indefinable look clouded Marcus's eyes. He gave a quick hunch of one shoulder and lifted his head to the older boy. Jamie gave a nervous glance back at his bodyguard.

"Let's all just settle down," I said, hoping to assert the authority I didn't quite feel. I regretted not having sent in Dr. Luchstein to "sensitize" the group to my current fragile state of mind. I stood surveying them a moment. The new plaid-jacketed uniforms had a weirdly parochial school look to them. I had gone to a Catholic school up to fifth grade, before my mother had been run over while crossing an icy road and my father began swinging between a manic pantheism and a depressive atheism; and now I had a sudden and eerie flashback to the chalky, dun-painted classrooms of Our Lady of Mercy in Six Elms, Minnesota.

But none of my fellow students back then had had three nannies to attend to them—daytime, nighttime and assistant—like little Nicola Graff now fidgeting in her seat in front of me. And none as far as I'd known had miniature castles built for their ninth birthday, complete with moat and remote-control-operated drawbridge, like Jonathan Schwickly, who was chewing on his knuckles at a back table. And though my best friend at the time, Margaret Gutreicher, had been second runner-up for Little Miss Smile Emerson County, it scarcely rivaled the worldwide celebrity of Jamie Alston.

The illusion abruptly vanished.

"Okay," I said briskly, "now you all know this is an animation workshop since that's what you all signed up for." Duh. Brilliant opening. I added hurriedly, "Can anybody tell me what the word 'animate' actually means?"

There was fidgety silence, punctuated by a sniffle coming from eight-year-old Dana Rich, whom I knew from Chloe's car pool and who suffered from epic hay fever. Then Marcus Barnes's soft voice piped up. "It means, like, to make something come alive."

"That's right! And how can we tell if something's alive or not?"

"If it moves?" proposed a freckled girl.

"Yeah, when it moves on its own. When it walks and talks and runs and does push-ups."

"When it farts." Thus spake Kerrin Granger. He shot a sidelong glance at his hero, Jamie, to see if this *mot* met approval. But Jamie appeared too preoccupied in gouging the soft wood of the table with his fingernails to have even noticed.

I decided that ignoring Kerrin was my best defense. I launched into a brief spiel about the process of making a drawn object appear to sing and dance. I'd made up a flip book for demonstration purposes. I squeezed between Dana Rich and the freckled-faced girl and set the book down in the middle of the table. "See, on the first page I've drawn Harrison the Frog." It was a character from the Amerinda series, a somewhat foppish amphibian in spats and top hat. A couple of the younger kids bobbed their heads in recognition.

"Now look on the next page," I continued. "It's Harrison again, but this time he's a little different. One of his hands is raised a little higher and he's bending a little forward. And on the page after that . . . see, his hand's up even more and his head is down even lower. Now look what happens when I flip all the pages quickly."

With a kind of ta da! flourish, I fluttered the pages: The animated Harrison doffed his top hat and took a comic bow. There were several squeals of delight matched by a prolonged sniffle of approval from little Dana.

"That is so lame," pronounced The Dreaded Spawn of Satan. He teetered his chair back onto its two rear legs and crossed his arms in a posture of almost cosmic boredom. "The last movie I did they animated a whole alien planet, cities and beaches and spaceports, and they put me right in the middle of it. Besides, you gotta be brain dead if you don't know it's all done on computer now."

"In our next session, I'll bring in my software and we'll work directly on computer," I said. "And then we can whip up entire galaxies if we want to. But in this session we're starting from basics. So please quit making rude and disruptive comments, Jamie, or you'll have to leave the workshop."

"Please quit making rude and disruptive comments," Jamie repeated, "or you'll have to leave the workshop."

It was a superbly professional mimicking of my voice, right down to the rather squeaking rise of inflection I acquire when I'm agitated. As I stared at him, he teetered his chair back again and hit me with an insolent I-dare-you-to-do-something grin.

Kerrin had turned almost purple with excitement. The rest of the class was tensely silent, waiting for my reaction. I wondered what would happen if I hauled off and smacked Jamie Alston's famous apple cheek, whether I'd be sued for assault by his mother, agent and president of his fan club, or whether Baldy the Bodyguard would simply rough me up on the spot . . .

I was saved by the bell.

Literally. An ear-splitting clanging noise suddenly shattered the air, making us all flinch and nearly causing Jamie to totter over backward in his tilted chair. It was the fire alarm. The School had lately been plagued with a rash of mysteriously set blazes. The last had been kindled in the faux Gothic assembly hall: Only by the chance fact of two fifteen-year-olds sneaking into the empty building for a brief makeout session had the fire been detected early enough to be put out before the building and possibly the entire campus had burned to the ground.

"Okay, gang, you all know the procedure," I shouted. "Everybody double file. And walk briskly, don't run."

Fire being always a cardinal hazard in Southern California, Windermere rigorously trained its student body to be prepared. The kids had already popped to their feet and were efficiently forming pairs. The bodyguard hustled Jamie out the door, no doubt prepared to use himself as a human shield against any encountered inferno. Kerrin Granger jostled past several bodies to scramble after them. The rest of us trooped into the hall and joined the stream of other double-filed classes stepping lively to the emergency exit. There were no flames that I could see, nor any detectable whiff of smoke in the air.

The heavy fire doors opened onto the edge of the soccer field: middle school players in crimson-and-blue jerseys froze in midplay postures, indignant at having their game overrun by their punier classmates. Nearby me, a teacher stood watching the disrupted match. It was Paul Lynch who taught middle school history, a handsome, soft-spoken man with a talent for making Napoleonic Wars and English royal successions as exciting as any action flick. He was one of the most popular teachers at The School. The fact that he was also openly gay was, I suppose, a testimony to our liberalness.

I moved toward him. He greeted me with a wry smile. "So where was the fire set this time?" I asked.

"There isn't any. It's just a drill. We're going to be enjoying a lot of them, thanks to our industrious little firebug."

"Do they have any leads yet on who it is?"

"No, except it's obviously an insider. A disgruntled janitor or some underpaid teacher's aide. Or maybe it's some maladjusted student." His smile tightened with irony. "This school's been known to have one or two screwed-up kids."

My eyes fell involuntarily on Jamie Alston. He stood at an imperial remove from the rest of the crowd, his bodyguard seeming to act as a barrier even to the faithful Kerrin who skulked nearby. "There's a kid who qualifies brilliantly in the screwed-up category," I remarked.

"Who, Jamie? Yeah, big time," Paul agreed. "But he didn't use to."

"I suppose he couldn't have been a totally hateful infant."

He gave a light laugh. "I'm talking just three years ago. I was a tutor for the kids in the cast of his first movie. It was a horrendous job—trying to cram some education into little heads that were already swelled to the bursting point with all the attention they were getting. Except for Jamie. He was eight then, the sweetest-tempered kid imaginable."

I made a face of disbelief.

"Believe it or not. As an actor, he was a dream. Learned his lines at a glance, took direction like a trooper. And during lessons, he was as attentive as a kid can be after a couple of grueling hours under hot lights."

"So what happened? Did he get replaced by his evil twin?"

"Uh-uh, it's still him. But what happened is he got famous and started to bring in the big paychecks. Those hillbilly parents of his realized he was their ticket out of a life of drudgery. Once a child's got to support his own parents, he gets pretty warped."

"I can imagine." I shuddered at the concept.

"I've told the administration I won't have him in my class. Not after what happened at his last school."

"What was that?"

"He kicked a gym teacher in the nuts. Afterward, Jamie said the man had tried to touch his penis and he was just defending himself. But this teacher had been at the school for twenty-five years with never a complaint. And other students reported that Jamie had it in for the guy because he gave him no preferential treatment—just made him get out on the soccer field and take his knocks with the rest of his classmates. There were lawsuits threatened on both sides. Then it was decided that young Mr. Alston would just withdraw from the institution and it was let go at that." Paul smiled grimly. "My advice is, if you've got to be around him, watch your private parts."

"Gee, thanks," I said.

Paul smiled again, this time a bit uncertainly. "Listen, I'm glad I've run into you. I wonder if I could talk to you a sec about Brandon McKenna?"

The picture I'd momentarily managed to drive from my mind, that grisly crater in place of Brandon's face, flashed vividly back.

"I'm really sorry," Paul said, seeing me wince. "I'm in quite a lot of pain about it too."

"I didn't know you even knew him."

"Well, yes. We were seeing each other."

"Seeing each other?"

"We'd had a couple of dates. In fact, we were planning to go out again that very night." Paul's voice broke. "I was becoming very fond of him, and I'm pretty sure it was reciprocated. Physically we were a great match, but it was more than that, we had acres of things in common. Didn't he tell you?"

I was too stunned to immediately reply. I just stared blankly, trying to process this information. Brandon McKenna was gay. The man I'd lost my virginity to. The one I'd been flaunting myself at the past few months. I thought with mortification of my ridiculous notion that he'd been equally lusting after me.

I wondered how Paul Lynch would react if I suddenly just sat down on the grass and cradled my knees to my chest.

"Are you okay?" he was asking.

"Yeah," I managed. "It's just that his death was such a shock. But no, he didn't confide in me about your, um, relationship."

"I'm not surprised. He was very concerned about being discreet, at least till we knew for a fact we were committed." Paul's lips trembled as he struggled to control his emotions. "Which is why I debated so long about talking to the police."

I looked up with surprise. "The police called you?"

"No, I called *them*. I was going to report something I thought might have been significant. They put me through to the officer in charge of the case, a somewhat gruff-sounding man with an Italian name . . ."

"Detective Langocetti?"

"That sounds right. He told me they'd arrested the men who killed him. I've always considered myself a liberal person, always anti–death penalty. But I have to confess that when I think of how these monsters just cold-bloodedly took Brandon's life, I find myself thinking . . ." He lifted a slender hand to his eye and brushed away a tear.

"I know," I said, "it's hard not to want some kind of revenge." For a moment we both stood silently contemplating just what forms of exquisite torture might suitably avenge Brandon's death.

"What was it you were going to tell the cops?" I asked abruptly.

"Oh, it was about something that happened the last time I saw Bran. The day before he died. It was probably nothing."

"Tell me."

"Well . . . classes were just letting out and the kids were all racing out to their car pools. I saw Brandon waiting in his car, your Volvo wagon, so I went over to chat. We made a date for the following night, I had tickets to *Traviata* and Bran said okay, though he wasn't much of an opera buff, Ella Fitzgerald was more his cup of tea. We were talking about what time we'd meet, when suddenly he went white as a sheet. He was looking into the crowd of all the kids and moms and nannies, but it was if he was suddenly seeing Godzilla stomping toward him. I said 'Brandon, what's wrong?' But then your daughter and another little girl climbed into the car. And he just kind of spat out, 'See you later' and next thing I knew he was taking off." He paused a moment, collecting himself. "I was so furious when I didn't hear from him the next day."

I felt a terrible chill. I was certain there could only be one reason for Brandon to have reacted like that—he had seen the child who had pushed the woman in Blahnik platform shoes to her death.

Which meant that one of Chloe's schoolmates was a killer kid.

My face had no doubt blanched the same color of bed linen that Brandon's had, since Paul was eyeing me in a distinctly startled way. I wondered if I should fill him in on my discovery of the murder-on-tape. But then the fire alarm started clanging again, signaling the end of the drill.

"Time to get back to class," Paul said. "Thanks for hearing me out, Lucy. I think I just needed somebody to know about Brandon and me."

Then he was rounding up his students and my own little group was flocking around me, and whatever opportunity I'd had to share my suspicions with him was gone.

I shepherded my group back into the art studies classroom. We seemed to have lost both The Dreaded Spawn of Satan and his sneering sidekick.

"Jamie's not coming back in," Marcus Barnes reported. "His bodyguard was concerned about smoke inhalation. He didn't seem to believe it was only a drill. And Kerrin's staying with them."

"Fine," I said with some relief.

Without the two, the workshop became fun. I gave each of the remaining children a simple line drawing of a cat overlaid with tracing paper, then had them trace the cat with a slight variation of its tail—so that when they flipped the two pages back and forth, the tail twitched. Finally I distributed blank flip books, instructing them to try their own animations as homework. "You can either start with my cat or come up with an original drawing of your own," I told them.

Then more bells, this time pealing out the tune of the old English rhyme: *Oranges and lemons, Say the bells of St. Clement's . . .*, the announcement that school was out for the day. The kids snatched up their flip books and charged out. I followed at a more leisurely pace to the front entrance, where a line of luxury vehicles snaked a quarter mile back from the gates.

When will you pay me, Say the bells of Old Bailey . . .

I stopped walking suddenly. Three days ago, Brandon had been at this same place at exactly this time—and he had seen something, or more likely someone, who had scared him to his marrow. I gazed out over the scene, trying to determine what it might have been. There was the unremarkable herd of plaid-blazered kids stampeding to their rides. And behind the wheels of the cars, the usual bored, frosty-haired moms taking swigs from sports-capped bottles of Vittel water; the Latina housekeepers bouncing to salsa on KMEX; European nannies and au pairs checking their mascara in rearview mirrors; the occasional dad thumbing through a script or surreptitiously copping glances at the au pairs . . .

None of whom seemed a likely candidate for cold-blooded murder.

In front of me, a Land Rover with a full contingent of eight-year-olds pulled away and a Rolls-Royce Silver Cloud glided into its place. It was driven by a chauffeur in a snappy cap, which was unusual—even the richest moguls among us usually avoided such Old Money ostentation.

The rear window whirred down, revealing a woman in her late thirties. She had a pale, querulous face, with pink-rimmed eyelids and long, ironed-looking hair that seemed to have faded to its present Dust Bowl brown from a more vivacious color. This was Myra Alston, mother of kid superstar Jamie Alston and, despite her post-hippie appearance, generally acknowledged as the hustling force behind his career.

I had actually known Myra years ago in New York. During my last year at film school, I had waitressed at an East Village dive called The Panic Café. My fellow waitress was Myra Brecker, a high school dropout from one of the bleaker towns of New Jersey, whose conversation had consisted solely of detailing her grievances against her landlord, her employer, all boutique clerks and an upstairs neighbor with a hacking cough. She had a snaggle-toothed, Fonzi-haired boyfriend named Randy Alston who sporadically drove a cab and who, three or four nights a week, dropped by the café for a bite of din-din, always ordering the skirt steak, medium rare, with shoestring potatoes. When the owner caught on to the fact that no check was ever presented with the order, Myra was given the immediate sack. I expected never to see or hear about either of them again.

But after Jamie Alston's first movie shot him into overnight-sensation status, there were my old acquaintances, suddenly become fixtures in the popular press—Myra still looking like a latter-day flower child with a temperamental stomach, Randy still rapacious of eye and in need of a good orthodontist.

And lately the Alstons had been scoring frequent cover space on every supermarket tabloid, due to the fact that they were in the throes of a savage divorce. The headlines screamed their respective points of view:

Myra: He's a tyrant when he's drunk!
Randy: She's so hard you could strike matches on her!

Both repeatedly stated that they absolutely, positively refused to even set foot in the same city as the other. Myra had staked out L.A. as her turf, while Randy held court in New York.

Myra's sharp little eyes now fell on me. No recognition—apparently she'd chosen to forget our earlier hash-slinging acquaintance. Then Jamie suddenly materialized on the opposite side of the Rolls, with his bald bodyguard in tow.

"This school bites even worse than St. Matthew's," I heard him proclaim as he scrambled in beside his mom.

Myra's window whirred back up, obscuring the Mother and Child Reunion from my view, and the silver car glided off.

I wandered onto the parking lot, retrieved my own car and headed for home. My thoughts were aswirl with the astonishing information I'd gleaned in the past hour—that a prepubescent killer might be stalking the halls of Windermere Academy; that someone related to that minikiller might have blown away Brandon McKenna; and that Brandon and Paul Lynch had been a two-on-the-aisle item. On automatic pilot, I glided into my garage, got out and opened the service door into the kitchen . . .

And then I dropped my purse and gave a shriek.

Brandon McKenna was standing at the wide-open refrigerator, chugging from a bottle of organic Cranapple juice.

7

Though his back was turned toward me, I was absolutely certain it was Brandon: there was his lanky, broad-shouldered frame; his small, neat ears; his way of slightly tilting his fair-haired head, as if somewhat puzzled by the proceedings at hand.

Except that the process of dying and being reborn seemed to have had a curious effect on his sense of style. He was now sporting a stay-pressed tan suit with tan moccasins and patterned yellow and green socks. It seemed the outfit of choice of, say, a rather jaunty term-life insurance salesman from Kansas City—a far cry from Brandon's old leather jackets and faded jeans. Plus somewhere in the afterlife he had managed to acquire a truly bad haircut, roughly shorn on the sides and cresting to a kind of Tweetie Bird peak on top.

He lowered the bottle and turned to me. He seemed to have also sprouted a furry blond mustache of the sort favored by cops and firemen in the early eighties.

"Hi there," he said. "Sorry if I gave you a scare."

The voice was that of a stranger, a flat Midwestern twang. The round, pale blue eyes fixed on me were also a stranger's.

"Who are you?" I asked weakly.

"Richard P. McKenna. You must be Lucy." He stuck out a hand, long and bony-fingered like Brandon's, but dominated by a very un-Brandonlike high school class ring. "Pleased to meet you. Your maid let us in, said we could go ahead and help ourselves to something cool from the icebox."

In a daze, I let him pump my hand. "I'm sorry, I just don't understand."

"I should've said right away. I'm Brandon's brother. I'm here with the missus, we got into Los Angeles this morning and made arrangements to pick up the body. And now we're here to collect his effects. The police gave us the go-ahead, and like I said, your maid let us in."

"Brandon didn't have any brothers," I said.

"I beg to differ. Four brothers and two sisters. He was the baby of us seven. I'm a year older, but everyone always said how there was a pretty strong resemblance between us. I suppose he told you something different? Which story did he give you, the one about the orphanage in Sioux Falls?" Richard McKenna gave a grim chortle. "Bran didn't like to be lumped in with the rest of us. We were a good deal too square for his tastes. But the fact of the matter is there's a whole clan of us McKennas in Lincoln, Nebraska. Including, I might add, eleven little nieces and nephews who'd of sure liked to have known their Uncle Brandon."

I sank onto a stool at the breakfast bar. At this point, if I had found out that Brandon McKenna had actually been a purple-clawed crustacean from the planet Rigel 4, I wouldn't have been overwhelmingly surprised. A wave of my strike-at-anytime morning sickness begin to undulate up from my stomach and I reached for a box of Stoned Wheat Thins to counteract it.

As I munched a dry, salty wafer, Richard P. McKenna began nosing around the kitchen. Poking his head in the oven door. Lifting the griddle top of the stove. Smoothing a palm down the stainless steel face of the refrigerator. "You've got some nice goods here," he remarked. "I'm in appliances myself. Wholesale. I used to tell Bran that when he finally settled down, got a house and family of his own, I'd fix him up with top of the line. Whirlpool. Amana. All at cost."

"Brandon wasn't the settling down type," I said, through a mouthful of cracker. I had a sudden vision of him setting up housekeeping with Paul Lynch, a little Craftsman cottage in Mar Vista with a date palm on the lawn. I wondered if his brother would have been still willing to ante up the kitchenware. "Were you in touch with him recently?" I asked.

"Recently, nah. Last time I laid eyes on him was three years ago. He actually paid us a visit, which was a rarity. Naturally it turned out he wanted something."

He was interrupted by the appearance of a tiny woman in a canary-colored jogging suit. Fittingly, she also had a canarylike face, all beaky nose and peering bright black eyes. Over one thin shoulder was slung a soiled canvas dufflebag that I recognized with a pang as having been Brandon's.

"That room looks like it's already been stripped," she pronounced in a peevish twitter. She broke off at the sight of me, cocking her head to fix me with a suspicious glare.

"Sharie, hon, this is Lucy, the lady of the house," Richard said nervously. "I told her as how we were here to pick up Brandon's stuff."

"Where's the rest of it?" Sharie demanded. "There's hardly anything in that room upstairs."

"Brandon traveled pretty light," I said. "He didn't like to be weighed down by possessions." It seemed that lately I was spending a lot of time apologizing for Brandon's deficient consumerism.

"I find it difficult to believe he traveled that light," his sister-in-law sniffed. "Just some ratty old clothes and an outdated computer?"

"What are you saying?" I shot back. "Do you think my husband

and I pawned all his valuables? Or maybe you think we've got them buried about the property till the heat's off?"

The tiny woman gave a slit-eyed look as if she were actually entertaining the possibility. "I suppose it wasn't you," she muttered, "but maybe that maid of yours helped herself . . ."

"If you say one more word against Graciela, you're leaving this house immediately!" I shouted. "She wouldn't steal a rotten apple from a tree even if she was starving to death!"

I had leaped off my stool in a way that must have been extremely threatening: Sharie backed up, cringing, against the dishwasher. "Awright, I'm sure I can take your word on that," she twittered. "But we flew down here from Lincoln at a considerable expense to ourselves, you know. And we've hardly had sight nor sound of Brandon since the time he borrowed four thousand dollars from Rich. We've got three kids, you know, you can't blame us for wanting to see that money back." She aimed an accusing look at her husband. "Of course I wouldn't have agreed to the loan in the first place, if I'd of been consulted. Which I was not."

"Is that why Brandon came to see you three years ago?" I asked his brother. "To hit you up for a loan?"

"Yeah, he needed help financing this movie he was going to make." Richard glanced fearfully at his spouse. "It sounded like a pretty good idea at the time. You know you're always hearing about these movies that get made for practically nothing and then they end up making millions."

His wife issued an eloquent snort. "You, Mr. Big Time Hollywood."

"It wasn't just about me getting rich," Richard went on sullenly. "It was more about helping out Brandon. I'd advanced him before. Nothing on that scale, a couple hundred at a time. He always paid back right on time, plus threw in a little kicker for interest even though I didn't ask. But this time, after taking the four thou he just kind of vanished into thin air. Practically the next time we heard anything was when we got the call from the cops down here."

I nodded, more to myself than the McKennas. It confirmed my belief that Brandon had been hiding out for the past two or three years. He didn't even feel safe enough to contact his family. "The movie he wanted to make," I said. "What was it going to be about?"

"It wasn't even a real movie," Sharie said sourly. "It was just one of those old documentaries of his." She zinged another of her *j'accuse!* glances at her husband. "I'd sincerely like to know how many documentaries you heard about raking in all those millions?"

"Did he tell you what it was going to be about?" I repeated.

Richard shrugged. "Some kind of thing about kids in show business. Brandon seemed to think it was a pretty hot topic. He got really worked up about the way these stage mothers will do anything to get their kids ahead, and well . . ." He shrugged again, more despondently. "It sounded like a good idea when he was talking about it."

Another snort from his devoted wife.

"Did he give you any more details?" I pressed on. "Like what kids he was going to document or where he was going to start?"

Richard shook his head. "I got one card from New York City saying everything was hunky-dory. No return address or phone number. Then that was that."

"And that was the end of four thousand of our hard-earned dollars," sniffed Sharie.

I decided to brighten her day. "You should be getting some of that back. If you look in that old leather jacket up in Brandon's closet, you'll see the lining's stuffed with money. At least a thousand dollars, probably a lot more."

The McKennas looked at me warily, as if I might be having some big city fun at the yokels' expense.

"It's where he kept his money," I explained. "You know, the way some people stuff it in a mattress."

The two exchanged glances. "Guess we better take a look, huh?" Richard said to his wife. Without further ado, she led the charge back upstairs to collect the loot.

The second they were out of sight, I yanked open a drawer

crammed with hodgepodge, rummaged for Terry Shoe's card and dialed her pager number. Graciela appeared hesitantly in the hallway. I assured her it was perfectly okay to have let in these people, unpleasant though they had proved to be. Then the phone rang. "Shoe," Terry's voice said tersely.

"It's me, Lucy Freers," I hissed. "I've got some information I think is relevant."

"Relevant to what?"

"To everything. The videotape and Brandon's death. I'm positive now they're very much connected."

"Hold on." There was static, then dead air, then Terry came back on a crackling connection. "Sorry about that. I'm out in the field."

"On a murder scene?"

"Don't think so. Elderly gentleman DOA, been dead for about three days on his living room sofa. My guess is probably a heart attack. A neighbor called the police to complain about his dog barking night and day. Welsh corgi." She paused, then added, "It had eaten part of the DOA's left thigh."

I could think of no suitable comment to this newsy item and merely said, "Oh."

Crackle-urp went the radio. "So what's this information that can't wait?"

"Brandon McKenna's brother is here, come to pick up Brandon's personal effects. He told me that Brandon had been working on a documentary about the world of child actors, which makes perfect sense. I'd had a strong feeling that video was made at a casting call."

"What, like an audition? For a movie or something?"

"Could be a movie. Or for a commercial or a play. It could be amateur, like for some school play. Though that woman looked pretty snazzily dressed for a teacher's salary. I think she was a professional casting director."

Terry gave a grunt. "That's fine, but there've been a lot of casting calls in this country over the past few years."

"I've got a strong hunch it was in New York City. That's the last place Brandon's brother heard from him, nearly three years ago, after which he just dropped out of sight."

There was a commotion in the background of the radio, voices, a sharp laugh and the yap-yap of a dog, presumably the snacking corgi. "I've gotta attend to this," Terry said. "I'll be back in the station in about an hour. Tell you what, I'll make some calls to New York. If I get anything, I'll let you know."

Her line went dead. I got busy downing my daily pharmacopoeia of pregnancy-formulated vitamins, minerals and herbs. Then I force fed Rollins the parrot his antibiotic pellet, put some romaine in the hamster's cage, carrots in the rabbits' and fresh water in the chinchilla's, removed a packet of frozen baby rats from the Sub-Zero to thaw for Ratty the spangled red rat snake's supper. I was opening a can of Fancy Feast salmon dinner, while the two cats, Howard and Furball, twisted around my ankles, when the McKennas trooped back into the kitchen.

"We found two thousand eight hundred and twenty-four dollars," Richard crowed.

"And there was a pretty decent watch in one of the pockets," put in Sharie. She now looked like a canary that had swallowed a vulture.

"What do you plan to do with the body?" I asked.

They looked puzzled, as if they'd momentarily forgotten the source of this windfall.

"The family all chipped in to bring him back to Lincoln," Richard said, pulling a solemn face. "We'll give him a darned right decent burial."

Poor Brandon! I thought. Ending up right back in the bosom of the family he'd tried so energetically to shuck off.

The McKennas finished loading up their rental car with the gleanings from his room. Richard presented me with a dun-colored business card, cozily assuring me that if I ever needed anything in the "appliance line" he could get it for me wholesale. With profound relief, I watched them sail out of my life.

I was suddenly exhausted. I staggered upstairs, collapsed on my bed and fell instantly unconscious. I dreamed I was taking a shower with Brandon, my wet skin slithering erotically against his. Then Paul Lynch was pressing his face against the streaming glass of the stall, contorting it like a stretched rubber mask. "You're out of shampoo again," he clucked. "Such filthy habits." I wanted Brandon to defend me, but when I looked back at him, the water was melting him away like the Wicked Witch of the West. The imagery was so obvious that even my former Jungian shrink, Dr. Postro, who reveled in dream interpretation, would have scoffed at wasting valuable session time on it.

Still, it left me when I woke up with a residue of arousal mixed with guilt, which I was still trying to shake off when the phone rang. Terry Shoe had been speaking for several moments before I focused on what she was saying.

". . . talking to a captain of one of the downtown precincts. Guy named Merle Washington. He IDed the case right away. Said two years ago last November, day after Thanksgiving, they had a DOA, a woman who took a fall down stairs at a casting call and sustained a fatal head injury. According to Washington, it was at an audition for kids to star in a movie version of that musical *Orphans*. I saw that show when it played here," Terry added. "Had some terrific tunes. But I never heard of any movie coming out."

"It never got made," I said. The cottony residue of sleep was finally beginning to clear from my head. "I remember reading about it in *Variety*. The studio decided it would be too expensive to produce and pulled the plug on it. So who was the woman who died?"

"Her name was Korshalek. Joyce Korshalek. Washington said she had something to do with the casting company."

"Did he say where the audition was held?"

"Yeah, in a loft in that downtown warehouse district, what's it called, Treblinka?"

"Tribeca," I corrected. "Treblinka was a Nazi death camp."

"Oh, yeah, you're right. Tribeca. Anyhow, the death was termed accidental and the case was closed."

"But now that there's evidence that it wasn't accidental, it obviously has to be opened again," I said.

"You're assuming that it *is* the same case—which we still don't know for a fact. All I can do is send the tape on to the NYPD. It's their jurisdiction, so it's their call whether they want to pursue it or not."

"They've *got* to pursue it," I waited. "I'm positive this is what got Brandon killed." I curled my legs under me and pressed the phone more tightly to my ear. "Listen, I know what stage parents are like. There's a whole clique of them at Windermere. They're like fanatics when it comes to their ambitions for their kids."

"So?"

"So think about it. You've got a parent, probably a mother, with nothing much going in her own life. So she focuses all her hopes and dreams, all her ambitions, on making her kid a star. Then, oops! the kid kills a casting director—that's a really bad career move. Even if it's found to have been just a playful accident, it's still not going to make this child wildly popular at future auditions. So this mom or dad will go to extreme lengths to keep their budding star from being exposed. And that could well include bumping off any inconvenient witnesses."

I expected some squelching remark from Terry. To my surprise, she gave a thoughtful grunt.

Since I was already out on a limb, I decided to climb all the way to the shakiest branch. "And I've got reason to believe that the child in the videotape goes to Windermere," I declared.

"Why?"

I described my conversation with Paul Lynch, tactfully leaving out details of the burgeoning relationship between the two men.

There was a moment of silence on Terry's end. "Not a hell of a lot to hang a hat on," she said at last. "I've got an uncle who's deathly afraid of wasps. When he sees a yellow jacket, he goes into a panic. Or maybe McKenna wasn't looking at anything at all. Maybe some awful thought just crossed his mind—like he forgot to turn the iron off before he left home."

"Except for one thing. Chloe told us that when she got in the car right after that, Brandon put on a hat and dark glasses. He said it was a disguise so the bad people wouldn't recognize him."

Another thinking-it-over pause. "There's still nothing I can do," Terry declared. "Except tell you to keep your eyes and ears open. If you get anything more, let me know."

I was thunderstruck. This from Terry Shoe, whose twin mantras were "Keep your nose where it belongs" and "Stop trying to do my job"?

"Are you actually giving me the okay to investigate?" I asked.

"I'm absolutely not giving you the okay," she snapped. "But knowing you, you're gonna plunge right ahead and do it anyway. So you might as well keep me up to date. By the way, elderberry tea."

"Huh?"

"It's supposed to be terrific for morning sickness." On this mid-wifey note, she hung up.

8

When you're married to a movie producer, you spend a lot of time sleeping alone.

Since hitting the big time, Kit was forever zipping off to meetings with fellow moguls in New York or Sydney or London, or else spending months at a time on exotic location sets. I, on the other hand, shuttled glamorously in and out of my home studio while holding down the home front: taking car pool, arranging termite control, battling rust on the roses and blight in the bougainvillea, hunting up an electrician who might conceivably show up at an appointed hour and day.

When we had first moved into this sprawling house, I had been rather scared to be by myself at night. But by now I was well familiar with its myriad of noises: the creaks and complaints of the joints and floorboards, the restless rustling of eucalyptus and acacia outside the bedroom, the occasional slam of a downstairs door or casement window in a gust of wind, the various scratchings and slitherings and meowings of Chloe's menagerie. And so at the moment it was not the unfamiliarity of finding myself solo in bed that kept me tossing fretfully all night, but the turmoil of my thoughts. At dawn I finally dragged myself up, padded downstairs and, having no convenient access to elderberry tea, sat slumped over a cup of Sleepytime. I began reviewing everything I'd learned so far about Brandon and the possible circumstances of his death.

Over and over, I revolved the notion that he had seen the killer child in my videotape at Windermere's gates—a kid who had possibly been at the audition for *Orphans*. Which hardly narrowed it down. At a school so steeped in show business as Windermere Academy, ninety percent of the kids had at least flirted with becoming actors at one point or another—casting calls were actually posted in the weekly school bulletin. Even Chloe had contracted the performing bug a couple of years back, coming home one day with the news that her ex-best friend Alwyn Rossner was going to be in an episode of *Home Improvement* and now thought she was so totally cool, and that *she* wanted to start trying out for things too. Kit had obligingly finagled a tiny part for her in a buddy's film. To my profound relief, after one day's work she had pronounced it "Bor-ing!" and spent the rest of her time on the set pestering the horse wrangler.

Okay, so looking for kids who'd ever been to a casting call would get me to nowheresville. How about the fact that the *Orphans* audition had been held in New York? Would that highlight any suspects?

Probably not. Lots of major children's casting calls were held in the Big Apple, particularly when producers wanted to attract more offbeat, and therefore supposedly "real-looking," kids. Besides, the families of Windermere students traveled extensively, particularly to the opposite coast: New York City was practically just another exit of the Ventura Freeway. Any of them could have made a visit to Manhattan that Thanksgiving.

My attention wandered to a tiny green spider as it scuttled to the edge of the table, then rappelled down the leg. It vanished, and my thoughts sluggishly returned to the problem at hand. Okay, I asked myself, so how could I narrow the field? I could hang around the Windermere campus, collaring kids as they passed and grilling them on whether they'd ever auditioned for *Orphans* or knew of any of their friends who had . . .

Or I could broadcast the same query over the parents grapevine . . .

Yeah, right. I could also just hang a sign on my back saying, *"Shoot Me, I Know Too Much."*

Okay then, what about a more subtle approach? What if I could obtain a list of all the kids who had showed up at the audition from whatever casting company had run it? I could then compare it to The School's student roster. But how would I go about getting such a list?

How about through another casting director?

The name Andrew Oberest wafted into my mind, at just about the same time a billow of sleepiness wafted through my body. I got to my feet, tottered back upstairs and this time fell into a deep sleep.

When I woke up, Andy Oberest's name popped immediately back to me. For a run of several decades, he had been among the top five casting directors in Hollywood. There was no disputing the fact that he possessed an amazing talent for matching a face to a role, for finding the actor or actress with the perfect idiosyncratic tic that made an otherwise insignificant part suddenly leap off the screen. At least a dozen stars owed their discovery to Andy's slotting them as junkies or society hookers, as gay best friends or stuttering losers—offbeat but vivid roles in which their talents and looks had been given an opportunity to shine.

Andy also had another invaluable asset—a seemingly supernatural memory. After one glance at a glossy of a craggy-faced fellow with a mole above the right brow, seven months later Andy could not only conjure up the face, but also the actor's name, his agent and the fact that his credits included Shakespeare in the Park, a Tums ad and the role of Second Klingon in *Star Trek III*.

But Andrew Oberest also had a sizable flaw—he happened to

believe that the old-time Hollywood tradition of the casting couch was still alive and well and at his disposal. For most of his career, he had freely propositioned the more physically gifted of the many starlets who had sashayed in and out of his office. For some time, none of these Julia Roberts wannabes had complained. Then a couple of years ago, a twenty-two-year-old brunette named Celia Moorhouse had filed a complaint with the Screen Actors Guild, stating that in a call-back interview, Andrew Oberest had double-locked his office door, zipped down his fly and exposed what, according to the complaint, he had referred to as "Action Jackson and the twins." He allegedly proceeded to propose that in return for certain oral services performed by Ms. Moorhouse on said Action Jackson, he could guarantee her a role in the movie. When word of the complaint got out, a sizable number of other actresses weighed in with variations of "the creep pulled the same thing on me," and the studio, having no choice, dismissed Andy from the movie.

Which, needless to say, had a less than salubrious effect on his career. His subsequent slide had been precipitous. No longer did he have swanky offices on the Universal lot; now he worked out of a hole-in-the-wall in a shabby Hollywood complex called Burleigh Studios. No longer did he cast multimillion-dollar Harrison Ford vehicles; daytime soaps were now his bread and butter.

Kit had used Andy's services on one of his earliest pictures, and for a time, Kit and I had been casual pals with Andy and his third wife, Kelly, a rabbity-mouthed blonde who did voice-overs for Huggies commercials. But the movie on which Andy waggled his thing at Celia Moorhouse also happened to be one of Kit's, and it was Kit who was obliged to do the actual firing, effectively ending their friendship.

But he was the only casting director I actually knew. Plus I suspected he had always been fond of me—he'd made a lackadaisical pass when we'd first met, seemed rather relieved when I shot him down, and from then on seemed to single me out at parties, where we'd trade wisecracks about the glamorous mob swirling around us. And after all, I wasn't the one who'd been the messenger of the "You're fired!" tidings. It seemed to me that if I could just see him, I'd be able to get him to talk to me.

There were three things I knew that Andrew Oberest had a passion for. The first being of course bounteously endowed young women. The second was a free meal. The third was the creamed spinach at Musso & Frank. The three together would be an offer he couldn't resist.

I hit the Rolodex on Kit's desk, twirling through names until I found one that fit Category A: Gwen Hauver, a young talent agent with a sultry face and a body that was just a tad overweight in all the right places. Then I rang up Andy's office.

"Oberest Casting, can I help you?" The voice was deepest San Fernando Valley, accompanied by a snap of gum—a long way from the upper-crust British accents that used to answer his phones. I identified myself as Gwen Hauver's assistant. Ms. Hauver wondered if Mr. Oberest would be free for lunch today, to discuss a new actress who would be perfect for *The Young and the Restless*, say Musso's at twelve-thirty? There was a pause, then Ms. Juicy Fruit came back on the line. Mr. Oberest would have to move several things around, snap, twang, but he'd be able to do lunch.

Musso & Frank, established in 1919, is a Hollywood Boulevard landmark, a place where generations of guys named Marty, Manny and Moe have come to satisfy their nostalgia for sand dabs and coleslaw served with attitude by cranky waiters well into their shuffleboard years. It has wood paneling, the kind of red leather booths that seem to cry out for a Rat Pack member, and a menu that apparently hasn't been changed since 1937.

Andy was already ensconced in a corner booth when I arrived, downing a martini with double olives. Lookswise, he was something of a time warp himself—though from an amalgamation of several times: the swinger's-style heavy gold chains that weighed down his neck spoke eloquently of the seventies; his auteur-look black turtleneck harked back to the fifties; and the hairpiece that rested uneasily atop his head was *echt* early Beatles.

He lifted his mop-top as I approached his table and gave a querulous scowl as he recognized me.

"Hi, Andy," I said brightly. "Long time no see." I slid into the booth beside him.

"Hey, I'm expecting someone," he barked.

"Yeah, I know. But Gwen Hauver couldn't make it. She sent me in her place."

"What is this?" He rose truculently, but his pudgy frame wedged between table and booth, making him momentarily captive.

"Look, I'm sorry I tricked you, but I felt I had to," I said, seizing the opportunity. I let my voice falter piteously. "I knew you wouldn't see me if I used my own name, but I really need your help. Please, let me buy you lunch so I can talk to you a little."

In a beseeching gesture, I laid a hand on my chest—a chest which, thanks to pregnancy, now sported a pair of C cups. I had set off my new cleavage with a vintage Diane Von Furstenberg wrap dress. Andy's eyes, naturally protuberant, seemed to pop a little further. "What the hell, I gotta eat," he mumbled and stuffed himself back into his seat.

A septuagenarian in a white apron shuffled toward us and hovered with an irritated air. "I'll have the hearts of lettuce with extra Russian, veal cutlets, side of creamed spinach and a Tanqueray martini, no-make-that-a-double," Andy rattled off. I requested a Cobb salad and a glass of milk. The waiter wrinkled his brow in unconcealed disgust, then shuffled off to the kitchen.

Andy swilled the dregs of his current martini. "How's that *pisher* husband of yours?" he said. "If this is got anything to do with him, you can forget about it."

"It's not about Kit," I said quickly. "It's about a casting call that took place in New York about two and a half years ago. For a movie version of *Orphans*. One of the casting directors had a fatal accident."

Andy peered suspiciously at me over the wide rim of his glass. "Whatcha want to know about that for?"

"You do remember the one I mean?" I said, evading his question.

"If it's the one where Joyce Korshalek took a dive downstairs and whacked herself dead, sure I do."

"How could I get a record of the kids who were there?"

"You can't." He smugly folded a slice of sourdough and slotted it through his lips. "There is no record."

"There would have to be something, wouldn't there? Sign-in sheets, tapes of the auditions themselves . . ."

Andy gave a bread-muffled guffaw. "Yeah, right, all bound in leather and filed in the Library of Congress. You gotta be kidding. If I kept sign-in sheets from every audition I ever held, I'd have to move into Buckingham Palace just to stack them up. And forget about tapes. They cost money, ya know. The production guys use the same ones twenty, thirty times over."

"Oh." I crumbled a crust of rye in disappointment.

"And besides which, nobody was looking to save anything from that particular call. The whole thing was a sham."

My interest perked back up. "What do you mean?"

"A *farcockteh* publicity stunt. The schmucks took out ads for an open call in *Backstage*, saying they wanted fresh faces, come one, come all. They got kids oozing out of the woodwork. There must have been nearly a thousand showed up, pros, amateurs . . . They were raking 'em in from all over the country. And publicitywise, it was a bonanza. Every *pisher* hometown newspaper ran a story about how one of their local-yokel kids was getting a shot at stardom." Another guffaw. "But the fact is they never had any intention of casting even a lousy extra from that zoo."

"How do you know?"

He reached for the fresh cocktail the ancient server plunked in front of him and swilled an eager gulp. "For one thing, I know because it's my business to know. I mean, for Chrissake, you think if they meant real business they would've used Korshalek?"

I reached for my own less-than-intoxicating glass of milk. "So

I take it you're implying that Joyce Korshalek wasn't top drawer."

"Hah, bottom rung. Cheap, yeah. You wanted to save some bucks, you got on the horn to Korshalek. Or if you wanted something done quick and nasty, she was your gal. She didn't waste her time with what you'd call stroking. Weeded out the unsuitables without even giving them a chance to read."

"You mean the kids she thought weren't right for the part."

"I mean any kid she thought wasn't right, period. Look, most of us, when we work with kids, we cut them extra slack. Even if they stink, we tell them they did great, they were fine, yadda yadda. Then later we call the agents, tell 'em their clients didn't make the cut. Not Korshalek. She'd line them up, six, eight in a row, and look 'em over, and then she'd start throwing them out, badda-ding! badda-da! right on the spot. The plug-uglies and the fatties, out. A little kid picks his nose—out. Another kid's trying to pass for eight but she's got breast buds—out. And so on and so forth." Andy paused for another draft of martini.

"That's pretty damned brutal, for a little kid to get rejected like that," I said. "The ones that did must have hated her guts."

"Not to mention the parents. On the circuit, they used to call her The Executioner. At a Korshalek audition, you'd always get a lot of shouting and kvetching and carrying on, people threatening to run her out of the business and the like."

"So there probably weren't rivers of tears shed when she died."

"If you're speaking about among the parents, there was rivers of rejoicing. The Wicked Witch is dead, ding dong." He finished his second drink and signaled to a passing busboy for a refill. "Stage mothers, though. Don't get me started on those babies. You want to know what's my definition of stage parent? It's 'child abuser.' "

"Come on, they're not all that bad."

"Yeah, only about ninety-eight percent of them. I'll give you an example. What's the worst thing that can happen to a kid actor short of dropping dead?"

I dutifully played straight man. "I don't know. What?"

"Puberty. A kid goes into puberty, suddenly your cute little tyke turns into a gawky teenager. You got acne, you got voices changing, you got the little button noses growing into schnozzes. Goodbye cute means good-bye career. How many kid actors you see ever make it as adults? Jodie Foster, that's it. And okay, Ron Howard as a director. The rest get cut loose, probably end up shooting drugs, living a fucked-up life, nothing ever living up to those glorious days when they were snotty little stars."

"Yeah, but puberty's inevitable," I pointed out. "You can't stop it."

"Sure, but these stage moms, when they see it coming, they start to panic and then they start thinking maybe there's something they can do to postpone it. So you get parents talking baby talk to fourteen-year-olds, dressing them like toddlers, practically keeping them in diapers. And did you ever hear about leptin?"

"Who?"

"Not who, what. It's a hormone. There were reports a couple of years ago, some scientific evidence that maybe it was what triggered puberty. So suddenly there's this big antileptin frenzy. You've got all these diets circulating that are supposed to suppress leptin, kids being force-fed strained kale and crap. Then some quack came up with an antileptin injection, and suddenly all these parents are dragging their kids for shots of this shit."

"What?" I burst out, sloshing milk onto my dress. "That's so horrible, I can hardly believe it!"

"Believe it, babe. Some of these moms I've had the pleasure to know, they'd have plutonium shot up the kid's *tuchis* if it meant keeping them working another year or two." Andy gave a grunting laugh. "Not only the moms, but the pops as well. And now you've even got grandmas in there pitching."

We were interrupted by the waiter who began plunking our food onto the table with the same irritable panache with which he had served our drinks. For some moments we were silent, Andy slicing, stabbing and chewing, me surreptitiously dabbing at the blotch of spilled milk on my lap.

"Why do you think the *Orphans* movie never got made?" I said at length. "Do you think it had anything to do with Joyce Korshalek's death?"

"Get real. The death of a nobody never stopped a studio from moving ahead with a project. I'll tell you the reason it was shut down. Two little words: Jamie Alston."

I'd been waiting for a mention of the Dreaded Spawn.

"Jamie caused it to be shut down?"

"Basically. The movie was contingent on him starring. He'd just gotten hot. No Jamie, no deal. Except somewhere down the road, somebody noticed the kid couldn't sing or dance worth a rat's fart. Since they were making a musical, that was seen as something of a problem."

"Not totally. They could have dubbed some other kid's singing voice for his. And he could have faked the dancing—there are some steps so easy that even a lamppost could learn them. It would have been worth it to still have the marquee value of Jamie Alston's name." I offered this wisdom a bit smugly. I hadn't been married to a producer all these years without learning a thing or two.

Andy swiveled his face toward me. There was a dribble of creamed spinach like the first dab of an action painting on the canvas of his chin. "Yeah, well maybe it wasn't worth it enough to deal with Mom and Pop Alston. They're nuts, those two."

"I've heard they're sort of difficult to work with." This was a purposeful understatement. From what I'd heard of the Alstons, it was like saying saber-toothed tigers would be sort of difficult to work with.

"A couple of junkyard dogs," Andy said, trumping my metaphor. "Now they're turning against each other. They're fighting over one big bone—who gets possession of the kid's career." He gave a kind of grunting laugh. "And I can tell you, it's gonna be a fight to the death. Only one of those two are gonna come out alive."

Two killer parents. And if there was ever a killer kid, it seemed to me it was Jamie Alston. "Was Jamie actually at the *Orphans* audition?" I asked eagerly.

"At a *farshtinkener* piece of business like that? Give me a break."

So there vanished that theory. Disgruntled, I returned to picking at my Cobb salad.

"Except now that I think of it," Andy continued, "he was part of the hype. I remember there was something about getting to read with Jamie if a kid made it to the final cut. So maybe he was hanging around at the time. I can't say for absolute sure."

The Dreaded Spawn of Satan immediately shot back to the top of my Suspects Hit Parade. "Do you know of any other local kids who were there?"

Andy shrugged. "If they were in the business two years ago, it's good odds they were. Like I said, it sucked in everybody from all over the country." He narrowed his gin-bleared eyes at me. "What's the big interest in this, anyhow?"

I muttered some barely coherent answer about trying to track down an old friend who was last spotted there, counting on all that Tanqueray Andy had lapped up to make it sound remotely plausible. He seemed to have stopped listening. Instead, he had begun to incline closer to me. His face was in fact now hovering just inches from my cleavage, which I was definitely beginning to regret having flaunted.

"You and me are old friends, aren't we?" he slurred. "You know, I could be a really big help to you."

"Like what, get me a part on *The Young and the Restless*?" I said lightly.

"I know everybody in this business, I could do a lot for your career." He started to kind of fumble at his waist. I had the horrified idea that Action Jackson was about to make a surprise appearance right here in the middle of Musso's, not to mention a cameo by the twins.

"Thanks, but my career's fine the way it is," I blurted and began to signal frantically for the check.

Back home, I raced to the answering machine, hoping to find a message from Kit and Chloe. But the only message was from our next-door neighbor, Dr. Pennislaw, complaining that our eucalyptus trees were dropping gobs of messy sap on his pool house roof and would we please have them cut back. I called the Aspen condo, but as I expected, there was no answer—at this time of day, everyone was naturally out on the slopes.

Though I'd just consumed a sizable Cobb salad, I was ravenous again. I wandered to the refrigerator, inspected the contents, and reached for a bowl of leftover fettucini. As I pulled it out, a sharp pain stung my forearm. "Ouch!" I yelped, dropping the bowl, which shattered on the floor.

Recently, because of what Terry Shoe would call my complete inability to keep my nose where it belonged, I had found myself running for my life from a crazy person firing a snub-nosed pistol. In the process, I had had my elbow bone winged by a bullet. Every so often, if I crooked my arm a certain way, the wound flared up again, which it had now. I stood rubbing the sore spot, noting with regret that the shattered bowl was of the increasingly rare orange Fiesta ware.

And then for some reason Brandon's videotape flashed into my mind. I vividly pictured Joyce Korshalek, aka The Executioner, giving that startled flinch of surprise at the appearance of the urchin-costumed kid behind her. I suddenly knew that something was wrong with that picture.

Or else something was wrong with my interpretation of it.

A surge of nausea racked me, momentarily driving everything else from my attention. I tottered to the sink and had an unpleasant revisit with my Cobb salad. When the nausea subsided, I knelt down to clean up pasta and pottery from the floor. It occurred to me that I was going to give birth in less than five months . . .

And it seemed all I could think about was death.

PART
TWO

9

The Harriet Ho Pregnancy Dynamics Center occupied the floor above a Victorian antiques shop on the Santa Monica shopper's paradise known as Montana Avenue. The Center had a pink-and-gold locker room with mirrors that slimmed and satin-tufted benches, an aromatherapy parlor, and a contingent of masseuses, your choice of facial, foot or full-body. The cost of a low-impact, muscle-toning but fetal-protecting workout was forty-two bucks a session, with all other services extra.

My starstruck mother-in-law Stacey had sent me a gift card of twelve sessions, having no doubt read in *Entertainment Weekly* that the place was chockablock with expecting movie stars and talk show hostesses. I now sat in the glittering locker room, pulling a less than pristine pair of sweat pants over my burgeoning waistline while checking out the other clientele. No famous faces. Just a dozen or so expensively burnished ladies, mostly clad in jewel-colored pregnancy leotards with coordinated leggings. For some baffling reason, most were also in full makeup, with freshly blow-dried coiffeurs, as if they were not about to stretch and sweat for an hour but rather pose for a photo shoot for *Vanity Fair*.

A honey blonde at the locker next to me misted her own perfect hair with a perfumed spray, then turned to me. "Have you reserved your nurse yet?" she asked.

"My nurse?" I responded blankly. For a wild moment, I wondered if the class I was about to take would be so strenuous I'd require medical attention afterward.

"The top-of-the-line baby nurses book up six months in advance," Honey Blonde elaborated. She shot an appraising look at my midriff. "You should start interviewing immediately."

"Don't speak to me about baby nurses!" shrilled a brunette down the row. She was as slender as celery except for what looked like a bowling ball in her tummy. "Mine just canceled, and I'm due in a month. I agreed to her full asking price, twenty-two hundred a week, but she said she had a better offer."

"I know someone paying three thousand a week," put in a voice across the room. "For a Jamaican nurse who had a reference from Meryl Streep."

"They're the worst snobs," pronounced Honey Blonde. "A girl-friend of mine got turned down by her first choice because the woman didn't like her repro furniture, can you believe that?"

There was a general murmur of assent.

"Actually, I don't plan to hire one," I piped up. "It's my second child, so I kind of already know the ropes."

A rather shocked silence filled the room, as if I'd announced my intention to give birth squatting all alone in a field.

"It's my second as well," said the celery-thin woman, "but I can't imagine going through those first few weeks without a trained professional."

"Have you arranged for your breast-feeding consultant yet?" Honey Blonde asked her.

"Yes, I just called the La Leche League about it yesterday."

I sat down on the tufted bench and applied myself to tying my Pumas, while my workout mates continued to compare notes on

the other personnel absolutely essential to childbirth: the gold needle acupuncturist; the technician to test the air in your home for
toxic emissions; the prenatal nutritionist . . . It began to seem extraordinary that some five and a half billion people had managed
to come into the world without benefit of such a comprehensive
support system.

At the dot of four, we filed into our various classrooms. For my
allotted fifty minutes, I leg-lifted, donkey-stretched and pelvic-
tilted to the strains of seventies chart-toppers like Fleetwood Mac.
It was concluded with a three-minute meditation, during which
we were exhorted to "peacefully commune" with our unborns.
Then off to the showers, each of us clutching a vial of a blackthorn
oil imported from Germany and guaranteed by Harriet Ho herself
to minimize stretch marks.

After a tepid douse, I headed back to my locker. I was dutifully
massaging my abdomen with oil while musing on the fact that I
needed to go up a size or possibly three in panties, the waistband
on the bikinis I was wearing being already stretched to the breaking point, when somebody slapped their hands over my eyes.

I let out a sort of yodel and whirled, effecting a quasi-martial
arts defense posture, to face my attacker.

"Jeez Louise, Lucy. I wanted to surprise you, not scare you into
premature birth."

Coolly amused black eyes, smooth brown skin, a pair of bizarro
earrings jangling under a curtain of heavy black hair . . . With a
surge of relief, I realized I was not confronting a hired assassin but
merely my old pal Valerie Jane Ramirez. "Are you okay?" she inquired with a furrowed squint.

"Yeah, fine. I'm just a little jumpy these days."

"I'll say. I thought you were about to knock me flat. Next time
I sneak up on you, I'll come prepared to defend myself."

I grinned, glad to see her. Valerie Jane was a costume designer
of considerable talent. Through her sartorial wizardry, a Danny
DeVito could acquire the regal command of a James Earl Jones,
and the flattest-chested of actresses could appear to flaunt a cleav-

age that would make Melanie Griffith rend her garments in de-
spair. She was rarely between films—I hadn't seen her for almost
a year. She still looked like a gorgeous Olive Oyl, all long, gangly
limbs and droopy skirts—albeit an Olive Oyl who had finally hit
the hay with Popeye.

I did a mental double-take. Why was Valerie Jane in the locker
room of the Pregnancy Dynamics Center looking a good eight
months cooked when she was an open Lesbian in a long-standing
relationship with the French sex symbol and defender of the rain
forest, Jacqueline Legère?

She giggled at my expression. "I guess you're wondering how I
happened to get myself knocked up."

"Well, now that you mention it . . ."

"Artificial insemination. Jacqueline and I decided we wanted to
be parents, so eight months ago I took myself to a sperm bank in
Paris. It actually took three tries, then bingo." She stroked the
huge swell of her belly, the universal gesture of pregnant women.
"I'm due in six weeks."

"That's terrific, congratulations," I said. "Do you know if it's a
boy or girl?"

"No, we want it to be a surprise. I chose a donor who sounded
a lot like Jacqueline. Sandy-blond, green-eyed and athletic. And
a botany student, which is kind of perfect, considering Jackie's
involvement with saving the rain forest. But tell me about you."

"Oh, I just took the more conventional route. I went to bed with
my husband."

Valerie let out a husky laugh. "No really, I want to know how
you are."

"I'm eighteen weeks and they tell me everything's normal. Except that at any minute of the night or day I can have the overcom-
ing urge to toss my cookies." I began to pull on the rest of my
clothes. "What are you doing here, anyway? I thought you were in
Barcelona, getting Brad Pitt dressed to fight the Spanish Civil
War."

"We wrapped last week. Jackie and I both agree the baby should be born in America , since I've got family here who'll want to be around for the event. She'll be over at the end of the month. I was going to call you today anyway. I want to ask you a favor."

"Shoot."

"I wondered if you'd fill in as my Lamaze partner until Jackie got here?"

"I'd be honored," I said, smiling broadly.

"Thanks, that's a real relief. I've been kind of nervous about this whole thing, if you want to know the truth." Valerie slipped her arm through mine, causing the some hundred or so bracelets she was wearing to clatter to her elbow. "Listen, are you busy right now? Why don't we do some shopping. You can tell me the story about why you jumped out of your stockings when I covered your eyes."

"Okay, you're on."

I stuffed my reeking sweats in a carryall and together we sauntered out onto Montana Avenue. If pregnancy had given me the appetite of Henry VIII, it seemed to have instilled in Valerie the shopping habits of Tori Spelling. Between us, we hit every store, me springing for banana frozen yogurt, Mrs. Field's cookies and passion fruit slush while Valerie scooped up picture books and dolphin-and-whale mobiles, hand-spun tiny blankets and hand-crocheted booties in sex-neutral colors like persimmon and jonquil. As our Visa cards flashed, we indulged in a mutual rigors-of-pregnancy kvetch: the heartburn, the leg cramps, the oh-so-attractive sprouting of spider veins.

At last we cruised into a little Provençal café, where I topped off my *grande bouffe* with a *pain au chocolat* and Valerie ordered an orange juice. I filled her in on my recent saga: from the summary execution of Brandon McKenna in Kit's BMW, to my inadvertent premiering of the videotape featuring the murderous *Orphans* auditioner, and my suspicions that the two deaths were related.

It was cathartic to be able to confide in someone I could com-

pletely trust. "If I'm right about all this," I said, licking bitter chocolate off my fingertips, "it means that someone connected with
Windermere Academy killed Brandon."

"Let me get this straight," Valerie said. "You think it was a parent covering up for their kid, who in turn had knocked off the
casting lady."

"I know it sounds unbelievable. I mean, to imagine a little kid
actually murdering somebody. If I hadn't seen it on tape, I'd never
believe it myself."

"Oh, I can believe it," Valerie said sharply. "At least when it
comes to child actors. Some of them are natural-born killers, and
the rest of them learn on the job. I'd rather work with rabid rats."

"They can't all be so depraved. There were a bunch of kids in
Kit's last movie, and they all seemed fairly well adjusted."

"Yeah? Maybe someone was giving them electric shock treat-
ments before they went on the set." Valerie blew a bit of orange
juice foam from the corner of her mouth, then gave a wry laugh.
"Don't mind me, I'm particularly cynical about them at the moment. On my last film, I had a biter."

"What do you mean? A kid bit you?"

"He bit everyone—director, stars, even one of the grips. He was
a regular little snapping turtle. See this scar?" She displayed a thin
brown hand. A mottled half-moon marred the base of the thumb.
"I was trying to fit him for his costume, a darling Eton jacket with
original buttons. Suddenly he was sinking his rotten little teeth
into me!"

"Ouch. Why didn't he get kicked off the film?"

"He did, as soon as he chomped on the director. It was Billy
Granger, one of those five albino Granger boys. Ever run into them?"

"As a matter of fact, yeah. The oldest one, Kerrin, made an appearance at this workshop I'm giving at Windermere. It's not often
I get the urge to garrotte a ten-year-old boy, but I've got to admit
that after five minutes with that one, I was entertaining the
thought."

"You've got plenty of company," Valerie chuckled. "I have to say though that after meeting the father, I can see why those kids are creepy. Seth Granger's a real piece of work."

"So I've heard. Kind of a tyrant about pushing his kids."

"Kind of! Picture Mussolini as a stage parent and you've got the idea. When Billy got fired, Il Duce Granger went storm-trooping in to Ellis, the director, and from all reports tried to do some serious damage to Ellis's testicles. Security had to forcefully remove him from the set, still kicking and screaming." She looked up at me suddenly. "Are you thinking what I'm thinking?"

"A violent daddy, a bunch of dysfunctional kids . . ."

"Sounds like a suspect, doesn't it?"

"What are the odds that at least one of the Granger boys was at the *Orphans* audition?"

"I'd say they were swell," Valerie declared. "But how can we find out for sure? Asking Señor Granger directly might not be too beneficial to our health."

"And I don't think I'd care to pump young Kerrin about it either," I agreed. I propped my elbows on the tiled tabletop. "I need to go to an audition. A major audition, one that would drag in a crowd of professional kids. I could check out who shows up from Windermere and maybe do some subtle inquiring about the *Orphans* call."

"I can arrange that," Valerie said. "This former lover of mine now casts a lot of national commercials. I noticed she's holding a call to cast kids for a new McDonald's campaign this afternoon. That's the kind of thing that'll bring them out in droves. I could give her a ring and have her slip Chloe onto the list. That is, if you really want to subject Chloe to something like that."

"Chloe's gone skiing with Kit. But I think I can recruit another little girl. She lives across the street from me, and her mother's been dying to break her into show business. Her name's Amanda Karpel."

Valerie scribbled the name on a napkin. "Okay, I'll set it up and ring you later with the where and when."

She began gathering the thickets of shopping bags from her

morning's forage. For a moment I had a strong inclination to blurt, "No, I've changed my mind. Don't make that call!"

Don't be ridiculous, I told myself. What could possibly be life-threatening about a bunch of grade-schoolers leaping for joy over Big Macs? And in a public place in broad daylight . . .

Of course, Joyce Korshalek would have said the same thing.

I pushed that thought firmly out of my mind and followed Valerie Jane on out.

10

The sprawling peach-painted Mediterranean manse directly across the road from our own had belonged to the beloved sitcom star Woody Prentice and his wife, Julia—the same Julia Prentice who had turned up one afternoon bobbing naked and dead in our swimming pool. Shortly afterward, Woody had followed his wife into that good night. For the better part of a year after their mutual demise, the house had languished empty and uncared-for, the landscaping reverting to hay under the searing sun, the branches of the eucalyptus trees drooping as if in lament. The only activity was the periodic arrival of sightseeing vans packed with those tourists who got macabre kicks from gawking at the former residences of the late and famous.

Finally the property was snapped up for a song by a wealthy tax attorney named Arthur A. Karpel, a robust sixty-something with simian arms, a moist-lipped smile and the requisite trophy wife. Lynette Karpel was a former Miss Arizona State and catalog model. She had been a ravishing twenty-seven when he had married her, but she was a birthday or two past forty now, and rumor had it that Arthur A. Karpel, datingwise, would soon be back in play.

As far as I could tell, Lynette now had only two interests in life. The first was to fight as hard as possible against the assault of physical decay, the longer presumably to hold onto her status as Mrs. Arthur A. She was first on line for every new procedure, from the chemical peel that left her face as red and raw as a tomato puree, to the "Super-Rolf," which was supposed to squeeze the fat out of your flab by pounding it under heavy weight. The week before she had been waxing eloquently about a new procedure in which—I swear to god—minute injections of botulism were injected into her forehead to freeze the frown lines.

Lynette's second passion was to break her daughter Amanda into what she called "the world of commercial acting." Lynette had an ear finely tuned to the ka-ching! of a cash register; she knew well that the residuals from appearing in one nationally broadcast ad could produce a lavish river of loot. And so I was fairly confident she'd be receptive to my call about the audition.

"McDonald's!" she breathed, pronouncing it with the same lofty reverence with which an art connoisseur might speak the name of Rembrandt. "This is just the break we've been waiting for."

"It's going to be a pretty big audition," I warned her. "About a hundred and fifty kids, and they're going to choose only four."

"My Manda's gonna make the rest of that crowd look like dog meat," was Lynette's response.

When I pulled up in their driveway several hours later, they were both waiting. Lynette, unsurprisingly, was fresh from a procedure—her chin and neck swaddled in bandages, giving her the look of a partially unwrapped mummy. I vaguely remembered she had been complaining lately about developing "turkey wattles."

She ushered Amanda to my car and bundled her into the front seat. "The very second after you called, I ran over and popped her out of school to get her ready," she announced to me.

My attention had been momentarily focused on Lynette's botulism-frozen forehead, wondering where they got the botulism—perhaps from old, dented cans of vichyssoise?—so that I hadn't yet focused on Amanda. Now I did and gave a start. Getting her ready evidently meant taking a perfectly average-looking seven-year-old and turning her into a cross between Dale Evans and a high-priced hooker. Her sturdy little body was encased in a fringed silver-and-blue cowgirl outfit with matching boots. Her heart-shaped face was rather luridly made up, and her hair was lacquered into a meringue of sticky dark brown curls. Her paler brown eyes gazed up at me apprehensively.

"You don't have to do this if you don't want to, Amanda," I said.

"Of course she wants to do this, she's raring to go!" Lynette answered for her. "Show that winning smile, honeybun."

The girl stretched her lips back from her teeth in a desperate grin and widened her eyes.

"That's a winner," her mother cheered. She thrust an eight-by-ten photo in my hand. "Here's her glossy. It's got her sizes and her special skills written up on back."

The photo could only be called steamy. Smudged, sultry eyes. Mouth glossed to a high shine and provocatively parted. I hastily jammed it into my bag, as if to protect it from any child pornographers who happened to be lurking in the vicinity.

"I'm gonna be right here holding my breath until you get back," Lynette declared. She blew a kiss-kiss in her daughter's direction and retreated into the house.

I took a packet of Wet 'N Dries from the glove compartment and turned to Manda. "Maybe we should take off just a little of that makeup," I said.

"But my mom spent a whole hour putting it on," she protested.

"Just a little bit," I insisted. I dabbed at her feverish-looking cheeks and crimson lips. "This is going to be lots of fun!" I said brightly.

Amanda gazed at me with a dubious expression.

Great, I thought, as I started the engine. I wasn't content with being a Totally Unfit Mother to my own daughter. Now I'd begun persecuting other people's kids as well.

*   *   *

The address Valerie had provided me was in the mid-Wilshire district, once the bustling retail hub of the city but now given largely to the kind of appliance stores that had perpetual *Lost Our Lease!* banners strung across the window. Amanda and I rode a shaky elevator to the third floor of a down-at-the-heels Art Deco office tower and walked down a malodorous hallway to a door marked *Westside Casting*. It opened onto a cavernous and jam-packed waiting room.

At first glance, it seemed to be jam-packed solely with women. Mobs of women. Most of them unattractive, either overweight or scrawny. Bra straps peeped slatternly from under frumpy tops, rolls of pasty flesh oozed over the elastic waists of cheap pants. For a moment I wondered if I had stumbled into the wrong casting call, perhaps one for an ad for problem-figure bras or dishpan hands.

Then I realized the women were all accompanied by kids. In contrast to their frumpy progenitors, they looked as if they had materialized off the pages of a Gap Kids catalog. They were big-eyed, button-nosed, immaculately outfitted in the latest in teenybopper chic: baggy cropped-at-the-knee jeans and Airwalk sneakers for boys, saucy little jumpers and backpacks in the shape of koalas or orangutans for the girls. And every single one of them had fantastic hair.

For most of these kids, this was a daily after-school routine—the long commute from their homes in Orange, or Thousand Oaks, or Rancho Cucamonga to wherever the sitcom or feature film or commercial was being cast that day. Then waiting to audition, sometimes for many long hours, hoping against the odds that this one, or maybe tomorrow's or the one the day after that, would at least lead to a call-back. Which would explain the air of tedium that drenched the room—the tedium of a backwater Greyhound Bus station, where passengers who'd been traveling for many wearying, uncomfortable days waited for the next connection in a journey that still had thousands of bleak miles to go.

I led Amanda to a table where a spiffy young man with Chiclet teeth was signing in new arrivals. I filled out a card with her vital statistics, cribbing from the back of her glossy—height, three feet ten; hair, "chestnut"; eyes, greeny-blue—and handed it to him. The Chiclet grin froze a split second as he got an eyeful of Manda's Vegas cowgirl getup. Then he quickly recovered his professional aplomb. "Amanda Karpel, age seven," he read from the card. "Okay, Amanda, what we're going to do is bring you into another room. And we're going to pretend you got a really good report card and now you're excited because you get to go to McDonald's. Can you do that? Let's see you be really excited."

Amanda gave a little flap of her hands and issued an anemic "Yea!"

"Super-duper." Chiclets snapped a Polaroid of her, then said to me, "We'll be taking kids four at a time. When you hear her name called, bring her over to that blue door."

Dismissed, we edged into the throng. Manda plunked herself in a chair and dug a Tamagotchi from her pocket. She was quickly engrossed in its beeping demands to be fed, cleaned up after, petted and amused.

I stood listening to the high babble of voices. A fat woman behind me was bragging about the commercial her son had just scored: "They needed kids with asthma, so I made him wheeze to beat the band." To my right, a mom with a face like a flour dumpling was lamenting about braces: "We've done all the hidden work we possibly can, and now it's gotta be metal. It's gonna put her out of work for two years . . ."

Then a familiar figure loomed out at me, a washed out–looking woman in a brown cardigan. It was Connie Meyers, who possessed the unfortunate distinction of being one of the poorest parents at Windermere. She lived on a small alimony check from a husband who had decamped from the marriage to move in with a young man who worked the bathrobe and pajama department at Barneys. The bulk of her income was now dedicated to furthering the show-business career of her daughter Theadora, as was in fact the bulk of Connie's entire existence. It was commonly known that Connie stumbled out of bed each morning at five to prepare to begin chauffeuring Thea to a regimen of acting and dancing classes, piano and elocution and ice-skating lessons. During the day, Connie passed the hours badgering casting offices, stuffing Thea's photos into envelopes, scouring the trades for upcoming auditions. She labored often till midnight ironing and mending her daughter's wardrobe—a wardrobe that boasted the labels of Neiman Marcus and Saks Fifth Avenue, while she herself shlumped around in Kmart's finest.

I waved. She peered with a quizzical frown, then lumbered over to me. "What are you doing here?" she said, her voice edgy with competitiveness. "I thought your Chloe didn't go in for auditioning."

"She doesn't. I'm just here as a favor, taking a friend's kid."

"Oh." Connie's eyes dropped to my stomach and gave it the unabashed once-over that was rapidly becoming familiar to me. "I didn't know you were expecting," she said.

"Didn't you see my full-page ad in the *Times*?"

"Um . . ."

"I'm joking," I said quickly.

"Oh," she said again. "Well maybe you'll get lucky and it'll be premature."

"What would be so lucky about that?"

"Don't you know? The laws say you're not allowed to use babies in movies less than fifteen days old, so there's a big demand for preemies who look like they're newborn. My girlfriend induced labor at eight and a half months. Right away she got her baby a feature and a *Chicago Hope*." Connie's voice went mealy with envy.

"My god!" I exclaimed incredulously.

Connie seemed to take this as awe at the sound of such a windfall. "Who knows, it could happen to you," she offered. Then she emitted a thin sigh. "We've been here for forty-five minutes already," she said. "When we have to wait too long, it gets hard for Thea to keep up her spontaneity. That's one of the main things they look for, you know, spontaneity."

I decided suddenly to try a gambit. "Yeah, but forty-five minutes isn't that bad. A friend of mine in New York said she once had to wait with her son for over seven hours. And then it all came to nothing. There was some kind of accident with the casting director."

Connie's no-color eyes wandered up warily to mine. "Are you talking about the *Orphans* audition?"

"Yeah. Were you there?"

For a second, she said nothing. My heart began to beat quickly, as I wondered if I had given too much away. Then she shrugged and said, "Yeah, we were there. Wasn't everybody? I scraped up my last dime so we could fly in special for it and pay for that sleazy hotel and our meals and everything. The only reason was because Joyce Korshalek swore on a stack of Bibles to me that Thea was going to get a part."

"Joyce Korshalek—is she the one who had the accident?" I pulled a face of bland innocence.

Connie nodded curtly.

"But according to my friend, that audition was all a rip-off," I went on. "Just a publicity stunt. The studio never intended to cast anybody from it."

Connie's mouth set in a stubborn slot. "That's bullshit. Joyce and I were really close, almost like sisters. She wouldn't feed me a lie. She promised she was going to give Thea her big break. And you know what I think?" She dropped her voice to a conspiratorial mutter. "I think somebody wanted to stop that from happening."

"What do you mean?" I muttered back.

"I mean, if you ask me, Joyce falling down that staircase was no accident, no matter what kind of bullshit they say."

"So you're saying you think somebody bumped her off to keep her from casting your daughter? That seems a little drastic, doesn't it?"

"You don't know the lengths some of these people would go to," she declared in a melodramatic tremolo.

"These people like who?"

"Shh." She flew a finger to her lips. "They're going to call more kids."

A second young man, even spiffier than the one at the sign-in desk, had appeared at the hallowed blue door. He rattled off a list of names, none of which was Theadora Meyers.

"I swear, someone in this company has it in for Thea," Connie whined. "Whenever it's Westside Casting, I can tell that she's being sabotaged. Somebody's bound and determined to make sure she can't get a break."

It struck me that Connie Meyers interpreted just about everything as a plot against Thea; it was probably the only way she could rationalize Thea's less than meteoric success. But if Connie saw saboteurs and assaassins lurking at every casting call, I reasoned, it pretty much put the kibosh on any value her dark intimations about Joyce Korshalek might have had. I tuned out as she continued to fulminate about her many enemies.

My attention was snagged by a little boy being led—or more accurately yanked—toward the blue door by a scowling, wiry-bodied man. The boy was so fair he was almost albino. I interrupted Connie in midwhine. "Is that one of the Grangers?"

"Yeah, Benny Granger," she said. "None of those kids are any good, but he's the best of the lot."

I watched them barge through the crowd. Benny had the same pulled-down mouth as his brother Kerrin, the same expression of perpetually smelling rotten eggs. The yanking man was, I presumed, the tyrannical Granger patriarch, Seth. He was medium-sized, with a blandly handsome face and short grayish-brown hair. There was very little Mussolini-like about him; if anything, he looked like Ward Cleaver, the Beaver's dad, minus the cardigan and with a good deal more attitude.

Connie Meyers suddenly tugged on my sleeve, a little-girlish gesture that was pathetically out of sorts with her used-up appearance. "I have to go tinkle," she said. "If they call Thea's name, see that she gets in, okay? She's over there by the bulletin board."

"Sure," I said quickly. An opportunity to chat with Thea alone was more than I'd hoped for.

I checked to make sure Manda was still absorbed with her Tamagotchi, then approached Thea. She appeared to be holding an animated conversation with the facing wall, while making repeated, exaggerated gestures with her arms, first flinging them over her head, then opening them wide, then gaily clapping them together. She's snapped under pressure, was my first horrified thought—the poor child's gone completely off her rocker.

Then I got closer and heard her exclaim, "Every day's like your birthday at McDonald's!" I relaxed, realizing she was just rehearsing for her upcoming shot behind the blue door. Some sixth sense informed her she had an audience. Without missing a beat, she twirled toward me, displayed a cheek-splitting smile and said, "Hi, I'm Theadora Meyers."

"I'm Lucy," I said.

"I'm very pleased to meet you." She put out her little hand and shook mine with just the correct amount of firm pressure. I suddenly felt even more chilled than when I thought she was crazy. Nothing about Thea Meyers seemed natural; every bit of her gave me the impression of having been carefully calculated for maximum cuteness. The ponytails that spouted like twin geysers from the top of her head. The artificially widened eyes and happy-almost-to-delirium smile. The just-so tilt of her head and hint of a lisp in her voice. Even the way she made comfortable eye contact with me seemed a long-practiced talent.

"Have you seen my work?" she inquired. "Most recently I was in a *Touched by an Angel* and a *Frasier*."

"I think I saw that one," I fibbed. "You were really good. But I've also seen you at your school. I'm Chloe Freers's mom."

Thea's glance sidled warily around the room. "So where's Chloe? Is she trying out for this too?"

"No, I'm here with another little girl. She lives across the street from me. That's her over there in the cowgirl outfit."

"That kid?" Thea treated Mandy to the kind of cool, disdainful appraisal that I imagined a veteran horse trader might allot to a swaybacked mare. "*She's* not going to get a call-back. They don't go for that kind of corny Western stuff anymore. And she's too skinny. If you're going to be in a food commercial, you've got to look like you like to eat."

This was indisputable logic. She sat in a chair and primly smoothed the bib of her jumper, a fetching garment appliquéd with nostalgia-for-the-seventies daisies and Happy Faces. I helped myself to the chair beside her.

"I was just over there talking to your mom," I said with studied casualness. "We were remembering that audition for *Orphans* that was held back in New York City. It was such a long time ago you've probably forgotten all about it."

She gave a blasé shrug. "I remember it. It sucked."

"Yeah? How come it sucked?"

"First of all because they made us wait around for hours and hours. And then it was like a hundred degrees, and we were all really hot and hungry, and there wasn't even a craft service table or anything. And then Joyce fell downstairs, and she was supposed to give me a part, so Mom got really mad."

"Did you see Joyce fall downstairs?" I asked lightly. Or, in other words, did you chance to see her being pushed to her death? Or happen to give her the fatal shove yourself?

Thea responded to my spoken question with a ponytail-bobbing shake of her head. "It didn't happen in the audition room. There were these stairs down the back way you could take if you didn't want to wait for the elevator. I never took them because they were totally gross, and I was wearing these new pink shoes with matching anklets."

"How do you know that's where it happened?"

"Because that is what they told us." Thea had begun to speak with the irritable precision of someone addressing a mental inferior. "This guy came in and said Joyce Korshalek had a bad accident, and wasn't that awful? as if we were all supposed to start crying or something. But we all hated her, so we didn't care."

I pictured a kind of *Children of the Damned* scene: a cluster of stony-eyed kids taking the news of the casting director's death with complete equanimity. The back of my neck prickled.

"Did you know any of the other kids who were trying out?" I pursued.

"Of course. I always know *some*."

"Do you remember any of the Granger boys being there?"

For an instant, Thea actually forgot to be adorable—she wrinkled her snub nose in a most unphotogenic way. "Yeah, that rotten Kerrin, he was there. He kept following me around with this stupid cap gun he had, saying if I didn't pull down my underpants for him, he was going to shoot me dead. It was so funny I forgot to laugh."

"Was Kerrin there with his dad?"

"I guess so. We all came with our parents. I mean, we're *kids*, so how else were we supposed to get there?" Her voice shrilled in exasperation at having to explain the obvious to the village idiot.

"You must have been pretty disappointed," I went on. "Losing a chance to be in a movie with Jamie Alston."

She rolled her eyes theatrically. "Big deal. None of us wanted to work with him. He totally sucked. I mean when he sang he sounded like a frog. And he couldn't even do a shuffle cramp roll. He can hardly do buffaloes!"

"Do what?"

She leaped to her feet and executed a rapid routine, tap, tappety-tap, shuffle tap. Then she plunked herself with a self-satisfied smirk back in her seat. "I could do that when I was four years old. But not that retardo, Jamie. And anyway, the studio was going to fire him. You know who they were going to make the star?"

"Who?"

"Marcus Barnes. He was really excellent. He made Jamie look like dog meat."

"Marcus Barnes?" I repeated with surprise. I pictured him in my animation workshop, his intelligent black eyes fixed somberly on me. "I didn't know he wanted to act. He's such a quiet, kind of shy kid."

"He's fabulous. He can sing anything, he just has to hear it once and he remembers it perfectly. The same with his dancing, he only has to see the steps one time to get it. When he auditioned for Miss Korshalek, she flipped out. She said he was the most talented kid she'd ever seen."

Her attention snapped away, instantly alerted to the fact that a fresh batch of names were being summoned to the magic blue door. She brightened as she heard hers included in the lineup. "You'll have to excuse me," she said. "I'm being called in."

From seemingly nowhere, Connie materialized. "They're calling for you," she said agitatedly. She squatted down and began making infinitesimal adjustments to Thea's clothes, aligning her jumper straps, perfecting the fold of an anklet. "Now remember, lots of energy and always keep up the eye contact. And don't forget to do something spontaneous."

"I'm going to scratch an itch on my back."

"Okay, great, that'll look good. Here we go."

The two scampered to the door where the previous clutch of kids were emerging, escorted out by a smiling, heavyset woman. I noticed Seth Granger charge up, grip his son by the arm and say something to the woman. She gleamed the kind of too-bright smile that usually accompanies lousy news, gave a brief reply, then hastily backed up and shut the door. Seth's face darkened to the ominous mottled purple of a prethunderstorm sky. His son stared up at him with terror. Seth seized his hand, pivoted abruptly and began yanking him back through the crowd, directly toward me.

"You tell me, what did she mean by 'a bit fidgety'?" I heard him barking.

"I don't know," Benny whimpered.

"You don't know what? Are you so stupid you don't know what fidgeting means?"

"Yeah, I know what it means, but I had to go to the bathroom."

"You went to the bathroom twenty minutes ago, so don't give me that crap. You think you're gonna get a call-back after this?"

"I don't know. Maybe."

"Maybe in a pig's eye! This is the third time in a row you've acted unprofessionally, and I've had just about enough."

To my horror, I watched him cuff the boy on the side of his head. All around them, mothers were suddenly studying their feet or fixing their eyes on distant points in the room.

Benny began to sniffle.

"You can cut out that blubbering," his father snapped. He jerked the boy forward, causing him to sniffle louder. "I said cut it out!" Seth hissed and delivered another cuff.

I couldn't watch this without doing something. They were almost directly in front of me now. Without thinking, I extended my foot, catching Seth at the ankle as he charged by. With a gurgle of surprise, he tripped and went sprawling chin first onto the cement floor.

There were gasps as he fell and someone cried out in alarm, but no one offered to help him up. He slowly collected himself into a sitting position. Blood stained his lower lip and chin; he touched the wound, looked at the blood on his fingers with some astonishment, then stared up at me.

"I'm so terribly sorry," I said, struggling to sound at least a little contrite. "That was incredibly clumsy of me."

A kind of growl seeped from the back of his throat. Little Bennie beside me gave a nervous giggle.

With a low-pitched bellow, his father scrambled to his feet. I moved to the boy to defend him. Then suddenly I felt two hands on my shoulders, shoving me roughly back up against the bulletin board hung on the wall. Pushpins dug into my shoulder blades and the back of my head, as I stared into the two pinpricks of fury that were Seth Granger's eyes. "You fucking bitch!" he snarled, and gripped my right arm.

A white hot pain knifed through me as he bent it to the breaking point.

11

The searing pain vanquished everything else from my mind. My eyes blurred with tears and a whimper escaped from my throat. For a moment I felt I was going to pass out.

Dimly, I became aware of other faces gathering in close to us. Someone shouted "Stop it, you're hurting her!" Another voice gasped, "She's pregnant, for godsake!" And then a dark-haired woman was clutching at Seth in what at first to my addled state seemed a strangely intimate way. "It was an accident," I heard her yell. "I saw the whole thing, she didn't mean to trip you, it was just an accident!"

The pain in my arm stopped abruptly. Seth took a step back, then swiveled his head left and right, as if bewildered to suddenly find himself the cynosure of a distinctly hostile crowd.

"Are you out of your fucking mind?" I burst out.

He slid his eyes back to me and a wisp of a smile flitted across his bloodstained lips. "That was no accident," he said in a velvety, almost caressing voice.

Then he turned brusquely and snatched his son's hand. "Come on, Benny, let's go."

The crowd parted, Red Sea–like, to let them pass, then roiled up around me again. I heard myself repeating that it was nothing, really, I was fine. Then one of the interchangeably spiffy young guys was hovering in front of me, shaking his clipboard like a tambourine. "I'm sorry but I'm going to have to ask you to leave," he sputtered. "We just can't permit this kind of disturbance. Sponsors are very sensitive. I'm sure you can understand my position."

"I understand perfectly," I said, relieved to have an excuse to get the hell out of there. I started back to pick up Manda, who I could see had collected her own little crowd of kids mesmerized by the Tamagotchi's importunate cheeping and blurping. Mercifully, she appeared not to have noticed the Disturbance. At least I'd be brightening her day by telling her she wouldn't have to audition after all.

"Excuse me." Someone tapped me on the arm.

I turned and recognized the woman who had deflected Seth Granger from doing serious damage to my humerus. "Hi," I said warmly. "Thanks for coming to my rescue."

"Oh, please," she said, with a dismissive wave. "I saw him smack his little boy. Parents like that ought to be crucified! I was delighted when you tripped him up."

"So you did catch that." I smiled sheepishly.

"Yes, and I nearly applauded. That man is a brute." She spoke with a society lockjaw accent. And in fact, here among the exposed-bra-strap set, she was something of an anomaly. Her dark brown hair was smoothed in an immaculate pageboy. Her apricot skin had obviously been the beneficiary of liberal amounts of moisturizer. Her small-chested, rather angular body was clad in a coral cashmere cardigan and tailored skirt. All in all, she looked as if she had set off to a bridge luncheon at the Greenwich Country Club in, say, 1962 and through some warp in the space-time continuum been deposited here instead. "I've run into him several times before at casting calls," she went on. "The last time I saw him, one of his sons, the youngest, I think, was in a sling. A dislocated collarbone. The father's story was that it happened during a game of catch. The boy had run to catch a wild throw and knocked himself into the side of the garage." She glanced meaningfully at me.

I tried to picture this frisky, Norman Rockwellesque game of catch between Seth and his son. The image wouldn't jell. The picture that did sketch itself in my mind was Seth, in a mindless fit of fury, slamming the little boy up against the garage and dislocating his collarbone.

"I can see we're thinking the same thing," my companion declared. "By the way, my name's Martha Beech. Though everyone calls me Muffer. It's from when I was a little girl and couldn't say Martha." She gave a lockjawed little chuckle.

"I'm Lucy Freers," I said.

"Yes, I know, you have a daughter at Windermere Academy. So do I. That's Holly, sitting over there with a textbook in her lap."

I glanced over and caught my breath. The most exquisite child I'd ever seen was perched daintily in a chair, turning the pages of a thick book. Rich brown hair shot with gold tumbled in rich waves to her shoulders; it framed a perfect oval face with enormous, deep-lashed eyes and an almost womanly full mouth. "She's stunning!" I exclaimed.

"Mmmmm," her mother responded; such tributes to her daughter's beauty were evidently commonplace.

"Funny, I've never seen her at school. I'd certainly remember if I had."

"Oh, she's new. We've just moved here, from New Canaan, Connecticut. My husband, Fred's a stockbroker, he used to work on Wall Street, but when he was offered a transfer to the L.A. branch, we decided to take it for Holly's sake. For the sake of her career, I mean. It's been a sacrifice. Fred now has to get up at four in the morning just to keep up with the market opening back East. We scarcely see each other anymore. And back in Connecticut, I had my finger in many different pies, the Junior League, Friends of the

Opera, the Cancer Association . . ." She ticked off the names of these worthy organizations on bony fingers. "Naturally I had to leave all that behind."

I gave a murmur of commiseration, vaguely wondering why she was sharing all this with me.

"But as I mentioned, for Holly to pursue her acting career, we really felt we needed to be on the West Coast," she rattled on. "Personally, I hate this whole process. The last thing in the world I want to be is a stage mother. The whole game disgusts me, the backbiting and the kissing up to agents and managers. But Holly loves performing, positively adores it. And she's so remarkably gifted, landed her first role when she was five and a half. It would be a crying shame not to give her every chance to make the top."

"With those looks, I'm surprised she's not famous already," I said politely.

Martha "Muffer" Beech's face darkened. "It's all politics in this business, you know. I can't tell you how many times some hideously unattractive child has been cast over my Holly simply because of politics."

The shock from my recent dust-up with Seth Granger must have clouded my thinking; only now did my brain begin to process the fact that New Canaan was just a short commuter hop from Manhattan. And two and a half years ago, the stunning Holly would have been the right age to be the straw-hatted dispatcher of casting directors in Brandon's video.

"You know, I think I have seen your daughter before," I said in an offhand tone. "A few years back I was doing the audition circuit in New York with Chloe, and I seem to remember noticing her." I scrunched my brow in feigned thought. "Maybe at the audition for the Campbell's Soup commercial? Or was it at that cattle call for *Orphans*?"

It seemed to me that Muffer's social-tea smile faltered for a fraction of a second. "Gracious, there have been so many," she said easily, "who could possibly keep track? I can hardly remember where we were even yesterday." A clenched chuckle. "You and I must get together and have a girls afternoon out," she went on. "I'm sure we have scads in common."

Yeah, right, I thought. Her idea of a perfect afternoon was to chair a fund-raiser for muscular dystrophy; mine was to catch a Felix the Cat cartoon marathon. I made a noncommittal murmur about keeping in touch. Muffer began to walk back toward her daughter.

I glanced once more at the girl. At the same time, she looked up from her book. Suddenly something hideous happened to her face: the eyes crossed, the nose flattened, the mouth contorted grotesquely. She's having some sort of fit! I thought with alarm. Then abruptly her face returned to normal, the serene, lovely visage of a budding Madonna. It had all happened so fast, I might have imagined it.

With a perplexed shake of my head, I turned to go collect Amanda.

I broke the bad news to Lynette that their mailbox was not about to brim over with residual checks. She looked momentarily crushed, but then, with the indefatigable perkiness that had no doubt scored her the Miss Arizona State crown, bounced back with a shrug. "There's always next time," she pronounced. "Oh, by the way, something came for you." She yelled into the house, "Juanita, where's that thingy that that guy dropped off?"

A tiny Hispanic woman trotted into view, a Dustbuster in one hand, a manila envelope in the other. She deposited the envelope in Lynette's hand and Lynette gave it to me. "Some messenger had the wrong house. I said leave it, I'd be seeing you later."

I took it distractedly. Messengers were forever dropping things off for Kit, usually scripts from aspiring screenwriters who were under the delusion that a home delivery would get their work more personal attention. I thanked Lynette and retreated across the street to my own house.

Just for a change, I was ravenous. I motored straight to the kitchen and began throwing together a Dagwood sandwich. Sawed two thick slabs from a loaf of slightly stale sourdough, added a slab of Gouda, a schmear of cream cheese, a few sliced Spanish olives, some romaine for the crunch, and then—to satisfy some bizarre craving—I sprinkled it all with soy sauce.

As I lit into this concoction, I began to mentally sort through the jumble of information I'd acquired at the audition. Specifically, the now-considerable roster of kids whose credentials of being both students at Windermere and veterans of the *Orphans* audition made them suspect-worthy.

First, there was Theadora Meyers. If there should ever be a telethon for the Prevention of Children in Show Business, the pitifully artificial little Thea could be its poster girl. She came aligned of course with her bedraggled stage mother, Connie, whose close personal friend, Joyce Korshalek, had dangled the promise of a part for Thea before inconsiderately getting herself dead. But what reason would little Thea have had to give her the coup de grâce?

Maybe she didn't want to get the part, I reflected. After all, her entire childhood had been robbed from her. She had been stripped of anything that was natural and turned into an all-dancing, all-singing, all-smirking little automaton. Shoving a casting director, with or without the intent to harm, might have been a last-ditch attempt to rebel.

No, I couldn't rule her out, I decided.

Juvenile Suspect Number Two was Kerrin Granger. Now here was a kid I could definitely feature in the role of assassin. What if Joyce Korshalek, fondly known as The Executioner, had already shot him down? Took one peek at Kerrin's Raisinette-sized eyes and pissed-off mouth and yelled, "Out!" Kerrin would then be facing the terrifying task of reporting back to his dad that he had flunked and made to bear the brunt of Seth's subsequent rage. So perhaps Kerrin comes across The Executioner poised conveniently at the top of a flight of stairs . . . I could see him lunge at her out of sheer fury at what she's set him up for.

Or maybe he pushes her because he figures that, if she has an accident, the whole audition will be called off, and his dad won't find out that he failed.

And I could certainly believe that if Seth Granger discovered his son had snuffed a casting agent, he would be fully capable of eliminating any witnesses to the event. The sunny thought flashed through my mind that, now that I'd definitively jumped onto his shit list, he was no doubt capable of eliminating me as well. I decided not to dwell on that for the moment.

Instead, I washed down a mouthful of sandwich with a swallow of Pellegrino, and moved on to Suspect Numero Tres. This would be Jamie Alston, aka America's Darling, aka The Dreaded Spawn of Satan. In his movies, he was the scourge of villains and authority figures, pushing them off catwalks, bonking them with bricks, etc., and it was considered adorable. At the time of the *Orphans* audition, he might have been too young to distinguish the difference between life and art. In a movie, sending a bossy lady like the Korshalek tumbling skirt over heels would be just the thing to get a good laugh and raise his salary another million bucks. So why not do it for real?

And if Andy Oberest was to be believed, my old pals Myra and Randy Alston would stop at nothing when it came to protecting their interests in their little golden goose—even to the point of trying to eliminate one another. So perhaps blowing away Brandon McKenna would have just been all in a day's work.

But I also had to consider the surprise suspect, Marcus Barnes. The shy genius who apparently possessed hidden talents—who according to Thea's coolly professional appraisal was so good he should have snatched the *Orphans* starring role right out from under Jamie Alston's adorably upturned nose. Could he have whacked Joyce Korshalek out of pique for being unjustly passed over?

And finally there was the dark horse, the exquisitely beautiful Holly Beech, with her lockjawed mom, Muffer. The two of them freshly relocated from New Canaan, Connecticut. Which meant, if Holly was the killer kid, Brandon certainly would have been surprised to see her pop up in the car-pool crush at Windermere. But I couldn't say for sure if she had even been at the *Orphans* call . . .

I finished the sandwich, mopped up the crumbs from the plate and devoured those, then took plate and glass to the dishwasher. As I did, my eye fell on the manila envelope that I had tossed onto the counter. For the first time, I realized it was addressed to me: *Lucy Freers* was scrawled rather crudely in green Magic Marker. I ripped it open. Inside was a smallish object wrapped in several layers of the L.A. *Times*. I tore away the newspaper.

It was a Willigher the Ghost key ring, with a single key dangling from it. It was the spare key to Kit's BMW that was always kept in the top drawer of the kitchen desk. I stared at it a moment, mystified by how it could have navigated on its own from the drawer out into the world . . .

Then the realization hit me with the force of a fist. This was the key Brandon would have been using the morning he was murdered in the car.

12

The fact that his case which had been so neatly wrapped up was now unpleasantly threatening to unravel was almost enough to draw a demonstrative response from Detective Langocetti. His Deputy Dawg face squinched in disgruntlement as he glanced at the key ring, then back at me, then once again at the offending key ring. He jangled it once or twice, pulled on one of his pendulous ears and regarded me again, this time with slotted eyes, as if suspecting me of trying to pull a fast one.

"How can you be sure McKenna was using this particular key?" he inquired.

"Because we have only three sets to the BMW," I explained. "Kit's got one on his key chain, and I keep another on mine. This one on the Willigher chain is always kept in the kitchen drawer. It's the only one Brandon could have had."

"How do you know that McKenna hadn't taken it on himself to make up a spare key? Maybe so as he wouldn't have to ask your permission every time he wanted to borrow the car."

I opened my mouth to protest that Brandon wouldn't have been that devious. Then I snapped it shut again, remembering that Brandon had *so* been that devious, and that when it came to making predictions about anything Brandon McKenna had or had not been up to, I was about the last person qualified to speak up. For all I knew, he'd been sneaking out in the Beemer after midnight every night, zipping down to Tijuana and whooping it up in tequila mills till dawn.

Langocetti was now scrutinizing the key ring's little plastic ghost, presumably for forensic relevance.

"If that's not the key Brandon had," I said, "then how did it get out of the house, and why has it been messengered back to me?"

"I could ask the same question if it *is* the same key. Why did it get sent back?"

"In my opinion? The killer wants to send me a message. He or she is saying that they're watching me."

"What for?"

I executed another open-then-shut-the-mouth movement. I couldn't very well tell Langocetti that I had been informally deputized by one of his fellow detectives to investigate a case that A, belonged to him, and that B, he had officially closed. I answered simply, "I guess just in case I started asking too many questions."

"Questions about what?"

"About Brandon's murder, of course."

He frowned. "There's still no real evidence it was a homicide."

I had the gruesome feeling I had slipped onto some kind of interrogatory Möbius strip—no matter how much we looped and twisted to reach another conclusion, we were always going to wind up back in the exact same place. "Aren't you going to reopen the case?" I wailed. "Maybe there are prints on the key ring. Couldn't you dust it or something?"

"It's been handled too extensively. I doubt it would do any good." He shot another disdainful look at the grinning Willigher. I wondered whether if the key had not been on a novelty ring but fastened to something more substantial, say a sterling silver chain from Tiffany, he'd have allotted it more investigative respect. "Now you say it was actually delivered across the street," he continued.

I nodded. "The messenger had the wrong house. My neighbor accepted the package for me, but unfortunately didn't get a look at the guy." The second call I had made after opening the package had been to Lynette, who had rattled on about having been on her bedroom phone trying to order some almond milk bath crystals from last season's Bloomingdale's catalog when the bell had rung and she had just shouted through the upstairs intercom. "She just talked to him through an intercom and told him to leave the package in the mailbox."

"I'll talk to her anyway," Langocetti conceded. "She might remember more than she thinks," He deposited the key ring in a glassine envelope and pocketed it. "If anything else gets sent to you, let me know."

"Believe me, you've just shot right to the top of my automatic dialing."

He nodded in approval, then lumbered on out.

Now I was alone in this sprawling house with the sensation that Chloe would have pithily called "the creeps." The rough-hewn beams on the living room ceiling cast shadows on the walls and furniture that I usually found romantic, but now seemed ominous. I had the crawly feeling that the old toys I collected — the biplane whirligig, the tin dancing bear, the painted train and the milk truck with its wooden red-capped driver—were about to start spinning and dancing and choo-chooing on their own, like the household appliances in *Poltergeist*. For company, I uncovered Rollins in his cage. He began to squawk out the repertoire of movie lines Kit and Chloe had taught him: "Show me the money!" "You talkin' to me?" "You talkin' to me?"

Then I remembered I hadn't checked my voice mail and picked up the phone. The first message was from Chloe: The skiing was cool, but last night she had a dream about Brandon, he was going up on the lift with her and wearing his Yankees hat backward, and when she woke up she felt really bad again.

Second was from Valerie Jane. Her first Lamaze class scheduled for tomorrow night, so glad I was going to partner her. "Frankly, Lucy, I'm feeling a bit abandoned right now. If you hadn't been around, I don't know what I'd do."

At least someone needed me. My spirits took a little lift.

I moved on to the last message. A woman's voice, low-pitched and elegant. "Hello, this is Helene Barnes. I believe we've spoken a few times at Windermere."

I felt a quick thrill. Marcus Barnes's mom! She must have found out that I was asking around about the *Orphans* audition and had something to tell me.

My wild thoughts were squelched as I refocused on what she was saying: ". . . heading up the school's fund-raising committee this year, and we have not yet received your donations for the auction. I realize that due to the recent tragedy in your household this has not been a high priority for you. But I'm sure you'll agree that it's vitally important that we maintain The School's funding." She stated her home number and coolly signed off.

Silly unfeeling bitch! I fumed. No matter if somebody near and dear to you had been brutally slaughtered—nothing must interfere with your making a contribution to the already bloated coffers of Windermere Academy. For a moment I was tempted to call her back and contribute a succinct "Screw you, lady."

"One-way ticket to Palookaville!" squawked Rollins from his cage.

I jumped at the sound. But the jolt made me think along cooler lines: Here was a perfect excuse to pay a visit to the Barneses and see what I could suss out. I picked up the phone again and dialed her number.

"Out of the Oven," her well-modulated voice answered.

This took me back a moment. Then I recalled that Helene ran a catering operation out of her home, providing artistic canapés to a select clientele at an equally artistic cost.

I identified myself, apologized profusely for neglecting my duty to The School. "If it's not hugely inconvenient, I could run over right now with my donation," I said.

"Well . . . I'm in the middle of a rush job," she said hesitantly. "We're a bit frantic." As if in corroboration, I could hear in the background the clank, rattle and blam of a pot hitting the floor, and somebody yelling, "Watch those squash blossoms!" "Perhaps you could have it sent . . . ?" she began.

"It's fragile, so I'd really rather bring it myself," I said quickly. "I won't get in your way."

She gave a kind of hum that I took for acquiescence. "See you shortly," I said and hung up.

I felt a surge of triumph followed immediately by a twinge of panic. How was I going to immediately come up with this fragile and valuable item I had promised? I cruised through the house, eyeing anything that looked remotely breakable, in desperation almost wrenching the mirror off my Art Deco dressing table. Then inspiration struck: I headed to the kitchen where I kept my cherished collection of vintage cookie jars displayed on a high shelf. After a brief but painful deliberation, I selected a Depression-era number—a hobo's head, sad-eyed and sooty-faced, the lid his tattered soft hat. It was a glorious piece of kitsch for which I'd coughed up fifteen bucks in a Glendale thrift shop some years before; but similar pieces now went for hundreds of dollars at auction. A sacrifice for dear old Windermere. I nestled it in an old Saks shopping bag and set off to see Marcus's mom.

The Barneses' address listed in the school directory was in Vanished Hills, a remote but swanky neighborhood of gated communities and horse compounds east of the Malibu Hills. I zipped up the Pacific Coast Highway, the ocean on my left a kinetic dazzle of diamonds and sapphires. I turned into Topanga Canyon, then veered onto the Old Topanga Road, with its rustic dirt off-lanes dotted with stuck-in-the-sixties hippie shacks. I had a strong feeling that if I switched on the radio, I'd hear the last refrain of "All You Need Is Love" followed by a bulletin from Vietnam.

Then it occurred to me with a shock that it was on one of these bucolic little remote byways that Brandon had met his violent end. I remembered from the police report that it bore the eerily resonant name of Forget-Me-Not Way. I drove slowly, checking out signposts. Three quarters of a mile farther, I found it, a rutted lane lurching off from the right. On an impulse I turned onto it.

It was hardly more than a path, with ramshackle wooden houses obscured by sycamores and dusty Christmas berry bushes. I slowed to a crawl, looking for . . . what? A mailbox bearing a name that might spark something?

But the police had thoroughly canvassed the neighborhood: none of the names of the occupants listed in the report had meant a thing to me.

The road bent sharply. I followed it around; a crow, startled by my approach, flapped wildly into the air, dropping the corpse of a dove. It seemed a sinister omen. I suddenly became aware there were no houses in immediate view, no sign of life at all. Then I heard another car coming up the road from behind. With a shudder of dread, I realized it was braking. I had the vision of myself occupying the slab next to Brandon's in the morgue, my face similarly erased. I gave a whimper of terror.

But then the car swerved to the left. I dimly noted an elderly lady behind the wheel of an old Caddie; she tapped an annoyed little toot of the horn to scold me for hogging the road, then zipped on by. I let out an almost maniacal laugh at my bout of sixties-worthy paranoia. Then I swung a U-turn and made tracks out of this Canyon That Time Forgot.

The Barneses' residence proved to be a large, square structure painted a nondescript earth tone, architecturally banal, with just a few startled-looking liquidambar saplings stuck in a sod lawn by way of landscaping. There were no visible personal touches to indicate the place was even occupied. I thought that if an alien species were to have the concept of a human house described to them and then be instructed to replicate it, this is pretty much what they'd come up with.

There was actually something replicalike about Helene Barnes as well, I reflected, pulling into the crushed-stone driveway. As if, as in *Invasion of the Body Snatchers,* the real Helene had been eliminated and a pod person insinuated in her place. Nobody human could be so consummately self-contained as she appeared to be. Nor so immaculately groomed, from the burnished copper skin that had certainly never been troubled with a pimple, to the formidable wedge of hair from which nary a scraggle ever escaped. Compared to Helene Barnes, Coco Chanel would have looked frowsy.

There was also the fact that nobody really knew much about her. She deflected personal questions with vague answers that revealed nothing. "Oh, I'm from the South," she'd reply, if you asked her where she was from. "A town you've never heard of." Even her husband, George Barnes, was a cipher; it was known only that he was white and had a job with some fuzzily financial description that kept him on a seemingly perpetual business trip to the Far East.

The perfect pod mate.

I had looked forward to seeing the interior of the house to see if it offered more personal information. But a sign reading *Out of the Oven,* written in a curling calligraphy, pointed to the side of the house, and that of course was where I'd find Helene. I followed its indication to a partially opened door and let myself into a vast kitchen. Some half-dozen young women scurried between brimming counters and stainless steel ovens. They were all either black or Hispanic, dressed in powder pink smocks and the kind of hairnets once favored by greasy spoon waitresses named Gladys. Smells so heavenly they made my knees weak permeated the room: a fragrant spice of orange-ginger, mixed with the holiday scent of almonds toasting in butter, and an earthy underlay of fresh-baked chocolate bread.

And over the din of young laughing voices, clanging pots, and the ping of a timer, a baby was strenuously crying.

I quickly located the source of the bawling babe—a bassinet

trimmed in white eyelet, placed in macabre proximity to a chopping block. Helene Barnes was stationed beside it, jiggling it rather perfunctorily, as if her Pod Person manual had described this as the preferred system for soothing human infants. Noticing me, she called out to the room at large, "Josefina, come tend to your son." A caramel-skinned teenager set down the cucumber she was peeling and took over the rocking duty.

Helene walked briskly over to me. She also had on a pink smock, but where the others were rumpled and stained, hers was as fresh and crisp-creased as if just plucked off an ironing board.

"So you made it," she said, with a slightly surprised inflection, as if she had not quite credited me with the intelligence necessary to navigate my way to Vanished Hills.

"It was a snap," I trilled. "Hardly any traffic this time of day."

She ignored my social platitudes and went on flatly, "I'm sorry to drag you into the middle of this bedlam. One of my regular clients decided to hold a cocktail tonight and gave me four hours' notice, if you can believe that. It'll be a sheer miracle if everything doesn't end up either burned or half raw."

As if to prove her point, one of the young women came up to us and presented a tray of pastries. "I think they got a little over-brown, Mrs. Barnes," she said diffidently.

I stared at them ravenously. "What are they?"

"Gruyère and green onion tartlet, to be garnished with a roasted Russian beet purée," Helene recited. "Maybe you could be our guinea pig. Taste one and tell me what you think."

I needed no urging to pop one in my mouth. The buttery crust flaked, then dissolved, on my tongue, giving way to a delicious tang of cheese and the sweetness of the caramelized onion. "Wonderful," I murmured.

"Then I guess it'll do." Helene nodded at the young woman who whisked the tray away. "Her Highness will just have to be satisfied. I don't know why I continue to supply Myra Alston, it's always such a drama."

The name of my old table-waiting crony immediately piqued my interest. "Is that who's throwing the party?" I said, unable to suppress a grin. Myra's culinary tastes had certainly come up from the old fried-porkchop-with-side-of-hash-browns days at the Panic Café. "I hope she tips well," I added. "She's a former waitress herself."

"She tips lavishly, as a matter of fact. A regular Lady Bountiful. Which if you ask me is exactly why she uses my service."

I raised a questioning eyebrow.

"As you can see, I employ inner-city girls. It's the whole basis of this company, to provide them with some vocational training. I supervise the food, but the service is sometimes a little rough-edged. Myra could afford to use a glitzier service, but I suspect she knows those gay cater waiters would be mocking her every time her back was turned. But with my girls, she gets to be Lady Bountiful."

"But I thought she was supposed to be such a tough cookie. Very difficult to deal with."

Helene's lips tightened slightly, an approximation of disdain. "The first affair I did for her, she tried a prima donna act. Demanding this, demanding that, throwing little snit fits if one of my girls so much as folded a napkin wrong. I quickly set her straight. I told her I didn't care how much she paid, or whether her son was the Messiah reborn, I would not stand for my girls being subjected to such abuse. She backed off immediately. Paper bullies like Myra Alston always do."

Do they? For some reason—perhaps because she had recited all this in her monotone Pod Person voice, I had the distinct feeling Helene wasn't quite telling the real story. Could it be, I wondered, that the reason the fearsome Myra was such a pussycat in Helene's hands was because Helene had something on her? Something possibly to do with her son? I searched for a way to unobtrusively roll the conversation around to Jamie.

But then Helene's face suddenly changed: the emotionless pod shell dissolved into a fairly human expression of pure delight. She was staring over my shoulder; I turned my head to see Marcus loping into the kitchen, a backpack slung over his shoulder.

"Hey, baby, I didn't hear you come in," his mother said, and kissed his broad forehead. "How was school today?"

"All right. They said I could skip ahead to solid geometry. They're going to let me take the class with the upper school."

"That's marvelous, baby!" She kissed him again.

"Hi, Marcus, remember me?" I cut in.

"Of course I do," he said levelly. "I enjoyed the workshop very much. Particularly when we examined the basic principles of animation. I'm looking forward to the next one."

"There's some Fruit Roll-ups in the pantry cupboard, if you want a snack," Helene told him. "Also honey grahams."

"I think I'd prefer the grahams."

It seemed odd to me that, with all this abundance of goodies, the adored son was allotted only packaged food. But Marcus seemed content to dump his backpack on the floor and head to the pantry, without even a glance at the sumptuous trays laid out all around him.

The baby, who had been taking a short breather, suddenly let loose with renewed gusto; at the same time, a huge pot began to overboil, causing several agitated little shrieks. Helene fixed me with an irritated frown, as if I were somehow the cause of all this commotion. "Forgive me if I cut our visit short," she said crisply. "That, I presume, is your donation?"

I'd almost forgotten what I'd ostensibly come for. I quickly thrust the Saks shopping bag into her outstretched hand. "People have been so generous," she murmured. "We've gotten some wonderful things in. A full set of Porthault linens, and airline tickets for two to Buenos Aires. Round trip of course. And admission for a group of a hundred to the Keystone Studios Theme Park."

My smile turned a bit sickly. Every item she'd ticked off had to be worth well over a thousand dollars.

"And wait'll you hear what Herb and Jeannie Gilman have donated!"

The Hope Diamond? Van Gogh's *Sunflowers*?

"What?" I asked sourly.

"A restored Silver Cloud Rolls-Royce that had once belonged to Cary Grant! We're predicting a mid- to high-five-figure bid for it."

On that note, she peered with great expectation into the Saks bag. Her elegant nostrils flared at the sight of the crockery hobo.

"It's a vintage cookie jar," I explained. "Made in the thirties."

"Oh, I see, a collector's item," she said faintly. "Well I'm certain it will fetch a good price." She peered at me meaningfully, a clear signal that I'd be expected to cough up the winning bid myself.

"The van's here!" someone shouted.

It was as if an elf had yelled out, "The sleigh's here!" in Santa's workshop. What had been a bustle of activity suddenly turned into a maelstrom. Last-minute garnishes rained down onto platters, sheets of cellophane sealed up trays, there were a few near-collisions as pink-smocked women raced purposefully around the room. Helene instantly forgot my presence and began field-marshaling her troops: "There should be three trays of salmon tartare. Where are the scallions for the halibut sashimi? Josefina, help Tanisha with the vegetable stack . . ."

I seized the opportunity of my sudden invisibility to gravitate to Marcus. He had pulled a stool up to one of the counters and sat solemnly munching his graham crackers while turning the pages of a book.

"So you don't get to sample the goods, huh?" I commiserated.

He shot me a somewhat superior look. "I don't really care much for fussy food," he said. "I'm more a plain and simple type of person."

"I guess that's healthier in the long run. What are you reading?"

He flipped the cover over for my perusal. I was relieved to see it was *The Adventures of Sherlock Holmes*; given the reputation of his I.Q., I was afraid it might be *The Critique of Pure Reason*.

"I loved that book when I was a kid," I remarked.

The huge green eyes regarded me again, this time thoughtfully. "The concept of deductive reasoning is very interesting," he said.

"Though of course in these stories we're only given fairly simple examples of the process."

"It's elementary," I said with a grin.

He didn't grin back, but nodded rather matter-of-factly. With those eyes and that golden skin, he'd be a remarkably good-looking boy if only he would lighten up, I thought. Then it occurred to me that I'd never seen him crack a smile or even display a hint of a twinkle—nothing altered that deadly serious expression. There had been hanging judges who'd been cheerier than Marcus Barnes.

"I'm sorry about Jamie and Kerrin the other day," I said. "I shouldn't have let them tease you like that. They're really nasty kids."

Marcus squirmed uneasily. "They're okay," he mumbled. "They're just kind of immature, that's all."

I was amazed to hear the sensitive Marcus defending the Satanic Two. But the mention of their names seemed to make him supremely uncomfortable, and so I changed the subject. "How are you coming with your flip book?"

"Okay, I guess. Though to be perfectly honest, I really haven't come up with a suitable subject yet. Drawing's not particularly my strong point."

"I guess acting is what you're better at," I said casually. "And I heard you're pretty good at singing and dancing too."

He gave the quick hunch of one of his thin shoulders that was evidently a nervous gesture. "I'm not that good."

"That's not what I've heard. Some of the other kids who were at the *Orphans* audition seemed to think you were the best one there. They said you should have been the one to have the starring role."

The green eyes lifted up to me again, this time with an expression that made me give a start.

"What's going on here?" Helene's voice snapped coldly at my back.

"We're just chatting," I said quickly.

"I heard you asking him about auditions. My son has no plans to be an actor. He's going to be a molecular biologist."

Marcus was now staring down at his graham crackers, which he was crumbling in his fingers. Helene laid a light hand on his shoulder blade. "We're extremely busy," she said to me. "Would you please leave."

I had the feeling she was prepared to chuck me bodily out the door. "I was just on my way," I assured her and promptly directed myself out.

I retraced my route back through Topanga Canyon, this time not thinking of Brandon. My thoughts were totally preoccupied with the Barneses, mother and son. The fact that Helene had given me the bum's rush at the mere mention of the *Orphans* audition was sufficient cause for rumination. But even more absorbing was that look in Marcus's eyes when I had brought it up . . .

A look I could only describe as sheer terror.

13

"Guess what, Mom," squealed Chloe on the phone, "I skied moguls today and I didn't fall down even once! Debby, that's my ski instructor, says I'll be ready for Ajax by next year."

"That's wonderful, sweetie!" I exclaimed. The phone had been jangling when I returned from the Barneses'. I raced for it and was rewarded with the sound of my daughter's voice. "I wish I was there to watch you." There was the thump, thump of a Latin beat in the background and a peal of laughter. "Where are you, back at the condo?"

"No, we're over at Annie's. She's got this really cool house, the window comes to a big point and you can see out all the way to the mountains. We've brought all our stuff here and I'm going to stay in Belle's room. Guess what, there's two canopy beds!"

"Who's Annie?"

"Belle's mom. We were all on the jet together and Belle's now my best friend. She gave me a cool silver charm for my bracelet and I gave her my panda bear necklace and when we go home we're going to have sleep-overs."

The background beat got louder.

"Annie's teaching Daddy how to cha-cha-cha," Chloe added.

This took me momentarily aback. Here was a guy whose idea of dancing heretofore had been to flail about in place to a seventies vintage Stones tune. "That's nice," I said, in a rather strangled voice.

"Did they catch the guys yet?"

"What guys, sweetie?"

"The ones who shot Brandon."

"Not yet. They're still looking for them. But don't worry, I'm sure they'll be caught." Even to myself, I sounded unconvinced. I added quickly, "Let me talk to Dad a minute, okay?"

"Yeah, okay. Dad-dy!" she yelled. "It's Mom."

The telephone dropped with a klunk. I heard the sound of footsteps retreating, then others approaching, and then Kit was on.

"What in the world is going on?" I demanded. "Chloe says you've packed up and moved to some stranger's place. Why didn't you tell me?"

"It was a spur-of-the-moment decision. Annie's got this fantastic huge place and Chloe's become joined at the hip with Belle, so it made sense."

"Just who is this Annie?" I heard a shrill Suspicious Wife note seep into my voice and struggled to eliminate it.

"Annie Manzano. You know, Charlie Manzano's wife. He's that big-time bankruptcy lawyer, the friend of the Steinmans . . ."

I could readily picture Charlie Manzano for the simple reason I had once surreptitiously used him as a model for a character in my Amerinda series—a back-thumping, stogie-gesturing ferret named Franklin. His wife was less distinct in my memory: I vaguely recalled a small, skinny person with spiky dark hair and a penchant for revealing what she had paid for her clothes. "So is Charlie there too?" I asked.

Kit gave an artificial laugh that made my heart sink. "They divorced over a year ago, don't you remember?" He lowered his voice to a confidential whisper. "She really took him to the cleaners, too. You ought to see this house, it's got to be worth three million at least."

"Are there any other guests?"

"Some geeky English writer and his girlfriend, but they're leaving in the morning, thank god. The guy's got permanent post-nasal drip."

"Let me get this straight." I reprised the Suspicious Wife Shrill. "You're going to be staying alone in a house with a divorcée who I scarcely know."

"We're hardly alone. We've got two extremely attention-demanding ten-year-olds, not to mention a staff of three or four. And I do have my own bedroom, naturally." He added in a teasing tone, "You're not jealous, are you?"

"Of course not," I said brittlely.

"That's good, since I didn't mind your little flirtation with Brandon."

I felt a stab of guilt, which vanished when he added, "You were like a teenybopper gaga over a rock star. And that didn't threaten me at all."

"Of course it didn't," I snapped back, "since Brandon happened to be gay."

Kit gave a burp of surprise. "He was? I didn't know that. I mean it wasn't obvious . . ."

"Why? Because he didn't walk with a sashay and spend most of his time critiquing the color scheme of our dining room?" We were in danger of getting bogged down in a silly squabble; I cut it short by adding, "There's a few other things you didn't know about him."

"Yeah? Like what?"

I took a deep breath, then launched into a quick rendition of my meeting with the network folks—how my Amerinda tape had acquired a new and distinctly unimproved ending, and how I believed it was all related to Brandon's death. While I was on a confessional role, I tossed in the news that he had had no documents, including a driver's license, and that an aviator jacket with a roomy lining had served as his personal banker.

There was a long moment of stunned silence on Kit's end. "Jesus, I thought you knew the guy," he said at length.

"I did, twenty years ago. And okay, I admit I should have realized people can change in that time. But I don't remember you suggesting we run any background checks on him either. He had you charmed right from the start."

"Okay, maybe we were both taken in. But whether or not Brandon was involved with anything shady, it's all over and done with. He's dead and can't be brought back and I'm horribly sorry about it, but that pretty much ends our involvement."

"Maybe not," I said.

Another wary pause. "What now?"

"Someone just messengered to me the BMW key Brandon was using."

"What are you talking about?"

"The spare key on the Willigher key chain." I filled him in on the mysterious messenger arriving across the street, and Detective Langocetti's stubborn resistance to take it too seriously. "It's all kind of creepy. Maybe I should get on a plane and come out there with you."

"Well yeah, sure," he said gingerly. "If that's what you want."

I began to calculate that I could hop a plane that evening, two and a half hours to Denver, arrive in Aspen before midnight. Except there were Chloe's animals to consider, with their complicated feeding schedules. Plus, I reflected, Valerie Jane was counting on me to be her Lamaze partner, she was already feeling abandoned, it would be rotten of me to let her down . . . "I guess there's no point," I said. "I mean, you'll be back day after next. And whatever those keys meant, I don't think it was an announcement that somebody intends to slit my throat." I attempted a brave little chuckle.

"I guess you're right, no sense in making the trip for just a couple of days." There was an edge of relief in his voice that I hated. "And I guess this means the network's not going to pick up your series," he added.

"I don't think so," I said crisply. "Unless they want to change the slant from flying hedgehogs to Kids Who Kill. And anyway, in view of everything that's happened, whether or not I get a show on the air is kind of insignificant."

"Yeah, of course," he said, without a thundering amount of conviction. We exchanged rather tepid "Love you" and hung up.

I listlessly began sorting through the couple of days' worth of mail that was stacked by the phone. A contingent of bills, a postcard from my stepsister Jilly in Minnesota, noting that my father's Alzheimer's seemed to be responding to massive doses of vitamin E—or at least he no longer thought she was his cousin Esther who'd been struck dead by lightning in 1962. And, thanks to Kit's fast draw with a credit card, zillions of catalogs. An emporium called Sensual Essentials invited me to forward thirty-six ninety-five for a vial of patchouli massage oil. Or, if I were in a friskier spending mood, I could command a pair of hand-lasted leather boots from an Italian concern for the price of twenty-four hundred smackers, plus applicable shipping and handling charges.

After browsing this consumption extravaganza, I reached for a remaining envelope that had almost been buried in the sea of glossy catalogs. It was a plain white business-sized envelope, hand-addressed to me. It contained a black-and-white photo, creased in half to fit. I unfolded it and gave a start.

It was a photo of myself, without question the most unflattering one ever taken. I appeared in extreme close-up, caught in the act of cramming a chocolate brioche into my mouth. My hair, hanging in damp, limp corkscrews, looked like overcooked rotelle and my pores seemed gigantic enough to swim in. My eyes were popping with the sheer exertion of gluttony.

I tossed the thing down in revulsion. Then I snapped it back up again and examined it more closely. With a shudder, I recognized that it had been taken just two days before, when Valerie and I had gone on our little charge-a-fest down Montana Avenue.

I scrambled for the phone to call Kit back, then realized that, like an idiot, I'd forgotten to ask him for the number of his new digs. No use trying Information—a social-climbing divorcée like this Annie would as soon amputate her right arm as have a listed number.

I had promised to notify Langocetti if anything else was sent to me. I pictured him clumping back through the door, perusing the photo with a stolid refusal to be impressed. Taking it with him to "check things out," but reminding me for the umpteenth time that the McKenna case was closed.

Terry Shoe on the other hand had exhorted me to keep her informed of any new developments. This was indubitably a new development; it was high time I kept her informed.

Despite its blue-eyed American name, Larry's Club Time, a storefront restaurant tucked into a Western Avenue minimall, was authentically Korean. It was spare as a luncheonette, with harsh, take-no-prisoners lighting, Formica-topped tables and plastic-backed chairs. On the plastered walls were hung several black-and-gold silk scrolls decorated with fabulous beasts. I made a mental sketch of one, a sort of cross between a unicorn and wild boar with ornate tusks and a horn that swirled fatly like a soft ice-cream cone.

The clientele was almost exclusively Asian businessmen in somber gray suits. The incongruous exception was the dumpy Caucasian woman in cranberry polyester seated with a handsome, snappily tailored African-American man at a table in back: Terry and her partner Armand Downsey. In the past, our powwows had always taken place in coffee shops or delis, over fat-and-sugar-bursting crullers and blueberry muffins: this was no doubt part of Terry's crash course in Korean ethnicity.

I slid into one of the two empty seats at their table. The surface was littered with bowls, plates and saucers of food redolent of pickled sauces and black bean pastes. But aside from the neat mounds of white rice, none of the dishes was familiar to me.

"Howdy," Terry greeted me. "You remember Downsey?"

I smiled somewhat tentatively. Pretty much the last time Armand Downsey had seen me, I'd been in handcuffs, on a forced march through the bowels of the West L.A. Police Station. But if he had any recollection of having witnessed the most humiliating moment of my life, he graciously gave no indication of it.

"Pleasure to see you again," he said in his rich purr of a voice. "And congratulations on your impending joyful event." I murmured my thanks. To Terry, I said, "Isn't this a little off your beaten track?"

"Yeah, but Frank's got some relatives coming to visit from Seoul in a couple of days. I figure I better get acquainted with what they're gonna want to eat."

Of course. Terry's husband, Frank, was a minister—Presbyterian, if memory served—who also happened to be a first generation Korean American. In a less frazzled state of mind, I'd have instantly made the connection.

Downsey pushed a pair of wooden chopsticks my way. "Do you use these? I've been trying to show my partner the correct way to hold them, but she still insists on handling them like a deadly weapon."

This was true: I watched her stab at a pork dumpling like Sharon Stone wielding an ice pick. "I hope you're hungry," she remarked to me. "We've got enough food to feed a town. I figured if I ordered enough different things, I'd find something I could at least get used to." She gestured to a wooden bowl. "This bip-bam-bop isn't too bad."

"It's called *bibambap*," Downsey corrected her gruffly. "It's a famous Korean specialty, a mixture of rice, vegetables, fried egg and chili paste. There's two flavors here, shrimp and this one's an herby mountain fern. That dish is *kalbi*, which is marinated short ribs, and that's grilled intestine, if you're up for something more adventurous."

"I tried it," Terry snorted. "I won't even mention what I thought it tasted like."

They waited till I had heaped my plate and had started hungrily sampling the food.

"So we heard about the special delivery you got," Terry began.

"The car keys from the BMW, huh? Langocetti said you perceived it as some kind of threat, but he's not so sure."

"I guess he just thinks Brandon was killed by a very considerate person," I said acidly. "Somebody nice enough to return our car keys so we won't be too terribly inconvenienced by his having slaughtered our live-in help."

Terry and her partner exchanged amused glances. I was thrilled to see I was living up to their anticipated level of entertainment.

"Aren't you rather jumping the gun?" Downsey put in. "You don't really know who sent the keys."

"No. And I don't really know who sent this either." I opened my crocodile clutch bag and took out the photograph. "This came in the morning mail," I announced and, with something of a dramatic flourish, handed it to Terry.

"Hee, hee," she giggled. "This is some picture! You're really pigging out." She giggled harder. "If somebody's blackmailing you not to show it around, my suggestion is to pay whatever they want."

She shoved it over to Downsey, who also couldn't resist a chuckle. "It's a humdinger, all right."

"That's not the point!" I burst out. "The point is it was taken without my knowledge. Two days ago, while I was shopping on Montana with a friend. Somebody must have been following me. And they obviously want me to know it."

Downsey lifted a brow. "Are you positive your friend didn't take it? He or she might have had a camera and snapped it when you weren't aware. And then sent it to you as a practical joke."

I considered the possibility that Valerie Jane might have whipped a Brownie from her pocket and immortalized me in a moment of looking disgusting. I shook my head. "It's not her style. My friend's a very forthright person, she never does things on the sly. Besides, even if she did take a picture of me looking like that, she'd never in a million years be cruel enough to show it to me."

Neither detective looked totally convinced. They evidently suspected that evil—or at least nastiness—could lurk in the heart of just about anyone. Disgruntled, I shoveled a chopstick-full of *bi-*

bambap into my mouth; then it struck me that I probably now resembled my pigging-out photo and yanked the chopsticks away as if they had suddenly caught fire.

Terry drowned her own plate with soy sauce, then stirred it into a loam-colored muck. "Okay, let's look at it your way," she said. "Somebody out there sent you both the keys and this photograph . . ."

"Brandon's killer," I cut in.

"Somebody who possibly was involved in a homicide," she amended. "Your theory is that both these items were meant to be a warning."

"Yeah. That this maniac knows who I am and is watching me."

"Why? Have you done anything that might attract a maniac's attention?" Downsey asked archly.

"Maybe," I said.

They both inclined slightly in my direction, an attitude I found weirdly flattering.

"You want to be more specific?" Terry demanded. Her eyes, which had the mood ring–like ability to change colors, from tawny gold to nondescript brown, now had a startlingly orange cast.

I began an almost babbling account of my investigations to date—from my enlightening luncheon with Andy Oberest, to my undercover operation at both the McDonald's casting call and the Barnes household. I finished, took a bite of cabbage kimchi, and waited for some acknowledgment of my brilliant legwork.

"Is that all?" Terry said.

My face fell. "All? Look at everything I've turned up."

"No hard facts, not one piece of corroborating evidence. It's only the most wild conjecture that any of these kids was that puppy in the videotape."

"But everything points that way. And you should have seen the look on Marcus Barnés's face. It was sheer terror. I've never seen a kid look that petrified before."

"Yeah, well I hate to break this to you, but scared looks aren't enough to reopen a homicide case."

I drew a breath of exasperation and almost choked on an acrid whiff of tobacco smoke. A party of businessmen at a neighboring table who had been boisterous over a bubbling hot pot, had now all lighted up, apparently oblivious to the news that L.A. eateries were supposed to be smoke-free. I glared futilely in their direction. "So what do I do now?" I asked, turning back to the detectives.

"You do nothing," Terry snapped sharply. "You stay out of the way of the whole goddamned thing."

"So you *do* think I'm under some kind of threat."

Neither said a thing for a moment. Then Downsey said, "Look, there's one thing that maybe you should know. Brandon McKenna was planning to skip town the afternoon he was murdered."

"What?" I exclaimed.

"He had a ticket to Vancouver, departing 1:15 P.M. on Air Alaska. Purchased in cash from a travel agent in Encino that morning. He presented a Nebraska driver's license as a picture ID."

"But that's impossible. He hadn't said anything about leaving. There wasn't a hint in anything he did . . ." I felt an irrational stab of betrayal, as if we actually had been lovers and I'd just found out he'd been planning to throw me over. "There was nothing packed in his room," I finished weakly.

"We've got to figure it was a spur-of-the-moment decision," Terry said.

I washed this information down with a deep draught of lemon-flavored water. "I guess it fits with what we already know," I acknowledged. "When Brandon dropped Chloe off at Windermere, he saw someone he was deathly afraid of—maybe someone he'd come here to hide from in the first place. So he realized he had to drop everything and run. So then he probably cruised down Ventura until he spotted a travel agent." I shook my head. "It still doesn't explain one thing. All he had to do then was head back home, grab his stuff and get out to the airport. So what was he doing meandering down a nowhere little lane in Topanga Canyon?"

"One possibility—someone could have forced him to drive there," Downsey said.

Terry nodded. "Say somebody's waiting for him when he comes out of the travel agency. They jump into his car, stick a gun to his head, and order him to drive to this secluded spot. That's where they blow him away."

"Sure, but the car was still there in this remote canyon street," I pointed out. "So how would this person have made his getaway?"

"Maybe there's an accomplice in another car waiting in the pre-arranged spot. Or, if it's a single perpetrator, maybe he simply walks away. Hikes down Topanga and grabs a bus on Sunset." Terry gave me a condescending smirk. "You Hollywood people might not realize this, but there is public transportation available in this city."

The cigarette smoke was swirling stronger. Every Surgeon General's warning about the effects of secondhand smoke on fetuses was trumpeting with the brio of a marching band in my brain.

"Are you okay?" Downsey asked me.

"You look sort of green around the gills," Terry put in.

"It's this smoke." I shot another dirty look at our puffing neighbors. "It's against the law, isn't it? Can't you go over and give them a ticket or something?"

Suggesting to two homicide detectives, the crème de la crème of cops, that they become the equivalent of meter maids was manifestly a faux pas: they both stiffened with affront.

"Sorry, stupid thing to say," I said. "I think I'd better get some fresh air." I rose somewhat unsteadily to my feet.

"Just remember what we told you," Terry said. "From here on, let things alone."

"No problem," I assured her. Then I staggered out to inhale the air of Western Avenue that was tainted only with a thin haze of winter smog.

14

The nine A.M. classes at Harriet Ho were always the most popularly attended. The aerobics class I'd been planning to take was a packed room, so I joined the low-impact that was mainly the province of the third-trimester ladies, waving to Valerie Jane warming up in a corner. After an hour of shuffling forward, shuffling back, and slo-o-owly stretching our leg muscles to prevent the heartbreak of varicose veins, we stumbled back into the roseate locker room.

Valerie sank heavily onto the changing bench. "That was some bitch of a workout," she wheezed.

"Actually I thought Deb was going easy on us," I said. With some concern, I noticed how much Valerie was sweating: her hair was soaked and her brown skin had an undertinge of deep red. "It might be time for you to cut out these classes," I told her.

"Maybe you're right." She mopped her face with a thick towel. "My grandma gave birth after a three-day hike from the slums of Guadalajara and swimming the Rio Grande. She popped my dad out in a dirt campground on the shantytown fringes of Laredo. And here I am, acting like some pampered *gringa*."

"You are half *gringa*," I reminded her.

"Yeah, the wimpy half." She gave a throaty chuckle and twined the towel around her long neck. "Anyway, I'm feeling better. It was just a little dizziness. Hey," she hissed suddenly, "check out that chick over there."

I finished peeling my damp tank top over my head and glanced in the direction. It was a girl in her early twenties with a pert, platinum-streaked ponytail, rather popping eyes bruised with purple shadow and a wide, thin mouth heavily greased with raspberry gloss. She seemed to fit in the struggling actress-waitress-whatever category, which made her a misfit among this coterie of well-heeled matrons. Her bun had been about five and half months in the oven, I thought, judging from the bulge in her tiger-print pregnancy leotard.

"What about her?" I hissed back.

"Notice anything peculiar?"

"If you mean she doesn't look like she's in a financial league to afford these classes, then yeah. But maybe the baby's poppa is footing the bill."

"There is no poppa," Valerie declared. "She's not really pregnant!"

I shot her a look. "Then she's got the worst case of water retention I've ever seen."

"Not that either," Valerie grinned. "It's padding. And a pretty crappy job at that."

"No shit!" I looked again. Nothing to me looked out of the ordinary, but I was willing to believe Valerie Jane—she had, after all, copped her second Golden Globe for a film in which she had made Alicia Silverstone go from virgin to labor, including a famous eight-months-pregnant bathing suit scene. "How can you tell?"

"Look at the way it's slightly more bulgy on one side than the other. Very sloppy work, I noticed it right away." Valerie shook her head with professional disdain. "And then in class, I was watching her. Every time her body moved right, her tum kind of jiggled to the left."

"Kind of against the laws of nature," I agreed.

"You bet. Hey look, she's not taking that sweaty leotard off, she's just pulling her shirt right over it. It's a synthetic fabric, she's going to stink like a barn." Valerie wrinkled her nose. "What the hell do you think she's up to?"

"Maybe she's planning to rob the lockers while everyone's in the next class," I whispered. Then I gave a low whistle. "Catch a look at those heels!"

The girl was squatting on a bench, strapping on a pair of black sandals that featured a fashionable four inches of stiletto heel. Valerie and I exchanged grimaces of imagined agony.

"A pregnant lady in stilettos. Yeah, right," Valerie snorted. "She must have one fucking miracle worker of a chiropractor."

The girl suddenly glanced my way. I quickly averted my own stare.

"That's the other thing," Valerie said. "She kept staring at you all through class. At one point I nearly sashayed right into her butt because she was so busy gawking at you and not Deb."

"I didn't know I was so irresistible." I gasped suddenly. "Oh my god!"

"What?"

"I just had a creepy thought. What if she's the one who followed us the other day. The one who took that photo I told you about."

Valerie sneaked another peep at her. "Could be. She's got enough room in that crummy padding job to hide a Nikon with a telephoto lens." She swiveled abruptly to her locker and began pulling out her clothes. "Hurry up and get dressed. We'll go stroll around again and see if she follows."

"What do we do if she does?" I asked nervously.

"Then we'll confront the broad and find out what the fuck she's up to."

"Do you think that's a good idea? I mean, we have no idea who she really is . . ."

"For godsake, Lucy, does she look like Jack the Ripper to you? Get a grip." Valerie spoke with the stern authority with which she habitually persuaded twenty-million-dollar-a-picture movie stars that the skin-tight black leather jeans they had selected from Wardrobe did not in fact make them look like a slightly more mature James Dean but only emphasized their bit of a paunch.

Without further argument, I shimmied into my chalk-pink sack dress, the one I'd bought envisioning myself looking like Jackie in the days of Camelot, but in my present state probably made me more reminiscent of Petunia Pig. I stuffed my grungy workout clothes in my canvas carryall and we both headed out to the street, turning in the foggy direction of the beach. We walked rapidly, talking in artificially animated voices.

After several blocks, Valerie said, "Is she there?"

I made an elaborate show of pretending to admire a passing brace of Scottish terriers, giving me the opportunity to glance back over my shoulder. The platinum ponytail was bobbing along some twenty yards behind. My heart skipped a beat. "She's there."

I watched her rather casually stop to window-shop an antique furniture store.

"Now she's checking out a Stickley couch," I reported.

"I wouldn't have thought Stickley was quite her taste, would you?"

"Uh-uh. She's much more the palomino-leather-trimmed-with-chrome type."

"Let's cross the street and see if she stays on our tail."

At the corner of Eleventh, we waited for a break in the traffic, then hustled ourselves across the road. The ponytail continued to bounce along amid the pedestrians on the opposite side. "She's not following," I said with relief.

"Guess again," Valerie said.

In the middle of the block, the girl suddenly made a sprint across the street.

"It still could be a coincidence," I said. "Maybe she parked over here."

"Coincidence, my ass. But okay, we'll give her the acid test. Let's go shopping."

She pulled me toward the nearest shop, a boutique called Sweet Nothings. Montana Avenue is as rife with lingerie shops as Marseilles is with fishmongers—there were at least a half dozen in the space of twelve short blocks, suggesting that Santa Monica women have far richer sex lives than you and me. Sweet Nothings was the largest and costliest of them: We pushed through the Baroquely etched glass door into a sprawling wonderland of satin and lace.

Valerie waddled the lead among racks and shelves of the sort of flimsy boudoir wear that, even when my stomach was flat, could make me feel like the Flab Queen of the West. A slinky young salesclerk with owlish glasses intercepted us at the end of an aisle. "Good morning ladies," she trilled. Her voice trailed off as her eyes settled on our midriffs.

Valerie plucked a wisp of a half-slip off a counter. "Does this come in a fifty-two-inch waist?" she asked briskly.

The owlish eyes blinked. "I don't think so."

"Damn, it's exactly what I'm looking for. I guess we'll just continue to look around."

The clerk blinked again. "Uh, fine," she managed and scuttled back to her register. With a giggle, Valerie and I turned to inspect a rack of frothy chiffon baby dolls.

"Two hundred and sixty-five bucks!" Valerie exclaimed, frowning at a price tag. "And look at the way it's made, crooked seams already starting to come apart. Some people have no concept of quality!"

I suddenly nudged her arm. "Our gal just came in."

The platinum ponytail hovered at the door. We edged to the other side of a rack of tap pants and peered at her through a curtain of peach satin. She ambled to a display of undies and began flicking through them with a nonchalant motion. Then she held up a pair of leopard-skin thong bikinis and studied them with the air of someone well accustomed to appraising sexy underwear.

"That gal's really got a jones for animal prints," Valerie remarked.

"Yeah, Sheena of Santa Monica."

The salesclerk now began to slink up to her with a "Can I help you" smile, then stopped dead at the sight of another bulging waistline. Her smile froze and she backed hurriedly away. Valerie and I smothered our laughter.

"Okay, this is it," I said, squaring my shoulders. "Let's go find out what this babe's all about."

"No, wait!" Valerie said. "If we confront her too suddenly, she's just going to bolt. What we need to do is get her alone someplace."

"What do you suggest, inviting her back home for a spot of tea?"

Valerie bit her lower lip contemplatively. "We're going to have to trick her some way."

I had a desperate idea. I opened my carryall and dug out a hairbrush.

"What are you doing?" Valerie snapped. "This is no time to primp."

"Primping is not what I had in mind," I replied crisply. "Just follow me." I grasped the brush by the bristle side, then strode quickly over to our ponytailed shadow and jabbed the hairbrush into the small of her back.

"This is a gun," I said softly. "Make one peep and I'll shoot."

She didn't make a peep but rather a sound like gargling with mouthwash and dropped the leopard skin thong to the floor. Valerie popped up at my side, grinning with approval. "So where should we take her, your place or mine?" she asked in a stage whisper.

Another and more emphatic gargle issued from the raspberry-glossed mouth.

"The dressing room," I declared, feeling a bit heady with power. I gave another jab with the brush handle. "Start walking!" I ordered.

We began moving *en groupe* toward the back of the store. Several customers stared in astonishment as we shuffled by. "What's everybody gawking at?" Valerie said loudly. "Don't they think pregnant women wear underwear?" She pulled open the swinging wooden door of a dressing room. I shoved the ponytail in and Valerie and I squeezed in behind her. The collective bulk of our three midriffs made the tiny cubicle a tight fit.

"What do you want?" the girl whimpered.

"We'll ask the questions here," Valerie declared. She was obviously drawing on her early years of working on B movies for the appropriate interrogatory technique. She was practically talking out of the side of her mouth. "What's your name?"

"Diane," the girl said in a scarcely audible voice.

"Pleased to meet you, Diane. Now strip."

"Huh?"

"You heard me, lady. Off with your clothes and make it snappy."

"I've still got the gun," I declared. I gave her hip a quick poke. With alacrity, she dropped her shoulder bag on the floor, yanked her shirt over her head, then shimmied the tigerskin leotard down over her stomach and stepped out of it. She was braless; two B-cup breasts jutted perkily above the cushion and thick pads of hospital gauze that were fastened to her stomach with surgical tape.

Valerie let out a loud guffaw. "Congratulations, you're about to give birth to a pillow. What did you do, fuck a Beautyrest mattress?"

"Should I take off my panties too?" Diane inquired in her teensy voice.

"No, don't!" I said quickly, hopping back.

"Hey, that's not a gun!" the girl squealed, getting a look at the brush in my hand.

"No, it's not," I admitted. "It's a travel-size Mason Pearson hairbrush with natural boar bristles."

She made a move as if to bolt from the dressing room, then suddenly realized she was half naked and shrank back up against the hanging mirror. She covered her bare cupcakes with crossed arms. "What do you *want*?"

"Where's the camera, girlie?" Valerie said, relapsing into bad noir dialogue.

The girl's eyes flicked to her shoulder bag on the floor. Valerie grabbed it and overturned it. A hail of stuff clattered onto the carpet, including a dollar-bill-sized Olympus camera. Also keys, wallet, Tampax, loose change, assorted cosmetics and costume jewelry and a shiny, flat-nosed gun.

The sight of a real gun made us all freeze, as if it were some utterly alien object that had just oozed out of another dimension. Diane made a sudden grab for it; Valerie body-blocked her with her enormous stomach, while I dived and picked the gun up with the tips of my fingers. "What's this for?" I asked in a shaky voice.

"Protection. I'm a single girl, and there are a lot of loonies out there."

"Yeah, a loony on every corner. I always have to beat them off with sticks." Valerie did a kind of Sumo wrestler squat, picked up the camera, and with a grunt, straightened back up. "Olympus with a zoom lens. She's our babe, all right."

"You took a photo of me the other day, didn't you?" I said. "And sent it to my house."

She seemed about to deny it. Valerie took a threatening step forward; Diane gave a whimper of alarm. "Yeah," she blurted. "But only because it was what I was told to do."

"By whom?" Valerie demanded.

"Her husband."

"What!" I exclaimed. "That's ridiculous."

"Excuse me, but that's exactly who it was." The thin lips set in a stubborn little slot.

"How do you know?" Valerie asked.

"I'm a serious actor, it's my *bus*iness to know who people like him are. He's Kit Freers, a producer of major motion pictures . . ."

"How do you know it was *Kit*?" I cut in.

"I met him. In one of those bars out on the boardwalk."

My stomach tightened. Kit's offices were in Venice, just a few blocks from the boardwalk.

"Describe him," Valerie ordered.

Her ponytail bobbled with indignation. "I knew perfectly well what he looked like, that's how I know it was really him. He's kind of medium tall with dirty blond hair and really light blue eyes. And his hair's kind of balding on top, right? And he's got this way of kind of patting the bald spot when he's talking?"

A pretty accurate description of Kit. The bones in my legs seemed to have softened to aspic; I propped myself for support against the dressing room wall. "When was this meeting?"

"Last Tuesday. It was five-thirty, I remember 'cause I came straight from my Pilates workout."

"And how did this important producer come to be having a rendezvous with a little Chiclet like you?" Valerie said.

"I did this low-budget horror movie last year, maybe you saw it? It was called *Touch Monkeys* and I played this, like, hooker? Who gets strangled on the subway?" She shot us hopeful glances to see if we'd caught this illustrious performance. "So anyway, the director was Dick Lopensky and he was the one who recommended me."

It was getting worse and worse—Dick Lopensky was, if not exactly a bosom buddy of Kit's, certainly an old-time acquaintance, dating back to the days when Kit was still toiling in the low-budget arena. "Okay, let's say it was Kit," I said. "Why did he want you to spy on me?"

"He wouldn't tell me exactly. He just said he was worried you were into something dangerous and getting in over your head. I figured it was drugs, like this girlfriend of mine who was dealing coke and got caught and now she's in this medium-security jail up near Mendocino . . ."

"So?" Valerie snapped impatiently.

"So Mr. Freers said he needed someone to follow her and get pictures of whoever she was with." Diane turned a sullen pout on me. "It was a lot harder than I thought, because I never knew when you were going to go out. And when I tried waiting outside your house, this mean old man knocked on my window and said what was I doing parking on this block, like he thought I was some kind of burglar."

I smiled. Old Mr. Goldenstein with his Cairn terriers—one-man security enforcer.

"But I was lucky your husband gave me some tips on where I could find you," Diane continued. "The one place was Harriet Ho's. So I started going there like I was a regular and nobody would be suspicious, and after that class the other day, when you didn't get right back in your car, it was the first time I could really follow you around. And I watched you two together . . ." She nodded to include Valerie. "And I thought that if you were into dealing, being pregnant would be a real good cover-up. So I took pictures like mad."

Valerie gave an amused snort. "She's got a point, you know."

"The photo you sent me didn't show me with anybody else," I said to Diane.

"*That* wasn't me. I mean, it wasn't me who sent you anything. I just left all the film where he told me, at this house in Santa Monica Canyon."

"What house? Do you remember the address?"

"Yeah, cause it gave me the creeps, Sixteen-sixty-six Warrick Drive. Six, six, six, like the devil, and Warrick sounds like warlock, so I was like, 'I don't want to go near this place,' but it turns out it was okay."

"No coven of witches inside?"

"Nobody inside. It was empty, all boarded up. Which would've been even creepier, except these two big boards in front made a cross, so I figured where there's a crucifix, it would cancel out any evil karma. And the mailbox was right there on the street, I didn't even have to get out of my car."

There are some moments in life that are so intrinsically absurd, you seem to be able to experience them only from the outside looking in. This was definitely one of those moments: I was crammed in the dressing room of a ritzy underwear emporium with a pregnant Lesbian and a starlet whose stomach was padded like a lumpy mattress and who believed that Satan's legions could be warded off by a couple of fortuitously juxtaposed two-by-fours, and I had just received news that someone who appeared to be my husband had hired this starlet to spy on me. I suddenly seemed to be not inhabiting my own skin, but hovering at some checkpoint near the ceiling.

"You're hyperventilating!" Valerie snapped. "Sit down."

I dutifully sank to the floor and put my head between my knees. My perspective gradually returned to normal.

"Can I get dressed now?" Diane mewled.

"Yeah, go ahead," Valerie told her.

She skipped the leotard and jammed her arms back into her shirt, then knelt to scoop up the junk that had spilled from her bag. "Can I have my camera back? I had to buy it myself."

With a shrug of acquiescence, Valerie flipped open the back of the Olympus, yanked out the film cartridge and tossed the camera back to the girl.

"Just how much did Kit pay you for this espionage?" I asked from my occupation of the floor.

"I'm not doing it for money." The bruised-looking eyes widened with affront.

"For what then?" Valerie snapped. "Practice for a future gum-shoe career?"

"I told you, I'm a serious actor. Mr. Freers has promised to give me a part in his next movie. He says there are several roles I'd be suited for." She glanced down at me pleadingly. "Look, it's the kind of big break I really need. And I'm real sorry if it caused you problems, but I figured if I didn't do it, somebody else just would've."

"Yeah, there's always somebody who'll stoop to anything to get a big break," I said acidly.

"Can I go now?" she inquired.

"Yeah, get the fuck out of here," Valerie said.

"What about my gun?"

With some surprise, I realized I was still clutching the revolver.

"We'll just hold on to it," Valerie told her. "If you have any objections, you can always go to the police."

Diane opened her mouth, as if to protest, then evidently decided not to push her luck and bolted out of the stall.

I got to my feet and stashed the gun in my carryall. "I think I'll show this to the police myself."

Valerie nodded absently. "This is making me very claustrophobic," she said. "Let's blow the joint."

She pushed out of the stall, her stomach sailing before her like a dirigible. We backtracked through the aisles of satin and gauze and burst back out onto Montana.

"Do you believe that broad?" Valerie said.

A brisk salt breeze was blowing from the ocean; as I inhaled its bracing effect, the oatmeal seemed to clear from my brain. "I believe somebody put her up to following me," I replied. "But it wasn't Kit."

"What makes you so sure?"

"For starters, he was already in Aspen with Chloe when that photo was taken. So how could he have been the one who picked up the film, had it developed and then messengered to me?"

"Maybe he had somebody else do the dirty work for him. Or this broad could have been lying about that part. She might be just smart enough to know about the trouble you can get into sending blackmail material through the U.S. mail."

I shook my head. "I could conceivably imagine he'd be crazy enough to pay someone to follow me, if he really thought I was involved in something. But promise some bimbo a part in one of his films? Not in a zillion years. He'd sooner pluck his still-beating heart out and offer that as a payment."

Valerie looked dubious. "He could have lied. Promised her the part with the intention of wiggling out of it when the time came. In my experience, men are pretty damned good at lying their tiny eyes out when they want something from you."

Kit wasn't like that, I started to protest. But then I hesitated. At least once before he had lied to me about an affair he'd had—a one-night stand some years ago on a location set with a starry-eyed reporter from *Vanity Fair*—so it wasn't as if he were completely incapable of deceit.

Valerie suddenly seemed to stop listening. Her eyes roamed the shop fronts on the opposite side of the road. "I'm parched," she declared. "I feel like I could drink a lake. Where's that place that has those huge mango shakes?"

"You mean Tropics? It's that pink neon palm tree across the street."

"Thank god." She darted out precipitously into the middle of the block. I was about to remind her that Santa Monica cops gave out jaywalking tickets with the zeal of Gideons stocking Quality Inns with Bibles; but then again, I reflected, even the most hard-ass cop wouldn't have the temerity to bust two pregnant ladies with desperate cravings for fruit shakes. Besides, the road was clear, the traffic was stopped both ways at lights. I followed Valerie's charge.

From the corner of my eye I saw it—a light-colored sports utility vehicle with darkened windows that was pulling out from the opposite curb. As if in slow motion, I watched it accelerate and come hurtling directly toward us.

"Valerie!" I screamed. Before she could turn around, I slammed her forward by the shoulder blades, and we both fell, tumbling hard onto the opposite pavement. The SUV blasted on by, then whipped around the corner to disappear down Eleventh Street.

Several passers-by scurried to our aid. "That jerk almost ran you down!" I heard a woman's voice exclaim. Someone else yelled, "Did anyone get a license number?" and yet another voice was asking, "Are you okay, ma'am?"

One of my knees and both elbows were stinging; other than that, all my body parts seemed to be functioning correctly. "Yeah, I'm fine," I said. I let a pair of hands grasp mine and rose wobblingly to my feet. I turned to Valerie, who seemed to be crouching rather dejectedly on the sidewalk. "Val?"

"I'm okay, I just had the breath knocked out of me. What happened?"

"You almost got run over, that's what!" a silver-haired woman stated indignantly.

We were collecting a rapidly expanding crowd of rubberneckers around us. Valerie tried to stand; with a deprecating little laugh, she sank back down to her crouch. Several men grasped her arms and hoisted her up. "I feel a little dizzy," she murmured.

I noticed with alarm that her face was flushed a deep scarlet.

"Oh my god, she's bleeding!" someone behind me gasped. It puzzled me a moment: then I heard myself shrieking, "Jesus, Valerie!"

Bright red streams of blood gushed from under the hem of her short smock dress and were running down the length of her legs.

15

"For godsake, somebody call an ambulance!" I could sense my lips moving, but my voice, cracked and shrill, seemed to be coming from somewhere else, as if projected onto my lips by a ventriloquist.

Hands began digging into purses, breast pockets, backpacks, and a thicket of cell phones suddenly emerged. The men who had helped Valerie up now began to ease her back down. A teenager with a shaved skull and a delicate silver ring in his left eyebrow stripped off his Tommy Hilfiger jacket and, with Francis Drake–like chivalry, laid it on the pavement for her. A stringy, pewter-haired woman with a Lhasa apso on a rhinestone leash proffered a plastic bottle of Vittel. "Drink, you need water," she commanded.

Valerie took the bottle, but instead of putting it to her lips, squeezed it compulsively in her hands. "My baby," she whimpered. "Please, get somebody to help."

"Paramedics on the way," somebody called out.

I crouched down and cradled Valerie in my arms, crooning reassurances that neither of us believed. The blood was gushing heavily now; the Tommy Hilfiger jacket was a gory mess. My own blood boomed like surf in my ears, merging finally with the wail of an approaching ambulance. The crowd seemed to shuffle like a pack of cards, then dealt out two briskly striding paramedics, who muscled me aside to attend to Valerie.

Then a police car cruised up beside the ambulance and its two occupants began to troll the crowd. The Lhasa apso owner pointed in my direction and they ambled over to me.

I rotely answered their questions: Her name was Valerie Jane Ramirez; no, actually I didn't know her exact age, late thirties I assumed but wouldn't be surprised if she were some years older. About thirty weeks' pregnant, no complications that I knew of, at least until now . . . Yes, we had both taken a tumble after I shoved her out of the way of a speeding car, but not a bad fall, just a spill, really . . .

"Did you say you pushed her?" asked one of the cops. He was young, with razor-burned jowls and the let's-get-to-the-bottom-of-this intensity of a rookie.

"A car was trying to run us down," I repeated. My attention was riveted on Valerie who was shaking with sobs as the paramedics ministered to her. "I had to push her out of the way."

The rookie's partner, a husky female with a wedge of strawberry-colored bangs, abruptly took command of the interrogation. "What makes you believe this vehicle was intentionally trying to run you down?"

"Subtle things," I said dryly. "Like the fact that on an otherwise empty road, it was aiming straight for us at about a hundred and fifty miles an hour. It even crossed a lane to get just the right angle."

The forehead beneath the strawberry bangs scrunched with suspicion. She was obviously leaning toward the theory that I had concocted this speeding-car story to cover up my own shoving-with-malicious-intent activities. But then the Lhasa apso lady popped up at my shoulder. "I saw the whole thing, officers" she declared. "One of those big four-wheel-drive cars almost hit those two ladies. And then it just kept on going without even a hi-de-ho."

"Did anyone get a description of the vehicle or a license number?" inquired the rookie.

There was an excited rumble of voices. Someone piped up that it was a white Land Rover, another insisted it was a Trooper and more of a cream color, someone else offered up a smoke-gray Chevy Blazer with dark-tinted windows. A beaky-nosed man put in that that was exactly the kind of car favored by drug traffickers, with a meaningful glance at my stomach, as if to suggest it was stuffed with several kilos of the purest grade heroin. No one had a real fix on the license, though one woman rather thought it had a K in it, and another was almost positive it was from out of state. Nor did anyone get a solid make on the driver through the darkened windows. The two cops exchanged scowls of disgust at our collective lack of observation.

The paramedics had strapped Valerie onto a gurney and were slotting her into the back of the ambulance. "I need to go with my friend," I told the cops.

"Sorry, you can't ride with the EMS," the rookie pronounced officiously. "They'll go ahead and take her to St. Michael's. You can meet up there."

"If you want to make a report of this incident, you can come into the station," added his partner, in a tone that implied I could also whistle scoobie-doobie-doo at the moon and it would be an equally valuable usage of my time. I muttered my thanks; then I slipped a few twenties to the bald teenager to make up for the sacrifice of his jacket and raced off to my car.

In the maternity wing of St. Michael's Hospital, I shared a beige-on-beige waiting room with three generations of an immense Filipino family who industriously snapped archives of photos of each other with disposable cameras, and a dazed-looking old couple whose daughter-in-law was in labor with triplets. An hour ticked by. Various personnel in white coats drifted in and out, but none could supply me with any news. At last I encountered a nun who seemed to be intimately working the floor—she was of a modern order, with a knee-length tailored habit and a veil that looked more like the kind of plucky caps assigned to World War II servicewomen. Her name was Sister Josepha; her pleasant, scrubbed face softened with concern when I inquired about Valerie. "That lovely dark-haired young lady. She was rushed to surgery for an emergency Cesarean, but she hasn't been brought into recovery yet. We should hear something shortly."

I thanked her, then decided to kill some time in the cafeteria, a cheerless, fluorescent-lit space a few floors below. I loaded a tray with a soggy grilled cheese sandwich, a wilted green salad and an extra-tall lemonade and brought it to a table. A couple of maga-zines had been abandoned by a previous diner: one, a *Ladies' Home Journal* featuring "Decadent Chocolate Desserts!"; the other an old issue of *Movie Time,* with a cover story on "The Uncivil War Between the Alstons." There was a mocked-up photo of Jamie being tugged in opposite directions by a snarling Myra and an evilly leering Randy, as if they were trying to split him in two.

I pushed the magazine aside—in my present state of mind, the last thing I wanted to think about was the Dreaded Spawn and his warring human progenitors. I took a bite of melted cheese and a slurp of sugary lemonade. Then I glanced at the issue again. Curiosity overcame my aversion—I flipped to the story and began to read.

The gist of the article was that Jamie Alston had once upon a time been a Good Kid. Even-tempered, sweet-mannered. A bit rambunctious at times, but no more so than any other healthy boy his age. But in the last couple of years, since becoming the prize bone in his parents' ugly junkyard dog feud, he had begun to act out.

And with a vengeance. I was quickly transfixed by the sheer scope of his nasty antics. He had graffitied the walls of his Plaza Hotel suite with blue, green and gold Magic Marker and started a food fight in a Denver steak house. On his last movie, he had peed on a napping assistant director, thrown roughly a tantrum a minute and employed a vocabulary that was, in the magazine writer's vivid phrase, "dirtier than a flophouse toilet."

And lately he had acquired a taste for personally firing people under his power. "You don't know the meaning of humiliation until you've been sacked by a nine-year-old," snarled his former agent. "The thing is, you can't shit all over people like that and stay on the top. He's got another six months, then he'll just be another washed-up child actor. Ten years from now, you'll be reading about him in some Where Are They Now? column and he'll be dragging his ass out of his twenty-sixth drug rehab, talking pathetically about how he's going to make a comeback."

And meanwhile, the uncivil war continued to escalate. Randy gave interviews depicting his spouse as an insatiable nymphomaniac who changed sex partners the way most people change underwear. Myra countered with portraits of Randy as a dangerous obsessive, sending her bouquets of dead roses and stalking her in his XKE.

The topper, according to Myra, came shortly after she had relocated to California. Randy had broken into her Malibu house under cover of night and kidnapped Jamie, spiriting him off to a dude ranch near Jackson Hole, Wyoming, where they were tracked down by local sheriffs some days later. Within weeks, Myra had succeeded in obtaining a precedent-setting restraining order, forbidding Randy to set foot within the city limits of L.A.

I slurped up the frosty sludge at the bottom of my glass, flicked a dribble of cheese from my chin and stared at a family photo of the Alstons taken in Happier Days: A stringy-haired Myra bore the infant Jamie in a sling across her breast; Randy grinned his snaggly dentist's-delight grin into the camera. They looked so very much as I had known them back at the old Panic Café that I was suddenly struck by a vivid memory. It was the night Myra had been fired for doling out free eats to her cabby fiancé. Some hours later, the owner Solly's beloved old cocker spaniel Alice somehow got out of the gated alley behind the restaurant and was hit by a car on St. Mark's Place. Reports were that it had been a cab. Nothing could ever be proved, but it seemed obvious that Myra and Randy had taken ruthless revenge.

My remembrances were interrupted by Sister Josepha appearing behind me. "I've been looking for you," she said. "Your friend's out of surgery."

"The baby . . . ?" I felt I could scarcely breathe.

"Stillborn, I'm afraid." The nun's pale lips curved with sympathy. "I'm deeply sorry."

I began to tremble violently. "It was my fault. I'm the one responsible, I pushed her and caused her to fall. I was trying to get her out of the way of a car, but I didn't have to shove her so hard . . ."

"It was not your fault," the nun interrupted firmly. "It wasn't anyone's fault. It was placenta previa. The placenta pulled away from the lining of the uterus, a natural occurrence. It would have happened no matter what." I expected her to add something along the lines of "It was God's will," but she simply continued to regard me with steady compassion.

"Can I see Valerie now?" I asked.

"I think so, yes."

I leaped up and rushed back up to the third floor, where I was directed to a semiprivate room at the far end of the wing. Valerie lay in the bed nearest the door. She turned a haggard, woozy face toward me. "My baby's gone," she said.

"I know. I'm so horribly sorry." I tightly grasped her hand. It felt boneless, a dry brown glove stuffed with something spongy.

"They did a C-section but it was too late. She was already dead."

I nodded mutely.

"The doctor said I didn't do anything wrong. But I didn't take care of her. I was jumping around in those stupid classes and running all over the place, and I killed her."

"That's not true!" I said, echoing Sister Josepha. "Listen. Even if you had spent the last six months in bed, not stirring a muscle, this would have happened. There was no way on earth you could have prevented it."

If she had understood me, she gave no indication. "Jacqueline's going to be just . . ." She squeezed her eyes shut, unable to even tolerate the thought. "She's been calling every day to see if the nursery's ready. She had me hire the best set designer in town to paint the ceiling, clouds and little angels and nightingales. She's going to hate me now."

"Of course she's not. And you can try again, the next time everything will be fine, I promise." All the empty platitudes. I shut my mouth and stroked her moist forehead.

Valerie was beginning to doze off. "My cats," she murmured. "They have to be fed."

"Don't you worry, I'll take care of them." Finally, here was something I could say with absolute conviction: animal maintenance had, after all, become my specialty. "Just get some sleep now, okay?"

I waited till I was sure she was sound asleep, then retrieved her keys from her bag and set off for her house.

Valerie Jane lived in a Hansel and Gretel storybook cottage on Crescent Heights, complete with a mock thatched roof and a Hobbit-sized red door that she no doubt needed to duck to enter. At my arrival, a herd of cats stampeded from perches on sofas and shelves and shot in through cat doors. With felines mewling and twining themselves around my legs, I found my way to the kitchen, raided the cupboards for cans and an opener, then dolloped fish-reeking food into bowls and saucers. While the cats greedily chowed down, I went to search out the nursery.

It was a small but gloriously sunny room in the back of the house, freshly painted the color of marigolds and crammed with baby goods, many still packed in their original boxes. I glanced up at the ceiling. It was indeed exquisite, painted in the trompe l'oeil fashion of Tiepolo. It depicted a sunlit, azure sky dotted with billowing puffs of pink and white cloud; the prettiest winged cupids peered down from the clouds with merry bemusement on us humans below, while fanciful birds dipped around their tilted heads.

It was as if the rafters of the house had parted to reveal a tiny slice of heaven itself.

Suddenly I couldn't stand to look at it. I bolted back out to the kitchen, collapsed into a chair amid the contentedly grooming cats, and began to violently cry.

16

For once I was glad to see Terry Shoe's mud-colored Caprice parked outside the gates of my house. Glad also to glimpse Terry's sturdy figure, in her sensible, squat-heeled shoes and equally sensible no-crease mulberry pantsuit. I swung into the driveway, hopped out of my Volvo and joined her.

She was standing by the vehicle's trunk, hands on hips, inspecting a large splotch on the rear window. "Some bird shat on my car," was her greeting to me.

"It was a great horned owl, and actually it's a regurgitation," I said didactically.

"You mean owl throw-up?"

"Yeah, it's how they get rid of what they can't digest from their system. Look, you can see, there's a little beak from some smaller bird that was part of its dinner. Chloe once collected owl regurgitation for a science project. In the stuff she found, there were feathers and claws and even a dog tag."

"Well, live and learn," Terry muttered. She took her first thorough look at me, and her brows lifted. "Crikes, you look like you've been through the wars."

"It's been a hell of a day," I admitted. "Come on in, I'll make you some coffee."

She trailed me inside to the kitchen. I selected a Kenyan high mountain roast, ground the beans and filled the Krups with filtered water, while Terry wandered over to inspect the painted Mexican sideboard. This was a recent acquisition to replace an Irish breakfront that had been shot to pieces by the same homicidal maniac who had winged my arm. It was decorated with Day of the Dead figures, frolicking, violin-scraping skeletons in sombreros and serapes. I waited for some sardonic remark from Terry, but she turned without comment. By now she'd no doubt come to expect that I'd festoon my kitchen with something like happy-go-lucky skeletons.

"I've got some news for you," she said, taking a chair at the pine breakfast table. "About your pal Seth Granger."

"Yeah?" I said with interest. "What?"

"He's in the slammer. Had an altercation last night with his next-door neighbor. The neighbor's one of your home-improvement types. He was making himself a birdhouse or what-have-you in his garage, running a jigsaw at ten o'clock at night. Granger went over to tell him to knock it off and the neighbor said, 'Kiss my ass.' So Granger goes back home, but comes right back with a revolver and starts waving it around. The guy's wife hears all the commotion and calls the cops."

I set a steaming mug of coffee in front of her. She dumped three teaspoons of raw sugar into it and stirred it with a clatter. "So the uniforms take him into custody," she continued. "They charge him with a 417, threatening with a firearm. A misdemeanor. Though as it turns out, the gun's legal. He's got it registered. It also turns out he's quite a collector, got himself a hefty collection of handguns. But all registered and totally aboveboard."

"And none of them, I assume, were used to kill Brandon?"

"You assume correct."

I went over to the counter on which I had dropped my carryall.

I fished out Diane the starlet's gun and placed it on the table in front of Terry. "How about this one? Could this be from Seth Granger's collection?"

She gawked at it from over the rim of her mug. "What are you doing with that?" she snapped. "Don't you know carrying a concealed weapon is against the law?"

"So what are you going to do, arrest me?" I snapped back.

"Why don't we start with where the hell you got this thing."

"From a superstitious starlet with a padded stomach."

She shot me an irritated look.

I sank into a chair opposite her, propped my elbows on the table and, almost in one breath, related the saga of my morning, beginning with spotting the ponytailed impostor at Harriet Ho's, through to my vigil at St. Michael's and ending with my final role as hash slinger to a gang of cats. "So if you want to slap the cuffs on me, be my guest," I concluded. "It would be the perfect end to a perfect day."

Terry regarded me with eyes that had mellowed to the color of thick honey. "Jeez, that's too bad about your friend," she said. "Losing a baby like that has gotta be tough. I feel for her, I really do."

I nodded mutely.

"But just what business did you have confronting that gal? I thought I told you to keep your nose where it belongs."

"She didn't look very dangerous," I said, bristling. "She just seemed like a silly young girl."

"Yeah, a regular Snow White. Who just happened to be packing a gun."

"It probably isn't even loaded," I said.

Terry opened the chamber and bounced four bullets onto the table. I flinched at the sight of them.

"Okay, so it was loaded," I conceded. "Do you think it could be the one that was used to kill Brandon?"

She gave a snort. "Please. That was a Smith and Wesson .44 Magnum. Your basic Dirty Harry weapon. This is just a little old Resolver. Italian-made 9mm. Hardly in the same class." She treated it to a quick once-over. "No safety catch. Meaning, one, it's doubly illegal, and two, you're lucky you didn't blow your foot off. Or worse." She aimed a meaningful glance at my midsection. I flinched again.

She resumed her inspection of the gun. "It's a weapon that means business, all right. It's lightweight, easy to tote around. All you have to do is point and shoot."

We both sat without talking for a moment, Terry slurping the dregs of her cup, me contemplating my brush with a ditzy starlet packing a gun fixed to point and shoot.

"Well one thing's starting to look pretty obvious," I said at length. "I think Seth Granger murdered Brandon."

By now I'd had enough dealings with Terry Shoe not to expect her to respond to such a declaration, either with an encouraging "Yeah, just what I was thinking myself!" or a derisory "Are you out of your skull?" She pinned me in the impassive amber beam of her eyes and let me chatter on.

"In the first place, we know he's violent," I began. "He attacks his neighbor, he beats on his own kids, and I can assure you, he was ready and able to snap my arm in two at the McDonald's audition. In the second place, he's obviously got free access to guns. And thirdly, he's a failed actor, so presumably he'd know enough about makeup and such to be able to impersonate Kit to this Diane."

"And he killed him because . . . ?"

"Also obvious. To cover up for his son Kerrin. From what I've seen of that kid . . ." I gave a little shudder. "He's the kind of kid who wants a BB gun for Christmas so he can take potshots at small animals. Pushing a casting director down a flight of stairs would have been all in a day's play for him."

I also knew Terry well enough not to expect a standing ovation for my brilliant Analysis of the Crime. "Any more coffee?" was her response.

I obligingly trudged over and refilled her mug.

"These Grangers, how long have they lived here in town?" she asked.

"I don't know exactly. I think Seth Granger grew up here, somewhere near Burbank. He started doing TV when he was a teenager. I remember seeing him on an old *Partridge Family* rerun . . ." I broke off. "Okay, I see what you're getting at. If Brandon was terrified of Seth, why would he even come within a hundred miles of the city where the Grangers lived?" I gave a dismissive wave of my hand. "Lousy theory, scratch the whole thing."

Terry sludged her coffee with sugar, stirred, then blew gently to cool it further. "There could be reasons," she said.

"Yeah? Like what?"

"Like maybe *he* dug up something on Granger. Something McKenna thought he could use to blackmail him into leaving him alone." She took a sip, then added, "Or maybe he had a plan to do in Granger first."

"Brandon planning to kill Seth Granger? That's ridiculous!" I blurted. "You didn't know Brandon, he was the kindest, most gentle person . . ."

"I don't care if you're Mahatma Gandhi. If you get scared enough, you start thinking in desperate measures." Her beeper sounded. She rummaged through her shoulder bag, pulled it out and peered at the number. "It's Downsey. I've got to hit the road." She looked wistfully at her unfinished mug. "You sure do make a fine cup of coffee."

"Glad to provide," I said disconsolately. Maybe that could be my next career: Lucy's Famous Coffee House. You'll know it's good because of all the cops who go there.

"So let me know if you have any more great revelations," Terry said, heading briskly for the door. "In the meantime, make sure you keep all your doors locked."

This breezy exhortation left me thoroughly shaken. I had a vision of Seth Granger, sprung on bail and hell-bent for revenge on anyone who had crossed him, turning up here with all four of his quasi-albino progeny. Scenes from *Lord of the Flies* played vividly in my mind as I scrambled through the house, bolting all doors and latching all windows. Then I activated the alarm system, figuring that if the Granger clan did come breaking in and slash me to ribbons, the tubby security officer from First Alert who would arrive a leisurely thirty or forty minutes later would at least be in time to prevent our pets from noshing on my remains.

With that happy thought, I pointed myself in the direction of the den. A little brandy was what I felt I needed. Just one sip or two of Courvoisier couldn't be harmful. I marched up to the wet bar.

"Hey, Lucy, what's shaking?" said Brandon McKenna behind me—exactly as he'd greeted me dozens of times before.

I let out a bloodcurdling shriek. My heart began to tom-tom, my legs quivered like plucked harp strings. I whirled, expecting to see Brandon's ghost. Or maybe Brandon himself saying the whole thing was one huge mistake, that hadn't been his body in the morgue at all. Or even nothing at all, proving that I was starting to dangerously flip out . . .

What I saw was Rollins the parrot.

"What's shaking?" he repeated in perfect mimicry of dead Brandon. "Hey, Lucy, what's shaking?"

I started to laugh, so hysterically that anyone coming upon me would have concluded I was definitely starting to flip out. It was partly from relief. But partly too because I had just realized one thing about Brandon: that gay or straight, crooked or not, dead or not, I was still more than a little in love with him.

17

Kerrin Granger was sitting smack in the center of the art class-room when I arrived for the next workshop session, his albinoish hair slicked back, his arms folded belligerently on the table. After my recent arm-wrestle with his father, Kerrin's appearance gave me a twinge of alarm and for a moment I hung back in the hall. "Don't be absurd," I told myself sharply. "He's a ten-year-old boy, not a Cosa Nostra assassin."

A second glance into the room assured me that Jamie Alston had not put in an appearance, nor the squat, scowling bodyguard. Without the Dreaded Spawn to play up to, Kerrin just might behave himself.

I walked jauntily in and greeted my group, noting with satisfaction that there seemed to be some half dozen more of them than the last time—the word must be spreading that this was a cool workshop to sign up for. At my request, the art department had set up a late-model Mac with a laser printer in the center table of the classroom. I began unpacking my animation software from my taffeta carryall.

"What we're going to do today is make an animation by drawing right on the computer," I explained. "This time, Harrison the frog is going to visit the rain forest and make some new friends."

A couple of late arrivals burst in. Among them was Marcus Barnes, his green eyes droopy, looking less at the moment like a near-genius than an ordinary child needing a nap; to my surprise, he chose a seat beside Kerrin, though a number of other places were available. To my further surprise, Kerrin looked distinctly uncomfortable at this arrangement. He twisted his neck to peer behind him, as if hoping to materialize Jamie; then, realizing he was definitely on his own, sort of scrunched down in his chair.

A freckled fourth-grader named Carrie Kienholz was energetically waving her hand. "What about our flip books," she called out. "Aren't we going to get to show our flip books?"

"I was just getting to that, Carrie," I said. "Those of you who were here last session and completed your flip books, take them out and we'll all pass them around." I became suddenly aware of a peculiar odor in the air—an acrid, yeasty smell, like burning cookies or bread. Somebody in the cafeteria wasn't paying attention, I thought. But the cafeteria was in the opposite wing: I'd never have guessed cooking smells could travel this far.

"I didn't get a flick book," Kerrin was whining. "It's not fair. Everyone else got one but me."

"When you cut a class, you've got to be prepared to suffer the consequences," said Marcus.

"Huh?" Kerrin irritably squinted his tiny eyes. "What's that supposed to mean?"

"It means sometimes you've got to take what's coming to you."

Kerrin's lips kind of twisted, as if silently trying out an appropriately intimidating comeback. Marcus gave that little hunch of his shoulder I had seen him do before—the nervous tick that looked as if he were about to take a slug at the nearest target. Kerrin clamped his mouth shut. He glanced behind himself again, but still finding himself Jamieless, opted to keep mum.

Flip books were appearing on the tables. Before we could look at them, we were interrupted by the now familiar clamor of the fire alarm. The kids groaned and called out complaints of "Not again!" and "Bor-ing!"

"Do we have to go?" piped up Dana Rich. "It's so dumb. They just make us stand around and then come back."

"Yes, we have to go," I said. "Everybody pair up and quick." There was a particular urgency in my voice, since I had just caught another whiff of badly burned cookies.

Chairs scraped back from tables, children shuffled to their feet and fell into a ragged double line. I swung open the heavy classroom door into the hall and gasped; instead of orderly streams of students and teachers there was bedlam—a crush of bodies large and small, running, pushing and shoving. And they were bewilderingly stampeding to the right, when the nearest exit was just several yards to the left. Above the raucous clanging of the bell, I heard screaming and shouting, and several very small children were crying.

"Do not run!" hollered a teacher, a chunky, bug-eyed woman who was herself setting a sprint pace. "Walk, but don't run!" She collided with a lagging fifth-grader, regained herself and continued to motor on by.

The air was rapidly acquiring a smoky haze, making my eyes burn. Blinking back tears, I saw Paul Lynch stationed in the midst of the streaming mob, helping stumbling children stay upright and moving. "Paul!" I screamed. "What's happening? Why is everyone going the wrong way?"

"We can't get to the fire exit," he yelled back. "There's a strong updraft of smoke rising from the basement stairwell that's cut off our access. We've got to go out the main doors."

"Where's the fire?"

"The custodian says it's in the basement. It started in that storeroom filled with papier mâché theater props and spread from there." He coughed harshly, then scrambled to assist a skinny boy who had fallen onto his backside and was in danger of being trampled.

The flour in the papier mâché—that would explain the bakerylike odor. I felt a loony sense of relief at having cleared that much up. It was followed immediately by a clutch of panic. I swirled around to face my little group who were solemnly waiting for instruction.

"Okay, guys, when we get out to the hall, we're going to go to a different door," I told them. "We're going to turn right and head toward the auditorium."

"Is it a real fire?" asked Carrie Kienholz.

"We're going to be burned up!" a girl wailed behind her.

Little Dana's hay fever sniffles fattened into teary snuffles. A boy at the end of the line began wailing loudly.

"We're going to be perfectly fine," I said. "We're going to go out in the hall and turn right, and we'll all keep moving until we get to the main doors. Okay?" I noted gratefully that the stampeding herd in the hall was beginning to thin out. "And we're going to sing," I added brightly. "Let's all sing . . ." Suddenly the entire repertoire of Western music had been erased from my mind. Show tunes, rock and roll, grand opera: all a blank. I racked my brain—the only tune I could summon was "Light My Fire."

And then a boy's voice, clear, strong and beautiful, began singing: "This old man, he played one . . ." It was Marcus Barnes; his voice was as stunning in its authority as it was in its purity of tone.

And then a second boy's voice chimed in: "With a knick-knack, paddy-whack, give the dog a bone . . ." A voice not of the same caliber as Marcus's, but well-pitched and pleasing. For a moment I couldn't place it; then with a shock I realized it belonged to Kerrin Granger. The two boys exchanged comradely glances as their voices blended and rose in the silly tune. A few other children joined in, tentatively at first. And then suddenly the entire group was belting it out: "This old man, he played two, he played knick-knack on my shoe . . ."

"Okay, gang, let's go," I said and led them into the hall. They marched right, coughing as they breathed the acrid air, but still carrying the song, led vigorously by Marcus and Kerrin. Others in the hall began to sing along. I heard Paul Lynch lustily, if slightly off-tune, take up the refrain: "This old man came rolling home . . ." And then miraculously, everyone seemed to be singing. I could actually feel the panic begin to subside, as the song's rhythm began to dictate our pace.

We kept marching and singing, past three grade classrooms, past a door marked NATURAL SCIENCES and another marked MUSIC, past both the Boys' Room and Girls' Room, and at last around a corner to the marble-framed main double doors, where we all poured out into safety and fresh air. Once outside, everyone began to run, as if the building were in imminent danger of exploding in a fireball.

I trotted a few yards onto the soccer field, but was suddenly too exhausted to go any further. I bent over, propped my hands on my thighs and sucked up deep breaths of air scented with a mélange of eucalyptus, sweet grass and smoke. Revived, I straightened up and gazed back at the gray stone mansion. Smoke was now seeping from most of the windows in the wing we had just vacated, curling like unruly tendrils of hair. My eyes searched the building for signs of flame. . . .

And focused on the face of a child in a window.

It abruptly vanished. For a brief moment, I wondered if I had imagined it: maybe I'd inhaled more smoke than I'd realized and was experiencing hallucinations. Maybe next I'd start seeing arch-angels or the figure of my dead grandmother beckoning from the eaves.

But then it reappeared, the pale, round face of a girl with her nose literally pressed up against the glass pane. I hopped up and down, waving and whooping at her. She disappeared again.

I turned to look for help, but everyone had by now scattered far from me. I raced over to the window where the child's face had appeared. "Hello, hey, hello!" I yodeled loudly. "There's a fire, you've got to come out."

If the girl had heard me over the clanging alarm, she did not respond. "Shit," I muttered. There appeared to be no other op-tion—I trotted back to the double doors and reentered the building, covering my nose and mouth with the sleeve of my jacket as I headed back into the smoky hallway.

I stopped and stared down the corridor. "Shit and double shit!" I muttered again. I had no idea which room the face had peered out from.

Okay, I told myself. Calm down and use a little logic. She couldn't have been in one of the restrooms—these had only two tiny ventilation windows near the ceiling, so I could skip searching them. And she had definitely been closer to this end of the hall than the other: which meant she must be in either the music room or natural sciences. Eeny, meeny, miney, mo—I chose the door marked MUSIC and pulled it open.

The class that had abruptly departed had left a CD playing, Gregorian chants that added a sonorous and ghostly counterpoint to the strident fire bell. "Anybody here?" I yelled. "Hello?" My eyes took in the walnut Steinway grand, the Moog synthesizer, the scrolled black music stands supporting listing pages of the Emperor Concerto. "Is anybody in here?" I yelled more stridently.

There was only the eerie Latin chanting in response.

With a grunt of frustration, I backed out, reshut the door, then headed into NATURAL SCIENCES. I repeated my call: "Hello, are you in here?"

This classroom too was empty. Empty of living creatures, that is; of the dead, it appeared to be chockablock. There was a gay contingent of stuffed small animals—a wolverine, a skunk, a red-tailed hawk—all preserved under glass. An array of beetles, roaches and grasshoppers were stuck with feathered pins to a display board, like unappetizing canapés toothpicked on a tray; their prehistoric cousins, fossilized in amber, had been allotted an entire cabinet. I gave a start at the sight of a skeleton dangling from a stand in one corner—a chimpanzee, one arm raised in a rather jaunty salute. It would fit right in with the happy bones on my Mexican sideboard, I reflected.

Streams of brown-black smoke were beginning to ooze in from the vents; both my eyes and throat were burning. I've got to get out right now! I decided and began scuttling toward the door. As I reached it, the alarm bells suddenly turned off: for a moment, the silence was as deafening as the cacophony had been. Then my ears became unstopped, and I heard a rustling movement.

I whirled and gazed back over the classroom. There was a cardboard replica of a beehive against the far wall: it was hardly three feet high—it didn't look large enough to fit a child over six, and the girl I had glimpsed in the window had been at least nine. But there seemed no other possibility. I hurried over to it, dropped down to my hands and knees and peered into the semicircular opening.

She was scrunched inside, her body compacted in a way that would have made Houdini stare with envy: knees tucked under her chin, arms flattened around her ankles. Tattered remnants of cardboard honeycomb tangled in her soft black hair and hung down around her face—a stunningly beautiful face, with a high white forehead and dramatically dark-fringed eyes.

"Holly?" I said.

She made no reply.

"You're Holly Beech, aren't you? You've got to come out of there. There's a fire, and everybody's left the building."

"I want to stay here," she said petulantly.

"It's not safe. We've got to go outside." I extended a hand to her. "Come on, sweetheart, come with me."

She drew her legs in tighter, as if trying to flatten herself into two dimensions. As she did, something dropped from her right hand. We both reached for it; my fingers closed around it first and drew it out. With a cold shudder, I stared at a box of matches from the Hard Rock Cafe.

"Did you start the fire, Holly?" I asked.

Her blue-gray eyes began to swarm with tears. She gave a tiny bend of her head.

"How come?" I pursued.

"I just felt like it."

I pulled my head out of the hive and rocked back on my

haunches, processing this startling news. Then I glanced back at the door. To my horror, smoke was seeping thickly from under it. Time after time I had coached Chloe in her fire preparation drills, endlessly repeating the slogan: "Smoke kills more people than fire."

Feeling like a mismade tortoise, I poked my head back into the beehive shell. "We'll talk about that later," I said. "Right now we've just got to get outside."

I reached for her wrist, but she jerked it away. "I'm not going," she declared. "If they find out it was me, I'll get into trouble."

"Holly, listen to me. There's a lot of smoke coming in under the door. If we breathe too much, we can get really sick. We could even die."

"I don't care. I want to stay here."

I tried to think. How do you reason with a nine-year-old pyromaniac who's holed up in a beehive and who would apparently rather be roasted like a Fourth of July wiener or smoked like a prize Virginia ham than "get into trouble" for torching some papier mâché?

I checked behind me again. The smoke had begun coiling into large black chrysanthemums which floated lazily in the space between us and the door. I experienced a new and improved rush of panic. The hell with reason! I told myself. I lunged into the hive, gripped the girl by her slender wrists and began yanking them forcefully. "Move your butt out of there this instant or I'll tear this thing apart and get you out myself!" I heard myself shriek.

The threat proved astonishingly effective. She came scrambling out immediately and gave a frightened little mewl at the sight of the swirling black haze. "It's smoky in here," she said.

"So you noticed?" I snapped. "And now we can't go back out through the hallway. We'll have to jump from the window."

I stood up, yanked her unceremoniously to her feet and half-dragged her over to the two large casement windows. I tugged at the heavy wood sash and it creaked open about fifteen inches; but the exertion in the tainted air sent me into a fit of hacking and coughing. To recover, I leaned my head out the opening, gulping in the fresh, clean breeze and blinking the stinging blur from my eyes.

As my vision cleared, I looked down to assess our situation. We were on the first floor, but the building had a raised foundation so that the drop to the ground was roughly about eight feet. It suddenly looked eighty. My head spun with vertigo.

"What the hell are you doing up there?"

The voice belonged to Paul Lynch. He appeared to be standing almost directly below me, his hands furiously clenched at his hips. I felt an irrational spurt of indignation. "What the hell do you think I'm doing, playing a last-minute game of Parcheesi?" I yelled.

He glared up with an are-you-completely-insane? expression. With an effort, I added calmly, "A little girl got left behind. I saw her at the window and came back to get her. And now the hall's clogged with smoke." Holly appeared beside me as if to corroborate my story.

"Holy Christ!" Paul exclaimed. "You'd better jump down from there."

"That's what I intended to do," I said in a rather aggrieved tone. I pulled myself back into the room and brusquely maneuvered Holly into place. "Okay, now I want you to climb out. Mr. Lynch is right down there and he's going to help you."

The girl had suddenly become the very model of docility: without protest or procrastination, she squeezed herself under the window sash, dangled first one leg over the ledge, then the other. I watched as Paul clutched her by the thighs and swung her easily down onto the lawn.

Now it was my turn. Which posed a knotty problem of logistics: to wit, the diameter of my tummy was larger than the width of the window opening. I strained at the sash again, but it wouldn't budge.

"Come on, Lucy!" Paul yelled.

"I can't," I yelled back. "I can't fit through the window, and it won't open any wider."

"Yes, it will. Put some shoulder to it."

I obediently put my shoulder to it and felt a sharp pain knife up the side of my neck. The window remained firmly put. "It's stuck!" I shouted.

The room was now totally diffused with an ugly tea-colored haze. It stung my eyes like nettles and had the effect of someone refinishing my throat with a medium-grade sandpaper. It's no use! I thought wildly. I'm going to be overcome by smoke inhalation and expire right here among the mounted dung beetles and Jurassic crustacea. With a jolt of terror, I imagined I could already hear the faint strains of a heavenly choir: perhaps I was dying already! I had the horrifying vision of my skeleton mounted in the classroom right beside the jaunty chimpanzee's.

With a yelp of terror, I gave a final shove to the sash.

To my astonishment, the window grumbled upward another six inches.

"Atta girl!" whooped Paul from below.

I flushed with an absurd sense of pride. Which turned abruptly to mortification as I realized that what I had taken for the advent of heavenly hosts was actually the strains of that Gregorian chant from the adjoining MUSIC room.

"What are you waiting for" Paul was shouting.

"Coming."

I folded myself under the window and, trying to keep as much weight as possible on my arms rather than my belly, eased my legs over the edge. A gust of wind billowed the skirt of my loose sack dress, giving Paul a splendid view of my pink-pantied crotch. He's gay, I reminded myself. Your crotch is about as interesting to him as a piece of chocolate layer cake to a cat. His arms wrapped around my naked legs. I pushed off from the window ledge, experienced a brief and rather heady moment of whirling through the air, and then my feet were blessedly touching the ground.

I sank down onto the grass and sat for a moment, doing nothing but breathing.

"Okay?" Paul asked, patting my shoulder.

I blushed deeply, thinking of our intimate little pas de deux. "Where's Holly?" I mumbled.

"Right here, safe and sound," he said.

We both turned to see nothing but empty lawn.

18

"What the hell?" Paul exclaimed. He looked wildly around. "She couldn't have gone very far. She probably just went around to join the others."

I heard a fresh batch of sirens come screaming up to the front of the building to join what must have already been a significant rally of fire, police and emergency vehicles.

"I don't think so," I said. "She's not particularly keen on hobnobbing with any authorities right now."

"Why not?"

I fished the Hard Rock matchbox from my jacket pocket. "She happens to be our little arsonist."

"Are you kidding?" Paul pursed his lips with astonishment. "That's so hard to believe. She seems so sweet. And such a beauty."

"Yeah, she could be the poster child for Firebugs of America."

"I guess we'd better find her," said Paul. "Do you think she could have gone back into the building?"

"Not with all that smoke. But she's a whiz at cramming herself into very small and secret places."

We surveyed the surroundings: the empty stretch of soccer field, the deserted bleachers. My eye fell on a machine left on the sidelines—the sort of glorified wheelbarrow used to lay the chalk lines on the field. Its funnel-shaped vat looked just about Holly-sized.

Paul spotted it at the same time. "The field marker?" he said.

We jogged in tandem to it. We were right—she had fitted into the vat by scrunching herself in a chalky ball. Paul grasped her under the arms and lifted her out. She had relinquished her Miss Docility crown and was now in active training for a title in improvisational martial arts: her feet kicked, her arms chopped, her fists punched. But Paul managed to both hold on to her and avoid all but a few glancing elbow chops. His experience tutoring on movie sets, where dealing with the tantrums of prepubescent stars had been all in a day's work, had obviously come to valuable use.

"Holly, stop it," he commanded. "Stop it right now."

"I don't want to go to jail," she screeched, kneeing the air.

"You are not going to jail. You have my absolute word on it. I will not let you down, understand. Not ever."

She executed some *tae kwon do*–ish footwork and threw a few fancy punches; then all of a sudden the fight went out of her. She sank limply to the ground, rocking back and forth and crying in convulsive little sobs. Paul crouched down to her and cradled her gently. "Hey," he crooned. "It's all right now. It's going to be okay."

He let her cry for a few more moments. "Why do you want to make things burn, Holly?" he asked gently.

"I just want to," she said in a tiny voice.

"Have you been doing it for a long time?"

She shrugged.

"Back in Connecticut?" I put in, keeping my tone as unthreatening as possible. "Did you start fires where you used to live?"

"Sometimes."

"Did anybody know about them?"

She shook her soft dark curls.

"Does something happen that makes you want to start them?" Paul inquired. "Does your mom or dad hit you?"

"No."

"Never?"

"Uh-uh."

"They never get mad at you ever?"

She pulled up her knees to compress herself. "Only when I eat like a pig and get too fat."

Paul and I exchanged glances. The girl was slender as a willow branch. "Who told you you were fat, sweetheart?" he asked.

"I used to be. I used to be gross. Then my mom put me on a diet so when I tried out for *Orphans* I'd be thin enough to get the part. I lost six pounds but it wasn't enough."

"So you did go to the *Orphans* audition?" I prompted.

She bobbed her head miserably. "We got there but the casting lady wouldn't even let me try out. She told my mom I was a little porker and the only acting career I could ever have was if they made another movie of *The Blob*. Or if Weight Watchers did a commercial, I could be the 'before' person. She went on and on saying all this stuff right in front of the other kids, and they were all laughing their heads off over me. You know that blond kid that goes to this school? That Kerrin? He kept calling me Crisco, Crisco." She shot us a miserable glance. "You know, fat in the can."

"He's just a stupid little boy," Paul told her firmly. "He likes to make fun of everybody, not just you."

She shrugged, not convinced.

"What did your mom do, Holly?" I asked. "Did she get mad at the casting woman?"

"Yeah, she got super mad and started yelling all this stuff back to her. Except that just made everybody laugh at me more, so I said I just wanted to go home. And then we drove home, and my mom wouldn't speak to me for the rest of the day."

"And did you start a fire that day, Holly?" Paul inquired softly. She bit her underlip.

"It's okay," he coaxed. "You can tell me."

She nodded.

"What did you do?"

"I had these Little Mermaid cutouts. And you know, Ariel's kind of fat too. If you look at her tail, it's really gross. So I took the cutouts to the backyard where nobody could see me and burned them up."

"And did that make you feel better?" he asked.

"I guess so. But mostly I felt better because I thought I'd never have to go to an audition again."

But Mommy Dearest obviously had had other plans. "Do you still think you're fat, sweetheart?" Paul asked.

"Sometimes," she said. "But I'm on a diet."

"All the time?"

"I guess so. I mean, I'm not allowed to eat anything fattening ever. That's why I'm not allowed to go over to anybody's house, because they might have cookies or M&M's and my mom says I'll just stuff myself."

"How would she find out?"

"When I got weighed. Every morning I have to weigh myself on the scale in the bathroom to see if I've gained more than two pounds. Except it could be because I'm growing, so then my mom gives me the pinch test."

"The what?" Paul asked brusquely.

"She pinches my waist and if she gets any fat, then that's how she knows I've been bad. And then I have to stay home from school in my room all day and not eat anything except some applesauce for dinner."

"Despicable," Paul muttered under his breath.

I agreed. Compared to Holly, Oliver Twist had been force-fed.

"Listen, Holly," I said as gently as possible. "Remember when you were at the *Orphans* audition? When Joyce the casting lady was being so mean to you, you must've gotten really mad. Did you try to hurt her?"

Holly blinked at me uncomprehendingly.

"Did you push her down the stairs?"

She shook her head. "I didn't do anything. I just went home with my mom. If she told you I pushed her, then she's a dirty old liar!"

"No, it's all right, I was thinking of somebody else," I said quickly. Unless Holly was the most superb actress I'd ever come across, she was telling the truth. She apparently didn't even know that Joyce Korshalek had been killed.

"What's going to happen to me?" she asked Paul tremulously.

"A lot of people are going to want to talk to you, and to your mom and dad," he said. "But remember, I'm always going to be there for you. It's all going to be fine." He coaxed her to her feet. "Come on, let's go watch the firemen."

He shot me a bleak look over her head. The hell it was going to be fine—at least not for a long time. What it *was* going to be was a nightmare of children's services bureaucrats, and family practice lawyers, and officious psychologists: Minna Luchstein was about to have a field day.

We wound our way to the front of the school, and Paul led Holly off through the milling throngs to search out the principal.

I was amazed at the size of the crowd. Word had apparently gone out that Windermere Academy was burning to the ground: there was a logjam of honking cars at the gates, frantic parents desperate to rescue their children from the conflagration. The local media seemed to have also pounced on the story; the whap-whap-whap of competing TV helicopters almost drowned out the sirens. A wedge-haired reporter holding a mike to her lips as if she were about to chomp on it wandered through the multitude with a peeved expression, evidently disgusted by the lack of both leaping flames and writhing, photogenically toasted victims. A man in a *Caroline in the City* sweatshirt made a sudden charge at the building, hollering, "My son Malachi's in there!" He was tackled by the soccer coach, who hollered back, "All the kids got out!" No one was thoroughly convinced by this statement: a phalanx of newly arrived moms appeared to be forming a human battering ram to break through the ranks of restraining firefighters.

Then an announcement came via bullhorn that the fire had been extinguished, the smoke dispersed, it was okay to reenter the building, which initiated a general charge toward the doors. I lingered outside till the crush had lessened, then made my way back toward my workshop room.

A stench of smoke still permeated the air, sending a residual tremor of panic through me. "The fire's out; there's nothing to worry about," I told myself firmly and busied myself collecting the stuff my group had abandoned. I gathered several backpacks, books and pads, and a solid gold charm bracelet one of the girls had dropped on the floor. A few flip books had been left on the tables. I picked one up and opened it with curiosity.

On the first page was a drawing of a woman's head. It was crudely stylized, with a wide, smiley mouth and a mop of wavy, below-the-chin hair. A peculiar semicircle bulged out from the right margin. What this was supposed to be puzzled me. I flipped all the pages to see the entire animation.

The semicircle grew into an enormous bullet which slammed into the woman's head, producing huge, globular splotches of blood as it struck. I dropped the book with a gasp.

Then I forced myself to pick it back up and I riffled the pages again. There was no mistaking it—this was a crude cartoon of a woman getting her brains blown out.

And then it struck me that the curly-mop hairdo was a lot like mine . . . And that my mouth was distinctly on the wide side . . . With a jolt of horror, I wondered if it was meant to be me.

My eyes whipped over the place at the table where the book had been left. I remembered clearly which child had been sitting there—the one who had drawn this gruesome cartoon.

It had been Marcus Barnes.

continued to stare at his now-empty seat for some moments. Was it a threat? I wondered. Was Marcus letting me know he intended to shoot my head off if I continued nosing around about the *Orphans* audition? Or was it a warning—his way of letting me know that someone else was aiming in my direction?

But I couldn't dwell on the ramifications of Marcus's message at the moment. I had a more immediate concern—to make sure my recent Escape from a Smoke-Filled Room hadn't affected my pregnancy. I pocketed the flip book, stashed the kids' belongings in the teachers' closet and hurried out to my car, where I called the office of Dr. and Dr. Tetweiller, declared that it was an emergency and that I would be arriving in twenty minutes. Then I attempted to navigate out of the traffic jam of cars both leaving and arriving.

The narrow road was further clogged with people who had jettisoned their cars and, like designer-clad refugees, were streaming toward the campus on foot. In their midst, I spotted the figure of Helene Barnes. She was rushing along in her stocking feet, swinging her high-heeled pumps in one hand, her Gucci bag in the other.

I honked and inched up to her. "Helene!" I yelled. "Everything's okay. The fire is out and all the kids are safe."

"Oh, thank god!" she exclaimed. She put a hand to the perfect butterfly of turquoise chiffon at her throat. "Have you seen my son?"

"He's with the others running around the parking lot. Listen, I need to talk to you about him. It's extremely important."

She narrowed her eyes. "Does it have anything to do about an audition?"

"As a matter of fact, yes." The driver of the car behind me gave a "Move it, buddy" blast of his horn. "Will you be home in a couple of hours?" I said hurriedly. "I could come by."

She glanced at a shimmer of gold watch on her wrist. "I need to buy produce for a benefit luncheon I'm doing tomorrow. There's a farmers' market in Malibu. It's on a side road just past Salty Dog Scuba. You can't miss it. I'll be there at five."

"Got it." I waved and stepped on the gas.

The doctors Raymond and Raymond Tetweiller were a father and son OB-GYN team, nationally renowned in the field of fertility. Or to be exact, Ray Jr. was the fertility mojo. "Every Lady Gets a Baby" was his informal motto; and it was a running joke among his patients that he would have the Statue of Liberty in labor within a year—assuming of course that Lady Liberty could swing his truly staggering fees. As befitting his role of Baby Maker Extraordinaire, he effected the look of a gigolo in a Thirties musical: slicked-back fair hair; smooth, plump face; and a perpetual, rather smarmy, smile. When he swept into your examining room, you rather expected to be invited to dance the Carioca; it was always disconcerting when instead he requested you to place your feet in the stirrups and began rummaging around in your private parts.

Once your pregnancy was a definite go, you were passed from the care of Junior to Senior; and so it was Ray Sr. whom I was now consulting. As obstetrician to the stars, Ray Sr. raked in several million a year, but had the folksy manner of the kind of country doctor who used to make house calls. He displayed red striped suspenders under his white coat, spoke in a down-home drawl and even walked with a bit of a shuffle, all of which was somehow superbly reassuring.

There was always a lengthy wait for either doc. By unspoken rule, the already-pregnant women sat in the sunny side of the room by the tall windows, while the wannabes occupied the opposite sofas in comparative gloom. Now I sank into a sun-drenched red armchair and surveyed the current crop of wannabes. There was a whippet-thin young couple in his and hers Calvin Klein, the husband compulsively cracking his knuckles—a clear case of Low Sperm Count. Also a woman who despite some excellent face work could clearly count her fiftieth birthday as a memory. She shared a loveseat with a russet-maned supermodel who was married to a three-time Wimbledon winner, and who had publicly confessed that years of bulimia had "messed up" her reproductive system. Phrases such as "donated eggs," "frozen embryos" and "surrogate wombs" ping-ponged among them, as if conceiving a baby were a team sport and they were discussing the possible plays. We on the safely knocked-up side tended to maintain a rather smug silence, as if the only communication we needed was with our unborn fetuses.

Some thirty minutes oozed by while I fitfully turned the pages of *Modern Pregnancy*. Finally I was ushered into an examining room by a crisp-faced Irish nurse. I donned a paper gown and sat shivering for another ten minutes until Ray Sr. ambled in. He listened to the tale of my recent adventure with much homespun clucking and tsk-tsking. "Don't sound to me like you did much harm," he drawled. "Why don't we do a little old ultrasound just to be safe?"

I thrilled as I saw my baby come flickering up on the monitor screen, heart visibly beating, tiny limbs curled up around itself. My own heart thumped wildly with excitement.

"We've got ourselves a little old boy," pronounced Ray Sr.

"Are you sure?" Somehow I had convinced myself I was having another daughter.

"Yep, you can see his little John Thomas, clear as day."

He assured me everything looked fine, awarded me an avuncular pat on the shoulder and shuffled on out. The Irish nurse handed me a Dixie cup for the requisite urine sample, and I drifted down the hall in my crackling gown to the bathroom. Another woman was just emerging from it. I was still in such a euphoric glow from having seen my unborn son that it was several seconds before I realized I was face to face with Myra Alston.

We stood gaping at one another for a moment, both of us bare-assed except for paper gowns, both of us clutching Dixie cups—mine empty, hers half-filled.

"So, Myra," I said at length, "long time no see."

She creased her forehead and squinted her eyes, an expression meant to convey a baffled lack of recognition, but looked more as if she were experiencing a sudden bout of indigestion. Obviously, Jamie had not inherited his acting talents from his mother.

"I'm sorry, but have we met?" she said in a flutey voice. .

"Well, yes," I fluted back. "We pushed smothered porkchops together for an entire year—as I think you well remember."

The indigestion cleared up, replaced by wide-eyed surprise. "It's Lucy Kellenborg, right? It's so marvelous to see you again. But I hardly recognize you. Have you put on some weight?"

"Yeah, tons. It's called pregnancy. Which just happens to be why I'm hanging around an OB's office. And come to think of it, what are you doing here? I thought you and Randy were split up."

"Well, obviously, I'm seeing someone else. And we want to have a child together."

"Togethah" was the grande dame–ish way she pronounced it. She'd picked up a few affectations of speech over the years, but underneath was the same nasal, South Jersey accent that used to cut through the clatter of dishes and diners back at the good old Panic Café. "We've got some specials today," I could still hear her say. "The soup's a mushroom-barley and it comes with crackers . . ."

"So Jamie's going to get a kid sibling," I said with a smile. "So if his career goes on the skids, you'll already be raising your next little meal ticket."

She flushed. I had the chilling realization that I'd hit on at least a partial truth.

"I don't know what you're talking about," she said brusquely. "But if you'll excuse me . . ."

She tried to sail by, but I blocked her path. "I want to talk to you."

She drew herself up indignantly; but then it evidently struck her that it was hard to maintain indignation when you're buck naked except for a peekaboo paper gown and holding a warm cup of your own pee. "What about?" she asked sullenly.

"I've had some pretty crappy things happen in my life lately. Maybe you've heard. A member of my household was shot dead in our car a week ago."

"Yes, very shocking. But what does it have to do with me?"

"I've also been followed, spied upon, and sent some threatening items in the mail."

"So?"

"So it all seems to point back to a movie audition two years ago. It was for a musical that never got made because the star couldn't sing or dance his way out of a used Kleenex."

"What do you know about it?" she flashed back. I noted with interest that she knew immediately which audition I was referring to. "It just so happens that the reason Jamie didn't learn the dance steps was because his faggot dance instructor molested him."

"Really?"

"Yes, really. This disgusting man touched him whenever they were alone in the rehearsal studio."

"How do you know?"

"What do you mean how do I know? Because Jamie told me."

"Just like he told you about his former gym teacher."

Myra stiffened. "Yeah. Him too."

"Isn't it funny," I said, "how your son seems to attract molesters?"

"Not really. He's a very adorable boy. People just naturally want to touch him."

Yeah, with a baseball bat, was more my observation.

"So when Jamie reported this fondling on the dance floor, was it before or after the studio decided to replace him with Marcus Barnes?" I pursued.

"I don't know where you got that from," Myra retorted, "but it's bullshit. The Barnes boy was just an amateur. My son's a superstar."

"Sure, but if he'd been kicked off a major motion picture and replaced with an amateur, it would have been kind of tough on his superstar status."

"Well, he wasn't replaced."

"No, the studio conveniently pulled the plug instead. Jamie certainly danced his way out of that one, free and clear. Left a couple of other people dead, but hey, I guess that's just the breaks."

"You are a horrible, vicious person!" Myra snarled.

"So shoot me!" I snapped back. And regretted it instantly—from the gleam in her eye I could see she considered this an attractive proposition. I took a cautionary step backward, nearly colliding with the Irish nurse who was bustling down the hallway.

"Mrs. Alston," she gasped, "you don't have to carry that! I'm happy to bring it to the lab for you." She whisked the Dixie cup out of Myra's hand and bore it down the hall, holding it in a weirdly reverent manner with both hands.

Which seemed to remind Myra that she was now a big wheel. She drew her stringy body up to its full height, tossed her lank hair, flashed her red-rimmed eyes. "Don't mess with me, Lucy," she said haughtily, " 'cause you have no idea who you're dealing with."

She pushed past me with a regal rustle of her paper gown and disappeared into an examining room.

I proceeded into the softly lit john, which had tinkling Muzak piped in, no doubt to facilitate the necessary functions. The unsettling encounter with Myra left me momentarily unable to perform my own function. But at last, to a jingly rendition of "Here's to You, Mrs. Robinson," I managed to fill my cup.

I dressed and left the office. With some hours to kill before my appointment with Helene Barnes, I wandered the shopping streets of Westwood Village and loaded up with gifts to bring to Valerie Jane—the latest fashion magazines, a bag of ripe mangoes, papayas and white peaches and another of sugar cookies, and beribboned bottles of scented lotions—then swung by the hospital. Her room was packed with friends, both straight and gay, and raven-haired relatives, most with Valerie's husky voice and easy laugh. The luminous Jacqueline sat on the edge of the bed, tightly clenching Valerie's hand, as if to transfuse hope or energy or even blood itself.

"We're going to try again," Valerie told me. "Just as soon as the doctors give the go-ahead."

"Terrific." I hugged her and was hugged in turn by all dozen of her extended family.

At a quarter to five, I returned to my car, turned west and whipped off toward the beach, blasting an Aretha Franklin CD so that my new baby would be born already familiar with the Queen of Soul.

Salty Dog Scuba was hard to miss: a ramshackle cottage with a double helping of Christmas lights still strung in its window and fronted by an eight-foot-high weathered sign of a Dalmatian dog in full scuba gear. I turned on the rutted road just to the north of it and jounced up into hills still scorched from the latest of the autumn infernos that habitually sweep through the Malibu Hills. At exactly a quarter of a mile, with Aretha belting out "Grapevine," I came to a field dotted with the white wooden stalls and makeshift tents of a farmers' market.

Which appeared oddly to be deserted. Of course! I realized— most of these markets were packed up and gone by midafternoon.

How could the preternaturally efficient Helene Barnes have made such a blunder?

But then I noticed there were a couple of cars parked at the edge of the field. Perhaps Helene dealt privately with one of the farmers, getting a special deal on her organic mesclun by buying after hours. I pulled my Volvo up behind a silver Ford Explorer, got out and walked into the maze of empty stalls.

The sinking sun cast long violet shadows on the well-trampled field and makeshift plywood sides of the stalls. A stench of decaying lettuce and fruit filled my nostrils—it was the first time in months the smell of food didn't make me salivate.

I heard a chatter of Spanish coming from a tent and directed myself to it. Two Mexican women emerged carrying large bundles of wilting gladioli. *"¡'Tardes!"* they called cheerfully and headed out to the road.

I sauntered a little farther into the marketplace. There was an enormous stall that evidently featured vine-grown produce. Several rotted hunks of watermelon were scattered on the ground and a large sunken pumpkin had been abandoned on the counter.

Footsteps pattered up behind me. I started to turn. There was a blam! and the pumpkin on the counter exploded into an orange and yellow mash.

hit the dirt.

Or more accurately, I performed my first squat-thrust since roughly the seventh grade. Two more shots, blam, blam! and this time a knobbly little green-striped gourd on the ground near my head met its maker.

Maintaining a prone position, I turned my head gingerly. Helene Barnes stood in the shadow of a spindly acacia tree. She wore a lemonade-colored pant suit with a double-breasted jacket, tastefully accessorized with discreet pearl earrings, a ruby and grass green chiffon scarf, and a gun.

This last appeared to be a flat, gray, old-fashioned-looking model, the kind that in World War II movies the elegant but ruthless S.S. commando would use to blow away Peter Lorre. I almost let out a laugh. For years I had trundled blissfully around L.A. never dreaming that most of the women I was encountering were packing pistols about their person. In fact, I seemed to be the only female in town without firepower—not counting, of course, those halcyon couple of hours I'd had Diane the starlet's Resolver nestled in my carryall.

"What are you grinning at?" Helene said, with something like affront. "Do you think this is funny?" Evidently Laughing in the Face of Danger was a human response not covered in her Pod Person manual. "Those were just warning shots, you know. If I'd wanted to hit you, I would have."

Who would have thought Helene Barnes, concocter of melt-in-your-mouth hors d'oeuvres, was also a crack shot?

"No, I don't think it's funny," I said quickly. "In fact, you've scared the hell out of me. For Chrissake, Helene, what are you doing?"

"Stay away from my son!"

"Okay, fine." The order mystified me, but I was not about to press for details.

She and her gun took a meaningful step closer. "If I ever catch you talking to him about acting or anything to do with it, I swear I'll shoot you dead."

"Okay, you won't, I promise. Just put the gun down."

"Just so we have it straight," she said and lowered her weapon.

"Can I get up now?" I asked.

She gave a curt nod.

I hauled myself shakily to my feet. "You really didn't need the gun," I told her. "You could have just told me to drop the subject and I'd have been glad to. I'm a mother too, you know."

"I needed to be sure," she insisted.

"Yeah, okay, now you're sure." I brushed some dried mud off the front of my dress. It was shaping up to be one particularly strenuous day. "Let me ask you something," I said gingerly. "Do you really think that just because you stop people from talking to Marcus about acting it's going to ensure he becomes a molecular biologist?"

"Do you think I'm a total fool?" she spat out. "I don't care if he grows up to be a biologist or a Buddhist monk. I'm just trying to make sure that he grows up. You just don't understand." She started to shiver uncontrollably.

"I think we should sit down," I said. I guided her to a large crate that didn't look too filthy. She sat on the edge, resting the gun rather primly on her lap. I perched beside her, thankful to be for once off my feet without ending up on my stomach. "Why don't you tell me what this is all about?" I asked.

She drew a breath. "Two years ago, Marcus tried to commit suicide."

I felt something cold squeeze inside my chest. "He was only nine years old."

"Exactly. A nine-year-old boy almost succeeded in hanging himself." The carefully controlled facade that Helene presented to the world suddenly became stripped away, replaced by a distraught and altogether human woman. A muscle above her right eye twitched and she agitatedly tugged at a wiry strand of hair. "We had just come back from New York City," she went on. "Marcus had auditioned for a movie, a big-budget musical . . ."

"*Orphans*," I put in.

"Yes, that one. We hadn't expected much, they were looking at hundreds of children, some of them with lots of experience and impressive credits. And Marcus was just starting out, he'd landed a couple of small TV roles, but that was it. I just thought it would be good exposure for him or at the least give him some practice in auditioning. And then once we got there, I thought I'd made a huge mistake. There was so much backbiting and envy . . . I heard seven-year-olds bragging about the size of their residual checks. I saw a grandmother screaming at a four-year-old for muffing a line. And all these mothers pushing and pushing their kids. I thought to myself I don't want to be like that, I never want to become a stage mother. I was ready to call the whole thing off."

"But then Marcus wowed the casting director," I said.

Her deep brown eyes fixed warily on me. "Right. Joyce Korshalek went crazy when she saw him perform. She told us the movie was in trouble because Jamie Alston was such a disaster, but Marcus could save it. And then she immediately started setting up meetings with the producers and studio executives. It was all supposed to be hush-hush till we got back here."

"Except then Joyce took a tumble downstairs."

Helene gave a fastidious little shudder. "Horrible accident. But she did wear very unsuitable shoes, I remember that."

Yeah, blame it on the Manolo Blahniks, I thought wryly.

"So when she died," I continued out loud, "that was the end of Marcus's chance at stardom."

"Not at all," Helene said crisply. "When we got back home, the phone was ringing off the hook. The producers wanted to assure us that they were still interested in him. It started happening very quickly. We had lunch with the studio people, and they were falling all over Marcus. It was very exciting. I thought Marcus was excited too. I mean, in a good way . . ." The little muscle in her forehead began to twitch violently. "I had just gotten off the phone with my husband, who was in Malaysia on business. We hadn't talked in several days, so it was a pretty long call. When I hung up, something told me, I don't know what, some sixth sense, to go up to Marcus's room. And I opened the door and . . ." She began to sort of hiccup, unable to get further words out.

"It's okay," I assured her. "You don't have to go on."

She caught her breath. "He had a belt. One of George's Mark Cross belts. He had buckled it to a light fixture on the ceiling and then knotted the other end around his neck. And he had stepped off a chair and he was dangling while being slowly strangled by his neck. And I could almost not get him down, because his legs were thrashing so much and he had knotted the belt so well. But I finally did and called an ambulance, and at the hospital they said another thirty seconds, just half a minute later and I'd have been too late." Her voice rose in an agonized shriek. "Even now when I think about it, I almost go insane. You have no idea. You can't possibly have any idea."

"No," I agreed in a low voice. "I can't even imagine."

I placed a comforting arm around her shoulders, briefly thinking how odd it was to be embracing the same woman who, minutes before, had expressed herself willing and able to blow me to kingdom come. We were silent for several moments. Then I said, "Did you ever find out why Marcus tried to . . ." I searched for an appropriate euphemism and finished lamely, "to do it?"

"The psychiatrists said it was performance anxiety. That he felt all this immense pressure on him, because he was being given the starring role and now it was up to him to save the entire movie. They said he was terrified of letting everyone down."

"Do you feel they were right?"

She shrugged. "We immediately pulled the plug on everything. Turned down the movie. No more acting or dancing classes, no more auditions. And he's never tried to hurt himself since." Her face hardened. "So you can see why I don't want any thoughts about performing put in his head. When I heard you talking to him about it the day you came to our house, I could have murdered you right then and there."

"Thanks for your restraint," I said dryly.

We lapsed into another unchummy silence. My eye fell on a ruby-throated hummingbird darting through a dusty hibiscus. I recalled irrelevantly that the Mayan word for hummingbird was *tz'unun,* which was exactly the sound it made in flight. The little bird sipped a blossom, then buzzed past my ear—*tz'unun*—and disappeared from my sight.

I had a sudden and disturbing thought. "Helene," I said, "did you ever say anything to Marcus about wanting to shoot me?"

"Of course not!" she said fiercely. "Why would you even ask me such a thing?"

"This is why." I reached into the pocket of my jacket and took out the flip book. "Marcus drew this for my animation workshop. I think you should take a look at it."

She accepted it with a puzzled frown and awkwardly fluttered the pages. Her face paled. "I don't understand," she gasped. "I didn't say a word to him. I mean, I didn't even plan on doing this until you pulled up beside me on the road. You said you wanted to talk to him about an audition, and I figured you were trying to get him for one of your husband's movies or something . . . I just kind of freaked out."

I made a sudden grab for the gun in her lap and flung it up onto the roof of a neighboring stall.

"Hey!" Helene protested. "That gun belongs to my husband. It happens to be a pre–World War II Mauser."

"So it's a collector's item," I said tartly.

She gave me a slit-eyed glance. "Why did you throw it up there?"

"Because I've got something I need to tell you that you might find kind of upsetting."

"What?" she asked warily.

"It's about the *Orphans* casting call. Joyce Korshalek's platform shoes didn't kill her. One of the children did."

"That's crazy!" she snapped.

"It's true. One of the auditioners gave her a fatal little push."

"I don't believe it. It's exactly the kind of malicious rumor those viper stage mothers are likely to start. They'll use anything to eliminate competition."

"It's not a rumor. It was videotaped and I've seen the tape. A kid in a big straw hat shoves her from behind, it's unmistakable. The only problem is it's impossible to identify the child."

At the mention of the hat, Helene had given a small but perceptible start.

"That's what Marcus had been wearing, wasn't it?" I pursued.

"So what of it? So were a lot of the others. They gave them out as props, you know, so the children could get into character."

"Was he wearing bib overalls as well?"

"I don't remember what he had on. But if you are even remotely implying that Marcus could do such a vicious thing, you must be insane."

"Obviously something very traumatic happened to him at that audition."

"I explained that. He was suffering under the stress of a tremendous performance anxiety."

"Yeah, and it was Joyce Korshalek who was responsible for putting him under that stress. Maybe he thought that if something happened to her, then the whole thing would just go away."

She gave a forced laugh. "That's ridiculous."

"Maybe," I admitted. "I could be totally wrong. But if I'm not, if he did push her, it would be a horrible thing for him to have weighing on him. Even if he seems okay now, it's bound to have consequences later."

"I'm not listening to this crap," Helene said, jumping to her feet. "And I won't have you spreading this kind of thing around." She glanced ruefully up at where I tossed the gun. The dying sun picked an ominous red gleam off its barrel.

I stood up as well and edged a few steps backward toward the street. "I'm only telling you this for Marcus's sake," I said. "If it turns out to be true, he's going to need some help."

"Somebody put you up to this, didn't they," she said belligerently. "Was it that bitch Connie Meyers? Her daughter was wearing a big straw hat that day too, I'll bet she didn't tell you that. And that little girl had plenty of reason to hate Joyce Korshalek. Joyce eliminated her on the first cut—called her a middle-aged midget in kids' clothing. And the girl threw a tantrum, using words I've never heard come out of a child's mouth before. So why don't you go accuse *her*?"

"I'm not accusing anyone," I said, backing further away.

"It sounds to me like you are," she said, keeping step with me. "And I'm not going to let you get away with it."

I had never really noticed how tall Helene was: coming at me full steam, she now seemed roughly the height of the Salty Dog Dalmation. "Okay, you've made your point," I told her. "So back off."

"I know your reputation," she said. "You never let things alone. You won't be satisfied till you've destroyed my son."

"Believe me, Helene, that's the last thing in the world I want to do." I broke into a sort of backward trot and smacked up against the side of a stall. Helene was still coming at me. Without thinking, I scooped a rotted tomato from the ground and lobbed it at her. It landed in a rather artistic red blotch on the jacket of her lemonade suit.

She stopped dead in her tracks, stared down at the defiled jacket and emitted a splutter of outrage. Evidently, she had been prepared to accept the consequences of killing me in cold blood, if need be, but the befoulment of her outfit was taking things one step too far. She bent down, grabbed a squishily decomposing head of lettuce and pitched it feverishly. It whizzed inches past my head, then spattered onto the boards behind me—apparently her aim with leafy vegetables was not as good as it was with a Mauser.

At the sound of footsteps rounding the tent, we both whirled. A stoop-shouldered man in a rumpled private security guard's uniform shuffled toward us. The sight of two women in a deserted and rapidly darkening open-air market obviously came as a disagreeable surprise. He took a wary step or two backward.

"Market's closed, ladies," he said. He gave his gray scribble of hair a nervous scratch.

"Thank you, we were just leaving," I said in my best social tea voice. Then, getting the jump on Helene, I turned and strode rapidly back to my car, dived into the driver's seat and peeled out.

Ten minutes later, I was wedged between a Starving Students moving van and a black Ferrari in a rush hour traffic jam, trying to wipe the fetid traces of decayed tomato from my fingers with an ancient Kleenex. My tête-à-tête with Helene had raised more questions than it had answered. I began to mull over my pack of underage suspects, trying to determine where they now were in the race to the guilty finish.

It seemed clear that the dark horse, Holly Beech, the former fatty tortured into svelteness, had to be scratched. She might have tried to incinerate everything in her path, but she had seemed genuinely unaware that Joyce the Casting Lady had gone tripping into that good night.

However, Theadora Meyers who had been lagging at the back of the pack seemed to be suddenly making an inside sprint. She had been brutally axed from the audition by Joyce the Executioner and had cussed like a longshoreman when it happened. Couldn't she have been capable of following up with an efficient little shove from behind?

And her mom, Connie, the bedraggled martyr to her daughter's career . . . Could she possibly have been the one to subsequently blow Brandon away? It was hard to picture the scrawny Connie Meyers wielding a .44 Magnum. But there were people you could pay to do that kind of thing. Connie's long years of being a stage mother had no doubt made her very resourceful when it came to hiring professionals: voice trainers, acting coaches, tap dancing instructors . . . So why not a hit man?

But galloping neck and neck into the stretch were still the favorites: Jamie Alston, Kerrin Granger and Marcus Barnes. All three had first-class motives: Jamie, about to give the entertainment media the scoop of the year by being replaced in his first big-budget movie with a complete unknown; Marcus, in mortal terror of not being able to live up to the frenetic expectations building around him; and Kerrin, in equal terror of having to report that he was a loser to his brutish pa.

All three came attached with parents who appeared capable of acting with complete ruthlessness should the occasion so call for it.

And all three of the above I had now actively antagonized. Maybe my best strategy would be to ring up Connie Meyers as well, baldly accuse both her and her daughter of having blood on their hands, and hang up. Then all I'd have to do was sit back and wait to see which one of the four actually showed up at my doorstep looking to permanently shut my mouth.

There was only one slight drawback to this plan—I wouldn't be around later to capitalize on what I found out.

I pictured Terry Shoe clomping through my house to examine my body. Explaining to her fellow officers of the law how she'd always warned me about being a Nosy Parker. Pointing out to them the various idiosyncrasies of my household decor—the cookie jars, my collection of windup and pull toys, my framed animation cels depicting skyscrapers with faces and hedgehogs with wings . . . Implying that she never did think I was operating on all six cylinders.

The traffic in front of me suddenly unclogged. I shot forward, shaking myself out of this macabre daydream. I reminded myself that tomorrow evening Kit and Chloe would be back home.

All I had to do was survive the day in between.

21

It wasn't the fact that Chloe had green hair that had me shaken—
these, she assured me, were just temporary streaks that would
shampoo right out. Nor was it the fact that her fingernails were
painted an industrial smokestack gray—from a line called Urban
Decay that she borrowed from her new best friend, Belle Manzano—or that she had acquired a new, high-pitched giggle, probably also on loan from Belle.

It was the way she referred to "Dad and Annie," all in a piece,
the way you'd say Ozzie and Harriet, or Heckle and Jeckle. "Dad
and Annie took us ice-skating last night and Dad fell down twice,"
she announced almost as soon as she got off the plane. "We went
shopping with Dad and Annie and Annie bought Belle a really cool
fake fur coat." "Dad and Annie said it was the best snow this year
they'd ever seen."

We had gone straight from the airport to a Mexican restaurant
called Chihuahua; it featured mariachis in frilly shirts and a *camp-
esina* with a round brown face and permanently pissed-off expression patting out fresh tortillas in a corner. Chloe loved it because

it also had a myna bird in an iron cage that could occasionally be prompted to talk in Spanish, including, rumor had it, several choice Mexican obscenities.

But so far tonight she hadn't even glanced at the myna. Nor had she asked about her own ailing parrot, or her cats or chinchilla or Ratty her rat snake. "There's this Tex-Mex restaurant in Aspen Dad and Annie took us to," she was saying through a mouthful of cheese, "and it used chocolate on everything, even the burritos. Remember Dad?"

"Mm," Kit replied.

The male half of the dynamic Dad-and-Annie duo sat in front of a margarita glass that could have doubled as a birdbath, absently licking the rock salt from its rim; so far he'd said almost nothing beyond distracted monosyllables.

The glorious reunion I'd been anticipating was threatening to be a fizzle. I fixed a determined smile on my face and mechanically chewed my *chile relleno*, wondering how I could get things back on track. I could talk about what I'd been up to the past few days— that the school had nearly burned down with me still hanging around a Natural Sciences classroom, and that a well-dressed caterer with a modulated voice had used me for target practice at a deserted vegetable stand . . .

I needed something more upbeat. It occurred to me that I hadn't sprung the news yet that the new baby was going to be a boy. Kit learning that he was going to have a son, Chloe that she could expect a baby brother—maybe that would snap their attention back to our own family life.

I tapped my glass of nonalcoholic sangria. "Hey, guys," I said cheerily. "I've got some news to tell you."

"Hello, Mr. Freerth," lisped a voice over my shoulder.

I swung around, startled, in my seat. Theadora Meyers was stationed right behind me, practically breathing down my neck. She was tricked out like a Montmartre tart: saucy velvet hat, striped boatneck shirt slipped provocatively down off one shoulder, twirly short felt skirt. Her little face was lifted to Kit, making what my stepmother Anna-Linda would call "goo-goo eyes" at him.

"Hi, Thea," said Chloe.

She remained fixed on Kit. "I'm Theadora Meyerth," she lisped on, batting her lids like a silent screen vamp. "I just had to come over and tell you that your movieth are my very most favorite ever."

"That's nice," Kit said with a strained smile.

Thea pouted her lips coquettishly. "If you will catht me in your next picture, I promith to work really, really hard."

She placed her hands on the crests of her hips and began to move toward him with what could only be described as a breathtakingly expert bump and grind. Kit and I stared transfixed with horror.

"I'm a very terrific actor and a real trooper, and I alwayth give my all to every part." She thrust out her little pudenda. Round and round went her hips: *boom-chicka-boom.* "I can dance and I can thing, and you'll never, ever be thorry if you uthe me." She moistened her lips with the pink tip of her tongue.

"Hey, Thea, why are you acting like such a dork?"

Chloe's no-nonsense voice snapped us out of our trance and put an abrupt end to Thea's grisly performance. For a second, Thea just stood there uncertainly, as if waiting for a director's cue.

Then she suddenly crumbled—no longer a miniature Gypsy Rose Lee, just a little girl in an absurdly seductive outfit.

"But I really need the work," she said plaintively. "I've only had one commercial since Christmas and it wasn't even national." Her lisp had vanished along with the burlesque routine. "Momma says if my checks stop coming, we're going to have to move out of our house and get some crummy apartment in Reseda or Tarzana!" She pronounced the names of these Valley suburban towns with the dread of an eighteenth-century English pickpocket facing exile to Botany Bay. Tears squeezed from the corners of her eyes and wobbled down her plump cheeks.

I picked out Connie in a far corner of the restaurant. She sat hunched at a small table, drab as ever in a linty mauve cardigan, peering hopefully in our direction. Ghoulishly waiting to see if her ten-year-old was going to score next month's rent.

"I'm not casting anything right now," Kit was saying uncomfortably. "I'm really in between projects at the moment."

Thea snapped into another persona, this time the seasoned pro taking disappointment in stride. "Please keep me in mind for the future, and thank you very much for your consideration," she recited. She flashed us all a dimpled smile, then retreated jauntily back to her mother.

"Christ almighty," Kit muttered, lunging for his margarita. "That is absolutely the worst kind of professional kid. She's about as natural as a Barbie doll. And frankly, I'd use a Barbie before I'd cast a kid like that."

"But the poor thing's been at it since she started to crawl," I pointed out. "It probably is natural for her to act like that now."

"Oh yeah? Where the hell did she get those moves? Some waterfront dive in Shanghai?"

"Nothing she couldn't have learned from watching HBO," I said. "And, Chloe, you didn't have to be mean to her."

"But look how she was coming on to Dad," Chloe protested.

Kit choked on his drink.

"Besides which, *she's* mean to other kids," Chloe went on. "Nobody ever wants her on their team in soccer because she'll shove and push you really hard so she can get to the ball, even when she's on your same team."

My attention sharpened. "Did you ever actually see her push anyone?"

Chloe nodded vigorously. "Sure, tons of times. Like this one time last year when Julie Fasserman was just about to kick in a goal, and then Thea came running up right behind her and knocked her down so she could kick it in herself. And when Julie fell down, she bit right through her bottom lip, and there was all this blood, and she had to have four stitches."

"What did your coach do?" I asked.

"Laurie? She started to yell at Thea, but Thea said it was an accident, because she was running so fast she couldn't stop in time. And then she started to cry, so Laurie believed her. But I saw her do it, and so did a lot of other kids. She did it on purpose. And I think she was faking her crying."

This was very possibly true—we'd just had a firsthand demonstration of how Thea could squeeze out crocodile tears on demand.

I noticed that across the room Thea and Connie had gotten up to leave. Thea sashayed ahead, sneaking peeks around the restaurant to see if any eyes were on her, while Connie shlumped a few steps behind, more like a faithful servant than a parent. In my horse race of kid suspects, Thea was pulling up at a gallop to the three front-runners.

Something nagged at the periphery of my mind. Something Thea had told me at the McDonald's audition and which I should have paid more attention to at the time, but hadn't. I racked my brain trying to bring it into focus, but it remained just fuzzily out of reach.

Chloe gave a cavernous yawn and drooped over her plate. I reached over and smoothed her vivid red-and-green-streaked ringlets. "I think it's time to call it a night."

"We're both exhausted," Kit said, echoing her yawn. "All that exercise in the fresh air really takes it out of you."

Not to mention all that exercise in the indoor air, I thought ruefully, cutting a rug with the gay divorcée.

A waitress in a sombrero slapped a check on the table. "What was the news you were going to tell us?" Kit said, reaching for it.

I felt a rekindling of that little inner glow. "I had an ultrasound yesterday. I found out the new baby is going to be a boy!"

"Hey that's great!" Kit said through another yawn.

"Yeah, cool," Chloe murmured. "Except I was hoping for a baby sister so I could give her all my old Barbies and stuff." Her head nodded; her eyes were already half-shut with sleep.

At home, Chloe rallied just long enough to conduct a quick inspection of all her animals, then crawled into bed still wearing her thermal socks and long silk underwear. While Kit undressed, I sat in a modified lotus position on the bed, tracing patterns in the Star of Bethlehem quilt.

"So tell me about this Annie," I said finally, striving for a breezy tone: it proved difficult between clenched teeth.

"I already did." He shimmied out of his boxers and pulled on a pair of drawstring pajama bottoms. "Besides, you've met her before, so what's there to tell?"

"Does she still insist on letting you know the exact dollar amount she paid for her clothes?" I winced at my own cattiness.

"I didn't notice. She does dress very stylishly."

As opposed to me, I presumed, who took wardrobe cues from the *Late Late Show*.

"So I guess you'd call her attractive," I said, intently studying the quilt.

"Extremely. She turns heads everywhere she goes." He pulled back the covers and slipped into his side of the bed. "Sensational body," he went on. "Stunning tits, a terrific ass. And in bed, she was a real wildcat."

I gave a start.

"She'd slip into my room at midnight and we'd go at it till dawn. Positions like you wouldn't believe! Old Charlie Manzano must have been one hell of a sexual acrobat for her to have picked up that kind of repertoire."

I let out a strained chuckle. "You're joking."

"But that's what you're getting at, isn't it?" he said petulantly. "And frankly, I resent the fact that you don't trust me enough to spend a couple of days with an old friend without jumping her bones."

"You're right, I'm sorry," I replied. "It's been such a crazy week that my imagination's been running wild." I added softly, "I'm really glad you're back."

"Me too." He patted my bulging stomach. "So we're getting a boy, huh? That's really terrific." He muttered again about being totally wiped out, then turned onto his side and in moments was asleep.

I stared at his gently heaving back. There were some scratches just below the shoulder, three roughly parallel, faint red lines. Probably meaningless, I told myself.

I was sure they hadn't been made by a wildcat's fingernails.

22

At ten A.M. the following morning, the road up to Windermere Academy was once more clogged to a standstill, but this time the atmosphere was festive rather than saturated with panic. We had all come for the gala fund-raiser, wallets and checkbooks ready for business.

The campus had been transformed wobblingly into a Renaissance fair. Jugglers juggled, jesters strode about the lawns on giant stilts, and minstrels in body-revealing tunics crooned "Greensleeves." All the performers beamed at us parents with the multi-kilowatt smiles of unemployed actors hoping to land a beam on someone who would prove beneficial to their careers.

Chloe had a hundred dollars to blow. She and two of her friends had agreed to pool their resources to bid on a basket full of Beanie Babies, which, rumor had it, included an extremely rare Peanut the Elephant in royal blue. The moment we found a parking space, she raced out of the car to go round up Lily and Sara Joan. Kit, muttering that he needed a stiff jolt of caffeine, tottered toward a stand selling caffe lattes in soup bowl–sized cups. I decided to go hunt up my hobo cookie jar to see how frenetic the bidding had been on it so far.

The auction loot was displayed on what at first sight looked jarringly like altars, but proved to be computer tables draped with white sheets of crinkly paper. This being a silent auction, each table also had a sheet of paper on which people were to record their names and bids, with each new bidder required to go at least fifty bucks higher than the one before. In the case of such items as the Porthault bedding and the round-trip excursion to Argentina, the competition was spirited: the list of names was long and the bids jumped in increments of a hundred or more.

For an entertaining moment, I watched a young matron in skin-tight jeans try to defend her lock on the bedsheets by hovering over the bidding sheet, only to be roughly shoved aside by a petite blonde who used her pocketbook as a kind of cudgel. Then I turned away and locked eyes with Helene Barnes.

My first instinct was to get as far away from her as fast as I possibly could. But astonishingly, she met me with a pleasant Return of the Pod Person smile. Nothing to indicate that just two days before we had been hurling rotten vegetables at each other, or that she had been firing a Mauser in my general direction.

"Hello there, so glad you could make it," she burbled. "I do hope you'll be generous and not skimp on your bids. It's all for the cause of supporting the school, you know." She had resumed her emotionless take-me-to-your-leader voice.

"I intend to spend till it hurts," I said with a nervous laugh.

I edged quickly away, hoping to take cover behind a gaggle of minstrels, but was instantly accosted by Connie Meyers. It was becoming a regular obstacle course of Aggrieved Mothers.

"Lucy, wait up," Connie said, even though I was standing perfectly still. "About the restaurant last night . . . I hope Kit didn't mind Thea coming over to him. In this business, you've got to be pushy if you want to get noticed. That's what I've always taught Thea."

"To push and shove?" I said bluntly.

"Whatever it takes."

"Does this extend to people as well?"

She eyed me suspiciously. "What do you mean?"

"Did you teach her that if someone gets in her way, she ought to shove them right out of it? Preferably down the nearest flight of stairs?"

If I had expected her to quiver with surprise and fear and possibly blurt out a confession, I was wrong. She set her mouth in a hard little slot and folded her arms over her concave chest. "I don't know what you're driving at," she said, "but I'm not going to apologize for making my daughter a competitor. I'm proud of that. And I'm proud of the fact that I sacrificed everything to give her every opportunity."

"How about the opportunity to be a normal kid?" I returned.

Connie creased her brow as if such a suggestion was too outlandish for her brain to even process. "Just you wait," she declared. "Thea's going to be a big star some day. And then none of you will be laughing so hard."

The notion that I'd been laughing came as something of a surprise. But before I could reply, Connie turned on her scuffed heels and shuffled away.

I resumed my search for my cookie jar. It had been relegated to a table on the far outskirts of the field. The bid sheet had only one entry, Carrie Bachelor, a liability lawyer who was known for squeezing a nickel until the buffalo bellowed. True to reputation, she had bid a tightfisted thirty-five dollars. With a sigh, I wrote down my own name, scribbled down five hundred bucks and turned back into the thick of the crowd.

Chloe came scampering up to me with what appeared to be a pacifier she was sucking on. "Mom, guess what!" she mumbled.

"What's that in your mouth?" I asked.

"Ring Pop." She pulled it out. The ring was attached to a bright blue hard candy that had stained her lips roughly the same hue as her Urban Decay fingernail polish. "But guess what?" she chattered on. "Jamie Alston bid on all these tickets to the Keystone Studio Theme Park, and our whole class gets to go tonight!"

"That's swell," I said. "Did you get the Beanie Babies?"

Her face fell. "Uh-uh. We only had five hundred and twenty dollars and some kid in the third grade put down two thousand."

An eight-year-old with two grand to drop on a basket of stuffed animals . . .

A gust of wind blew up, causing the eucalyptus trees to rustle and paper cups and plates to dance across the field. But it was a hot, dry wind from the desert and it wasn't what made me suddenly shiver.

The auction was followed by a parent-child softball game. I sat in the bleachers, where I hollered myself hoarse when Chloe walloped a triple and groaned theatrically when Kit was tagged out. Their side won by one run; we jubilantly returned home to get ready for the night at the theme park.

I sat in front of my dressing table mirror appalled at my reflection. I had lost that first rosy flush of pregnancy; now my skin was dry and flaky and covered with a fine film of dust from the softball field. Plus the dry wind had sucked out almost all the humidity from the air, producing an interesting prunelike effect on my complexion. I looked like Georgia O'Keeffe, the Later Years, I thought glumly. I began slathering my face with great gobs of moisturizing cream.

The phone shrilled: after three rings, when neither Kit nor Chloe had picked up, I reached for my extension with a greasy hand.

"Lucy? It's Roxanne."

I felt a stab of alarm. Roxanne was the elder of my two stepsisters. After getting her degree in surgical nursing from Michigan State, she had married her high school sweetheart and settled in St. Paul, fifty miles from the semirural town in which we'd grown up and in which my father and stepmother still lived. Roxie and I had never been very close; the only reason I could imagine her calling out of the blue would be to relate some bad family news.

"Is it Dad?" I asked quickly. "Did he have to go back in the hospital?"

"Huh? No, he's fine. We saw them last weekend and they were both in great fettle. The reason I'm calling is because I just saw that thing of yours on TV."

"My thing?" I repeated blankly. How could one of my animations be airing completely without my knowledge?

"Yeah, the real-life video that was just on that news show, *Deadline U.S.A.* They said it was taken by a Los Angeles filmmaker, Lucy Freers. That's got to be you, right?"

My brain seemed to be functioning with all the agility of sludge. "I'm not following, Roxanne. What video?"

"The one with the little kid pushing that woman down those stairs. It's amazing stuff! When we heard your name, Lou and I got really excited. I mean, wow!"

"You saw that on TV?" I exclaimed. The realization was surrealistically beginning to sink in: somehow Brandon's video had managed to appear on a sleazy syndicated news show, with my name attached to it.

"Well, yeah. Didn't you know? The reporter said that they couldn't show the entire tape because the last part of it was too graphic and violent for family viewing. So what *did* it show? Did she get impaled or something?" Roxie's voice was fairly quivering with prurient interest. I'd have thought a nurse would get a sufficient helping of blood and gore on her job without needing an additional dose of it after-hours.

"Let's just say you could tell her dancing days were over," I said brusquely. "And anyway, I didn't take that video, Brandon McKenna did."

"The guy who worked for you who got killed?"

"Yeah. And I have no idea how it got on that damned show."

"Wow," she breathed again. "Everybody from back home has been calling, they're all really wild. Wait'll they hear this part of it."

Glad I could brighten up an otherwise gloomy prairie night, I thought acidly. I told her I couldn't talk any longer, I had to go, and hung up.

The phone rang again almost immediately. Probably somebody from "back home"—maybe my old high school principal, Mr. Ringstrom, or the postmistress with the jiggly underarms—all panting to be told the delectably gory details that had been snipped out of the videotape. I was startled to hear Terry Shoe's voice.

"I'm fit to be tied!" she spluttered. "Some blazing A-hole in the NYPD slipped a copy of that videotape to a news program."

"Yeah, I know," I said. *"Deadline U.S.A."*

"How did you find out? It hasn't been on yet."

Of course—I had forgotten the fact that Minnesota was in Central Time—meaning everything was broadcast there two hours earlier. "I just got the news from somebody back east," I said. "Why in god's name would the New York cops do such a thing?"

"I certainly don't think it was authorized. My bet is somebody got a juicy little payment under the table. Could've been a cop or could've been a janitor. I'd just like to get my hands on the bastard."

I glanced at the bedside clock. "This means that sometime within the next hour, everyone in L.A. is going to know this tape exists—probably including Brandon's killer. And they're also going to hear my name attached to it."

"Which, all in all, might not be so bad an eventuality."

"Excuse me?"

"Let's just say you're right. I mean, that McKenna was killed by somebody—some parent—trying to protect the kid in that tape."

"So?"

"So maybe that somebody had thoughts that McKenna had spilled the beans to you. And so maybe, and I'm not saying this is true, you were next on their list for removal. But now this tape has hit the air . . ."

"Confirming all this maniac's suspicions," I cut in. "He or she is probably right outside my house this very second, waiting to plug me the minute I step out."

"There you go again, leaping to your extreme conclusions."

Kit came padding in from the bathroom swaddled in towels. He glanced at me quizzically, picked up some grooming aid from his dresser and padded back out.

I lowered my voice into the phone. "So what's your take on it? That they'll be waiting to present me with a Truth in Journalism award?"

"My thinking is that now you're home free. It's obvious that if McKenna had told you who the kid is and you had the tape as evidence, you'd have wasted maybe two nanoseconds before spilling it all to the authorities. So they're going to have to figure you *don't* know who the kid is. And now they'll leave you alone."

"That's a logical assumption," I said. "There's only one teensy flaw in it. You're presuming that Brandon's killer is a logical person. My experience is that a parent trying to protect a child doesn't exactly act in a completely rational manner. They'll act more like a grizzly bear protecting its cub."

"Well I guess we'll just have to wait and see what happens," was Terry's less-than-comforting summation. She yelled something unintelligible to someone on her end, then came back on the line. "Frank's family blew in from Seoul last night, and I've been running ragged showing them the sights. We went to the Chinese Theatre this afternoon. His uncle found out his footprints were an exact match for Mel Gibson's, which pretty much made his day. Now they want to eat Italian." She gave a dry chuckle. "Just when I was starting to get a taste for that bippetybop."

"What if something does happen and I need to get hold of you?" I asked plaintively.

"You've got my pager number. But Frank's made it very clear that this gang will think it's hugely disrespectful if his wife waltzes out on them. The fact that he's married a non-Korean gal is already hard for them to swallow. Me being also a homicide detective—well, let's say they couldn't be more perplexed if he had married a sumo wrestler. So if you go bothering me tonight, you better make sure your life's in immediate danger. Otherwise," she deadpanned, "I'm gonna have to kill you myself."

"Don't worry," I assured her. "If you hear from me, it will only be for an excellent reason."

"You're white as a sheet!" Kit exclaimed, appearing back in the room as I hung up. "Who was that?"

Before I could reply, Chloe slouched in, chicly attired in a cropped black-and-white sweater I had never seen before—no doubt booty from one of those Dad-and-Annie shopping sprees.

"How come you're not ready?" she demanded. "It's almost seven o'clock."

Almost time for *Deadline U.S.A.* I had a sudden idea.

"I'm feeling a bit queasy," I said. "I just need to rest a little bit and I'll be fine. You two go on ahead and I'll catch up with you."

"You sure?" Kit hesitated.

"Positive." I lay back languorously on the bed. "A little peace and quiet is really all I need."

The moment they left the house, I leaped up and stuck a tape in the VCR. I tuned the TV to Channel 5, hit "record" on the VCR as a Nissan ad gave way to the fatuously heroic credit montage of *Deadline*. Brandon's tape was given the dubious distinction of the lead story.

"We're about to show something that many viewers may find disturbing," the show's host intoned. "An actual video recording of a fatal accident that's perpetrated by a small child. The footage was shot by the Los Angeles filmmaker Lucy Freers, who passed it on to the New York City Police Department. Police there have been as yet unable to determine the identity of the child." He burbled on about how they had to edit out the last bit of the tape as being too graphic for public consumption.

And then suddenly I was once again watching those images that had become so searingly familiar to me. Joyce The Executioner Korshalek, in her power suit and tottering platform shoes. Her startled grimace as the urchin pops up behind her. The efficient little shove, her pop-eyed expression of terror and ungainly somersault down the stairs. The crack of her head on the sharp metal ledge.

But instead of the zoom in to the bloody porridge of brains and skull on the cement floor, the program cut back abruptly to the smarmy, sun-tanned reporter. "If any of our viewers have information as to the identity of this child . . . ," he began, in a tone of hushed importance.

I wasn't interested in hearing the rest of his spiel. I clicked off the TV, ejected the tape and ran with it downstairs.

The phones were already eagerly jangling as I hit the bottom floor, both Kit's two lines and my own. Many inquiring minds wanting to know. It was interesting how many people we knew who evidently had nothing better to do of an evening than hunker down in front of a cheesy TV magazine show.

I ignored the ringing and continued on to my studio. I dug out a blank flip book and soft lead drawing pencil, then took them into the den where we had a large-screen Mitsubishi. I snapped the cassette into the Mitsubishi's built-in VCR; then, with the flipbook open on my lap, I rewound the tape to the beginning of Brandon's footage.

Back in my second year of film school, I had taken an advanced animation class called "Techniques of Motion." The instructor, an elegant and high-strung refugee from Prague, would harangue us time and again on the importance of making the action in our work look natural. "Is okay if your characters are only stick figures," he would declare, spiraling a thin hand in the air. "Simple mouse, stylized cat, no problem. But if stick figure or simple cat runs, or jumps or twirls around on toes, it must be real running, real jumping, real twirl. Otherwise is good for nothing, your work."

To this end, he took sequences from old movies—Judy Garland and the Scarecrow skipping down the Yellow Brick Road; Gable sweeping Vivien Leigh upstairs in his arms; Fred dipping Ginger—and looped them over and over, freeze-framing at selected spots, until we students could break down the action into a series of simple movements and reproduce them in our drawings. This is what I now planned to do with Brandon's footage: break it down into simple, sketchable movements and see if it yielded any discoveries.

I ran and rewound the sequence three times over, concentrating only on the movement of the two figures. On the fourth time, I freeze-framed the tape at the moment the straw-hatted urchin first became fully visible behind Joyce. I drew a quick, rudimentary sketch of the child's body posture on the bottom page of the flip book. I advanced the tape several frames, then stopped it again and whipped off another sketch on the next-to-bottom page. I continued to the point where Joyce turned to discover she had company, making about a dozen sketches in all.

Then I riffled the pages of the flip book to animate the sketches.

And drew a shocked breath. What was scarcely noticeable on tape was clearly visible in my crude animation: the child's left shoulder rose and fell in a quick little hunch.

The unmistakable nervous gesture of Marcus Barnes!

My hands and feet felt cold and clammy, and a metallic taste of horror lumped in my throat. I realized I'd been desperately hoping he wasn't the one. But here was hard proof that he was.

I forced myself to press the "play" button. I needed to see the rest of the sequence now that I had the knowledge it was Marcus. There went Joyce, turning fatefully to meet her own executioner. Once again her start of surprise, and Marcus darting forward to pounce.

I quickly hit "pause." There was something wrong with this picture.

Or more probably, with my interpretation of it.

But what? I lifted the remote for an instant replay. "Ow!" I yelped, once more feeling a twinge of pain in the place my arm bone had been winged by the bullet. I rubbed it with annoyance: it seemed to be flaring up more and more frequently these days.

Particularly, I realized with a jolt, whenever I thought of this exact sequence of the videotape!

With a surge of excitement, I reran the scene to where Joyce gave a start and freeze-framed it. Seeing it on a fifty-two-inch screen, I suddenly had a whole new take on her expression and body language. She was not acting startled . . .

She was flinching in pain!

I had a dizzying flashback to the moment when I had been shot. I could vividly hear the crack of the gun and feel the sting of the bullet. Reliving the memory, I flinched.

In exactly the way Joyce Korshalek was now frozen on my Mitsubishi.

I leaned back into the sofa and shut my eyes, trying to put it all together. Joyce on the top of the stairs, Marcus appearing behind her . . . She suddenly feels pain. It could have been from any number of things—a sudden toothache or bout of heartburn, or a bunion from those ridiculous shoes of hers . . .

But it was her head that had jerked. And it kept stubbornly reminding me of my own near-date with death.

Marcus Barnes's flip book swam into my mental vision. I pictured the bullet the size of a martini shaker exploding the head of a woman with a curly hairdo like mine . . .

My eyes flew open. It looked even more like Joyce Korshalek's fashionable frizz!

At the same second, I remembered what I'd been straining to recall the night before—what it was that Thea Meyers had told me at the McDonald's audition.

"Oh my god!" I breathed, my heart thumping wildly. I leaped up and raced for my car keys. I was suddenly positive of two things:

Marcus Barnes had not killed anyone.

And his life was in terrible danger.

PART
FOUR

23

"So let me guess." Terry Shoe's voice crackled acerbically over the receiver of my cell phone. "There's a guy with a stocking over his face trying to break down your door with an assault rifle."

"Wrong," I snapped back. "I'm not the one in danger. A ten-year-old boy is. I'm in my car, trying to get to him before anything happens."

"You got a name for this ten-year-old?"

"Marcus Barnes."

"The genius one, right? So who do you think's out to get him?"

"If I'm right, and I'm pretty sure I am, it's Seth Granger."

"Go on."

"Marcus was a witness to Joyce Korshalek's death," I blurted. "I figured it out from watching the tape. And now that it's been on national TV, it stands to reason that others are going to figure it out as well. And once it becomes known that it was Marcus, the killer's going to want to get rid of him the way he got rid of the other witness, Brandon." I blasted my horn at a poky purple Neon that was hogging the left lane.

"Maybe I'm being particularly dense, but I'm not following this," Terry said, sounding more and more grumpy by the moment. "Backtrack a little."

"I taped the *Deadline* segment and then reran it and did a frame-by-frame analysis," I explained, tailgating the Neon. "I saw the kid in the straw hat make a kind of hunching movement with his shoulder. It's something I've seen Marcus do a number of times. Kind of a nervous gesture. Once you notice it, it's unmistakable."

Terry gave a not-quite-convinced grunt. "So saying that's true, it seems to me that makes him a perpetrator, not a witness."

I thumped my hand on the steering wheel in frustrated impatience. "No, it doesn't. Because he didn't push her. He saw her start to topple and fall, and he was trying to grab on to her and save her!"

"So you're saying she for no reason at all just started to topple and fall."

"There was a pretty good reason. She'd been shot."

"Oh come on!" Terry blurted out. "I saw that tape. There was no indication of any . . ."

Her voice on my cell phone abruptly conked out. "Hello?" I yelled into it. "Terry, are you still there?"

A crackle, then "Yeah, I'm here."

"I'm on the 405 heading into the pass, so I'm going to lose you completely in a minute. But once I explain everything, I think you'll see . . ."

The signal died out completely. "Shit," I muttered. I stamped on the gas pedal, shot around the poky Neon and had accelerated to a making-good-time eighty when a motorcycle cop flagged me over.

I sat fuming, while for what seemed the better part of a light-year, he scrutinized my license and registration, then radioed into headquarters to make sure I didn't occupy a prime slot on the Ten Most Wanted list, and finally wrote out a summons with the meticulousness of a medieval monk illuminating a particularly meaty passage of the Gospel. He handed me my ticket with an obnoxiously pleasant "Have a good evening, ma'am," then hopped back on his motorbike and roared away.

I maintained a law-abiding speed the rest of the way to Glendale, where the theme park sprawled in the yellowing foothills. I spent some time winding through the Coliseum-scaled parking structure, finally locating an empty spot on the highest floor and most remote back corner. It had been over forty minutes since I'd left home when I finally hurried out onto the boardwalk of shops and cafés that led to the entrance of the park itself.

Under normal circumstances, I'm a big fan of the Keystone Boardwalk. I love its over-the-top gaudiness, the crazy quilt of neon and plastic signs depicting gorilla-sized rabbits, three-story-high guitars and immense, rocking men-in-the-moon, all in the berserk colors of the forties and fifties: sunburn pink, pond scum green, Cadillac convertible aqua. But at the moment I was in too frantic a hurry to appreciate any of it. The only reason I noticed the rather dumpy female figure halfway down the strip was that she was wearing a dress the exact shade of fuchsia as the gigantic neon date palm she was hovering beneath. Only when she began to walk toward me, her feet splayed like a duck, did she metamorphose into Terry Shoe.

I scurried up to her. "What are you doing here?" I exclaimed.

"What do you think I'm doing, early Christmas shopping? I'm waiting for you. What the hell took you so long?"

"I got a speeding ticket," I said. A splutter of mirth escaped her lips. Ignoring it, I went on, "How did you get here so fast? I'd have thought it would take at least an hour from your place."

"I wasn't home when I returned your page. We'd just gotten to this restaurant, LaGuardia's, right over here in Studio City. They do a fettuccine with white clam sauce that would make you weep." For a moment her eyes did mist over at the thought of this passed-up pasta.

"So does this mean you believe I'm right?" I asked her.

"I wouldn't go so far as that. But what I do know is that Mr. Seth Granger has a tidy little record of assault and seems to need precious little provocation. So if you go waltzing up to him and start throwing around accusations, he's apt to start throwing something back." She shrugged. "Maybe I can keep you from ending up in the trauma ward."

"And maybe we can both keep Marcus out of the morgue," I added.

We had reached the end of the Boardwalk and were now engulfed in the swarm toward the ticket window. "Hell of a lot of folks," Terry remarked.

"It's Presidents' Day. A holiday always brings out the crowds. Schools are closed. And post offices. All those mailmen looking for a good time."

We took our place in a line that seemed to be moving at an inchworm's pace.

"How about explaining to me just why I'm here and not back with my family ordering a zabaglione?" Terry said.

"It's kind of a long story."

"Give me the five-cent encapsulation. What makes you so sure Korshalek was shot?"

I briefly described Marcus's flip book and my analysis of Joyce's flinch of pain from watching it on the big screen. "I've been shot myself," I reminded Terry. "I'm almost certain Joyce Korshalek was shot in the head."

"Even the most incompetent M.E. would've noticed a bullet in the woman's brain."

"Not if it just grazed her skull. That would have been enough to make her flinch and lose her footing. And then because her skull got so mangled when it cracked against that sharp ledge, all traces of a bullet wound could have been lost."

Terry gave a dubious grunt. "That's still a lot of assuming."

"I've got more. I was told by Theadora Meyers that at the *Orphans* audition, Kerrin Granger had been waving a gun around. She thought it was just a cap pistol. But my bet is he had swiped a real one from his daddy's extensive collection, just to act like a big shot. But then, when he saw the wicked witch casting director who had given him the boot, he decided to take a potshot at her."

"Jeez Louise. You're talking about an eight-year-old kid."

"So what are you saying?" I asked her. "That no child has ever shot anybody before?"

"They have," she admitted glumly. "The statistics go up every year. But when you tell me a little kid deliberately takes aim at somebody . . ." She shook her head. "It's hard to even think about."

"Maybe he wasn't intending to kill her," I suggested. "He might not have been really aiming at her."

"Just got a lucky bull's-eye, huh?" She looked at me, her eyes shifting to the color of baked mud. "Here's another possibility. Korshalek wasn't even his target."

"You mean Marcus might have been?" I shuddered at the thought.

"He was the kid they were all drooling over, right? The one who was gonna be an instant movie star? It had to make the Granger boy sick with envy."

"So you think I'm right then," I said. "That Joyce was shot by Kerrin Granger."

"I'm exploring it as a possibility," she corrected me, with professional hauteur.

We were in the thick of the crush toward the admission window now. Progress was stalled by a man with a Texas accent who was loudly wrangling with the ticket seller over the validity of his credit card. I made a sound of exasperation, then turned back to Terry.

"Let's take my theory one step further," I said. "Knowing Brandon, I can imagine that after witnessing the whole thing, he'd have gone straight to Seth Granger and told him what he saw—though not necessarily mentioning that he also had it on tape. He'd have wanted Seth to be the one to go to the authorities and probably just assumed that's what would happen."

"You mean he thought he would be dealing with a decent man," Terry remarked dryly.

I nodded. "Brandon was so thoroughly decent himself, it would have been hard for him to imagine anybody different. Particularly someone like Seth Granger, who, instead of doing the honorable thing and reporting to the police that his son had caused a fatal accident, went haywire on Brandon instead. Either threatened his life or tried to kill him right there and failed. And so Brandon was forced to go on the run."

Terry thought a moment. "There's still a couple of holes in your theory," she said. "Like for one, why didn't we hear a shot on the videotape?"

"Brandon was using a zoom lens. He could have been thirty feet away or more."

"Right, the sound was recorded where he was, not where the action was." She sucked in her lower lip in a disgruntled I-should've-thought-of-that-myself grimace.

"So what are the other holes?" I asked.

"Why did he come to L.A.?"

It was my turn to do some lip-sucking. I had forgotten that rather inconvenient detail. Southern California, home of the Granger clan, would seem the last place in the world Brandon would want to have migrated to. "Maybe he just got tired of running," I offered. "Maybe he had some idea of confronting Seth. Or of collecting evidence he could use to back up his tape, so he could finally go to the cops himself." These explanations sounded feeble, even to myself. "Maybe when we find Marcus, we'll have the answers," I concluded.

The Texan versus ticket seller confrontation appeared to have been resolved. The line surged forward, getting us close enough to see the posted admission prices.

"Thirty-eight bucks!" Terry exclaimed. "Highway robbery."

"That does include all the rides," I pointed out.

"Fat chance my trying to justify this on my expenses report. Come on." She broke out of line and strode directly to the entrance turnstile. The tickets were being collected by the kind of fanatically clean-cut young man who, in another time and place, might have spent his formative years as an enthusiastic member of the Hitler Youth.

Terry flashed her badge. "Official police business," she barked.

True to his Hitler Jugend appearance, he seemed to possess a profound respect for authority: he instantly released the turnstile lock.

"She's with me," Terry told him, pushing through.

I received a more wary scrutiny. For a moment I had the uneasy feeling he was going to demand to see my "documents." But then there was a click, and I was also admitted into the promised land.

"This place is humongous," Terry said, gazing around with dismay.

I had forgotten how big it was, sprawling over some dozens of acres. Music blared, cartoon figures cavorted, and everywhere people milled and sauntered. "We'll just have to cover as much ground as quickly as possible," I declared.

We began traveling briskly, weaving among flower barrows in a New Orleans courtyard, traversing a Spaghetti Western piazza, emerging in 1920s Chicago, with a backdrop of gangsters and Model Ts and machine-gun fire. For some minutes I became entangled in a massive group of seemingly all-overweight Germans. I struggled my way out of their midst and found myself at a stage where a doo-wop band dressed as presidents past was belting out "Earth Angel": Honest Abe had the falsetto lead, with the Roosevelts, Teddy and Franklin D., doing backup, and a red-wigged Jefferson wailing on sax.

I looked around for Terry and saw her come flailing out from the German mob.

"This is hopeless," I said, throwing up my arms. "We haven't even got to any of the rides yet. He could be anywhere."

"You're right, we can't keep meandering around like idiots," Terry replied. "I'm going to go talk to Security." She nodded toward a purple-painted electric cart manned by a thickset guy with a security badge. There were bevies of these carts around, I realized. All were painted in blend-into-the-gaiety gumdrop colors, the idea being, I supposed, that you weren't supposed to actually notice that your every move was under surveillance.

"Great idea," I said. "Maybe they can put out an APB on him."

Terry grunted. "Asking to find one kid in a place like this is your basic needle in a haystack."

"The uniforms!" I exclaimed. "A lot of the Windermere kids will still be in their plaid-jacket uniforms. That should make them more visible. And I think I've even got a picture . . ." I opened my bag, dug for my wallet and flipped out a recent snapshot of Chloe with three of her friends doing a mock cheer in front of the school gates.

Terry snatched it from my hand. "Wait here," she commanded in a this-is-a-job-for-a-professional voice. I remained watching our Chief Executives get down, segueing from "Earth Angel" into "Poison Ivy," while Terry went to confab with her fellow professional. After several minutes, she trotted back to me.

"We got a report that a bunch of them just went into the Prehistoric Jungle ride," she announced. "Here's a map."

We scrutinized the brightly colored folder. "We're not too far away," I said. "We cross through the Arabian Nights bazaar and it's opposite the pagoda."

We resumed our brisk pace. "By the way," I said, "they recommend that pregnant women don't get on these rides. So if we need to, you're the one who'll have to go."

"Me?" She shot me a sidewise glance.

"Is that a problem?"

"I kind of have a thing with claustrophobia," she said sheepishly. "Being in those tunnels and locked in those little trams kind of brings it out."

"No shit?" I grinned. I'd finally found a chink in Detective Shoe's seemingly impregnable armor. "So what happens if you have to inspect a body that's in some tight and confined place?"

"It's a bitch." She shuddered at the concept. "A couple of weeks ago there was a headless torso dumped in a crawl cellar in a house in Brentwood. I went in okay, but when I came out I was sweating like all get out. The uniforms thought it was because of the decapitation aspect." She made a contemptuous face. "As if I'd never seen one before." Apparently the fact that anyone would think her unnerved by something as humdrum as a headless corpse still rankled her.

The torch-lit gates of the Prehistoric Jungle now appeared in front of us. From behind them came the squeals and shrieks of people and the amplified roars and coos of dinosaurs. Inside the attraction, an ersatz river ran along banks of polyurethane outcroppings. Twenty-seater rafts pushed from a rough-hewn dock into a patch of white water to the left and disappeared from view. On the right, returning rafts were spat out with a splash from a "raptors' den" every thirty seconds.

Terry and I pushed our way through clots of people, some heading to get onto a raft, others rather shakily regaining their bearings after getting off it. I suddenly clutched Terry's sleeve. "My god," I cried. "There he is!"

"The kid?"

"No, Seth Granger! In the corduroy jacket, standing at the railing. He looks like he's waiting for one of the rafts to get in."

Terry peered at him. "Yeah, so he does."

"Aren't you going to do something?"

"Such as?"

"I don't know. Take him in for questioning."

"Is that all?" she deadpanned. "How about if I rough him up a little while I'm at it?"

I gave an exasperated look.

"As far as I've heard, this country hasn't switched yet to a police state. I can't just drag somebody in on the kind of fuzzy evidence you're talking about."

"But he killed Brandon! Are you just going to stand around until he goes for Marcus as well?"

"At this point, yeah."

"Well, I'm not," I said firmly and began moving in Seth's direction, not quite sure of what exactly I intended to do.

Plash! The raptors' den spat out another raft of shrieking satisfied customers. The spectators at the railing scurried back to prevent themselves from getting drenched. As they parted, I could see that the raft was packed with children, most of them wearing maroon plaid jackets. As it began puttering toward the landing dock, I picked out Marcus's dark curls in a middle row.

I looked back at Seth Granger. He was walking purposefully toward the dock. I quickened my own steps.

Two young hunks in rakish safari hats were helping the kids out of the raft. One gave a hand to Marcus, and the boy gracefully leapt onto the landing.

"Marcus!" I yelled and charged forward, nearly colliding with a teenager in a Death Row Records sweatshirt. I darted around him. Seth was almost in reach of Marcus, only steps away. I began to run.

To my utter astonishment, I watched Seth move right past Marcus without even a glance in the boy's direction. He continued to the edge of the dock, where kids were still rambunctiously disembarking from the raft. One of them was a boy with white-blond hair and a pinched face, aggressively shoving to get off. A safari guy hauled him onto dry land, and Seth marched up and took him by the arm.

I let out an abashed cackle of laughter. I'd had it stunningly wrong! Seth had been heading not to abduct Marcus Barnes, but merely to collect his own son.

I looked back at Marcus. At the sound of his name he had glanced up. Now his face wore that look of stark terror I had seen once before. But it clearly wasn't Seth Granger Marcus was scared of.

It was me.

Terry bounced up beside me. "Granger didn't go near the kid," she chortled.

"I noticed," I said.

"So there goes that theory. Who's the next guy you want to convict without a trial?"

I barely listened to her gloating. "Wait here a sec," I told her. "I want to talk to Marcus, and I don't want to spook him."

"So what do I look like, the Bride of Frankenstein?"

"No, though he seems to think I do." Marcus had started to edge nervously away from us. "Just wait here, okay?"

"Fine with me."

I composed my features into what I hoped was a nonthreatening expression and began gingerly moving toward Marcus. "Marcus, hey, it's me, Lucy," I called.

He shrank back, as if I were coming at him with a ten-inch carving knife.

"I know that all this time you've been afraid somebody would find out what happened at the audition. Up till now, everyone thought it was an accident. They didn't know you were with Joyce when she was killed."

He glanced at the water behind him as if considering it as a possible escape.

"Hey, it's all going to be okay," I said quickly. "Honest. I know you weren't responsible." I took another step closer. "Joyce Korshalek was shot. You were trying to save her, you didn't push her."

He looked at me with wary surprise. "How do you know that?"

"I saw a videotape. A friend of mine was nearby with a video camera when it all happened, and he got the whole thing on tape."

He hesitated. "So you can see her getting shot?"

He was too smart for me to try to bluff him. "Not exactly," I admitted. "Unless you look at the tape very carefully the way I did, it seems like you pushed her. But I can make everybody understand what really happened."

"No one's going to believe you," he declared. "They're going to think I killed her, and then they'll send me away to a juvenile facility." He hunched his shoulder with extreme agitation. "Do you know what happens to kids like me in those kind of places? They get beaten up and gang-banged. And they get held upside down with their heads in toilet bowls filled with turds until they almost drown."

I sucked in a sharp breath. "Where in the world did you hear stuff like that?"

"Everybody knows. I'd rather be dead than sent away there."

"That's why you tried to hang yourself, isn't it?" I asked softly. "Because you were afraid of getting sent away."

He didn't reply.

"You're tired of feeling scared all the time, aren't you? That's why you drew that flip book. You want to tell everybody the truth." I was close enough now to touch him. I extended a hand. "All we need to know is who did shoot Joyce," I said. "Was it Kerrin Granger? Or did he give his gun to one of the other kids?"

Marcus's response was swift and succinct—he kicked me hard in the shins. I howled and drew up my injured leg. Marcus began to run.

"Marcus, wait!" I yelled, but he was already shooting through the gates. Terrific, I thought. Now I've scared him so much, he just might try to kill himself again. I had visions of him leaping from the Alpine roller coaster or throwing himself under the wheels of a stagecoach. Ignoring the throbbing pain in my ankle, I took off after him.

I hobbled through the gates in time to see his slight figure weave swiftly through the throngs. The boy was a triple threat, I marveled: intellectual whiz kid, song and dance man supreme, and Olympic-caliber cross-country sprinter. Within seconds he had vanished from my sight.

I heard the welcome electronic rumble of one of the ubiquitous security carts. This one was raspberry-colored; the guard had salt-and-pepper hair and the kind of mirrored sunglasses that were once de rigueur for Third World military strongmen. I shot up my arm in a kind of hailing-a-taxi gesture, and he obligingly swung his cart over to me.

"Get on," he barked.

This seemed more than obliging, but I had no time to puzzle over it. "A ten-year-old boy has run off from his school group and is somewhere in the park on his own," I blurted out. "It's urgent that I find him."

"Name of the boy?"

"Marcus Barnes. He's got light black skin, dark curly hair, and he's wearing a maroon plaid school uniform jacket." I added stridently, "It's an emergency—he could be suicidal. He attempted it once before. He's very upset right now so there's a possibility he could try it again."

"Then we'll just have to round him up."

Something about the reedy voice sounded familiar. Before I could determine what it was, I noticed Terry Shoe's moon face among the crowd emerging from the gates. I waved frantically to her. She waved back and began trotting toward us.

"Stop!" I told the guard. "We need to pick up that woman."

"I don't think so," he said and stomped on the pedal. The cart shot forward.

I saw Terry come to a halt and stare after our retreating cart with a baffled frown. I swiveled angrily to my escort; my own frazzled face reflected back to me in his dictator's shades.

"Why didn't you stop?" I demanded.

His lips parted in a smile, revealing a set of distinctly snaggled teeth. With a shock, I realized I was in the company of my former acquaintance, the ex-cabby and avid consumer of shoestring potatoes, Randy Alston.

24

No wonder he'd responded to the taxi hail, was my first ridiculous thought.

Get the hell out of here, was my more lucid second. I moved to hop back out of the cart, but Randy grabbed me by the arm.

"No you don't," he said. Something cold snapped around my wrist. I looked down to see the silver gleam of a pair of handcuffs. "I might need you once we find the little pisser," he said. He snapped the other cuff around his own wrist.

There was something eerily familiar about this situation. Then it hit me—it was exactly like in *The 39 Steps*, when Robert Donat handcuffs Madeleine Carroll to himself to prevent her from going to the police; the only difference being that Robert Donat had been witty, gorgeous and noble, while I happened to be shackled to an orthodontically challenged goon.

And possibly, I realized, with a crawl of dread, a murderous goon. Some hard facts began to snap into place: 1, that Randy Alston was under court order to keep his ass out of L.A., so 2, if it had been Randy that Brandon was trying to hide from, Los Angeles would have seemed the safest place in the country to come to, but 3, here was Randy's ass indisputably within city limits, meaning that 4, he might well have been at Windermere ten days ago and encountered Brandon, which 5, would explain Brandon's look of shock and terror . . .

And had to mean that it was Randy Alston who, later that morning, carved a grisly moon crater out of Brandon's face, with one efficient blast of a Smith & Wesson .44 Magnum.

Very possibly the one now housed in the shoulder holster that poked beneath Randy's open jacket. Panic constricted my lungs; for a moment I could hardly breathe.

When I regained my breath, I decided the chatty old-friends-reunion approach would be my best bet. "So, Randy, it's been a long time," I said, struggling for a breezy tone. "I'm surprised you even remember me."

"I remember you all right," he snarled. "I remember you always acting high and mighty, like you were born with a solid gold rod up your ass. Snotty college bitch. I guess you thought you were too good for a cab driver."

It wasn't snobbery, I felt like explaining, *it was pure and utter loathing. You could have been chairman of General Motors and I'd have felt the same way.* But at this particular point, honesty hardly seemed like the best policy. "We've all come a long way since then," I said, attempting an insouciant laugh. "You and Myra especially. You must be incredibly proud of what Jamie's accomplished."

"I'm fucking proud of myself, is what," he declared. He barreled the cart past an antebellum plantation manor; a hoopskirted belle waved from beneath the portico. "The press loves to shit on me," he went on. "Randy Alston's the hanger-on, Randy Alston rides his kid's coattails. Screw that." His monologue escalated into a rant. "Who do you think, back in the beginning, was the one knocking on all the doors, not taking no for an answer? Me, that's who. Who was the one who made sure he took the right parts, not threw himself into just any shit they offered?"

"You?" I ventured.

"Damned straight. It was me every step of the way. Jamie had a photo session, I checked out every single negative, made sure they didn't use none that made him look like a gimp or a frigging crybaby. Every interview he had, I sat in on it, so's they didn't throw no crummy questions at him, just kept everything on the up and up. You ought to hear some of the stuff these media assholes will throw to an eight-year-old. Stuff about sex and do you believe in God? and all sorts of crap." He shook his head at the unconscionable venality of the press corps. "I'm the one got Jamie where he is. Myra was just there for the ride. So don't you fucking forget it."

"I won't," I promised.

He shot me a sidewise glance from behind his shades. An *urp, urp* sounded in his breast pocket. He braked the cart and, with the hand that wasn't inconveniently manacled to mine, extracted a cell phone. "I got her," he said to the caller. "Yeah, we were right, it's the Barnes kid. Just alert the central office you're looking for him, they'll track him easy. Where the fuck are you, anyway?" I heard an angry squawk emanate from the phone. "Okay, don't have a sheep. I'm on my way."

He set the phone on his lap, stamped on the pedal, and we began to roll again. I remembered reading how Houdini managed to escape from shackles by contracting his body parts, so now I tried contracting my hand to see if I could wriggle it out of the cuff. The effort only seemed to make the metal bite harder into my wrist. I gave a murmur of pain.

"I strongly suggest you relax," Randy said. "Those are the kinds of cuffs that tighten up with movement."

"Thanks for the tip," I said in a surly tone. "So where did you get this cart from?"

"The studio gives me the total run of this place. Jamie Alston's last flick put a hundred and eighty million on their bottom line, so you better believe they kiss my ass." He gave a sharp laugh. "Hey, you know what happens if me or Jamie want to go on one of the rides? They shut it down to everybody but us. As many times as we want. All the rest of you assholes have to wait outside till we're done." He chortled like a six-year-old who's kicked all the other kids out of the sandbox. Then he aimed another sidewise glance at me. "What did you think, I stole this cart? You think I'm a common thief?"

No, I just think you're a common murderer was my unspoken reply.

"I'm no thief," he declared, answering himself.

I couldn't resist. "What about all those dinners you stole back at the Panic Café?"

"Hey, we were entitled to that food. The old dude that owned that shithole, he was the thief, man. He paid slave wages. Myra was being exploited and I told her so."

"So in return, you just had to liberate all those strip steaks and shoestring potatoes."

"Shut the fuck up!" he snapped. "I'm sick of hearing you yap." The phone urped again. He flipped it open, said, "They locate him? Where the hell's the Alien Planet? . . . Yeah, okay, got it."

He swung the cart in an abrupt U-turn, causing me to lurch against him. The tabloids had been apparently accurate in reporting that Randy Alston was a fan of neither shower nor bathtub: he stank like old cheese. I wrinkled my nose and shrank as far from him as the handcuffs would allow.

I tried another tack. "I really don't understand what this is all about," I said, in an innocent high voice.

"You don't, huh? Well I'll tell you. A couple of days ago I happened to get a call from the producers of this TV show. They said they got this shocking videotape showing a murder at the *Orphans* audition and was Jamie going to have any comment? The second I heard your name connected to it, I figured you'd probably lead us to the right kid."

Which of course, I promptly did, I thought with deep chagrin. Lucy Blabbermouth Freers.

We were passing through the Fairyland Pavilion, where a gossamer-winged ensemble was delivering an up-tempo rendition of "Young at Heart" while other fairies milled through the crowd tossing handfuls of golden sparkles. One of the milling-around fairies tripped up to us. "Fairy tales can come true," she chirped and showered Randy with gold.

"Ah shit!" he snarled, slapping at his jacket. "I'm gonna look like a friggin' faggot." He shook his head and a flurry of sparkles snowed onto his shoulders like golden dandruff. With a whinny of disgust, he aimed the cart toward the entrance to the Alien Planet ride that now loomed to the right.

Another electric cart, this one painted a bright tangerine, was waiting in front. Out of the driver's seat climbed Myra Alston, clutching a walkie-talkie. She hurried over to us and squinted at the besparkled Randy.

"What's with you?" she giggled. "You look like Tinkerbell."

He slapped at his jacket again. "Friggin' fairies."

Myra sniffed fastidiously. "Jeez, would it kill you to take a shower once in a while?"

"Hey, I take plenty of showers, don't give me that."

"Myra and Randy, together again," I spoke up. "It's starting to seem like old times."

Myra turned to me with a simpering smile. "Yes, we decided that deep down we did truly love each other, so it was crazy to stay apart. And also for Jamie's sake."

"What the fuck are you explaining to her for?" snarled her True Love.

"Funny," I said. "I was under the impression this was strictly a business venture."

"I don't know what you're talking about," Myra said. She blinked her rabbity pink eyes.

"I'm talking about how you saw Brandon McKenna show up at Windermere and freaked out. So you and Randy declared a truce long enough for Randy to come to L.A. and get Brandon out of the way." It seemed I couldn't help being a blabbermouth.

"I didn't know he was going to shoot him," Myra mewled.

"What did you think he was going to do, sweet-talk him into staying quiet? And what do you think he plans to do with Marcus?"

"What are we standing around yakking for?" Randy cut in. "Do they have the kid?"

Myra blinked again, then poked a thumb at the entrance. "He's in there. I've told them we're responsible for him and they should hold on to him till we get there."

"Okay, out," Randy barked at me.

The two of us shimmied in a kind of mini–chain gang out of the cart. "Don't you think our being handcuffed together is going to look a little peculiar?" I said.

Randy frowned, as if he really hadn't considered this aspect. With his noncuffed hand, he slid the gun out of his holster and held it out to Myra. "Keep her covered while I unlock us," he ordered.

"I don't know how to handle that," she said.

"So I gotta do all the dirty work while your highness keeps her ass clean."

"I'm *sorry*," Myra protested. "I never learned how to handle a gun, okay?"

"Okay, okay. Then get the key out of my back pocket."

With a fastidious grimace, Myra dipped her hand into the buttocks pocket of his filthy jeans and tweezed out a small silver key.

"Speaking of keys," I said to Randy, "it was so considerate of you to send ours back to us."

"That was me," Myra volunteered. "I sent it to you."

"You did *what*?" Randy exclaimed.

"But that girl you had following me was a lousy photographer," I went on. "I've had passport pictures more flattering than the ones she took."

Randy's eyes bulged apoplectically. "What's she talking about?"

"I didn't want her to get involved," Myra said. "I thought if she knew she was being watched, she'd stay clear."

"You are so goddamned dumb! Dumb as a frigging dog!" His

eyes flicked to me. "And she's the one that gets the credit for Jamie's career, can you believe?"

"Life is so unfair," I commiserated.

"Don't call me dumb," Myra pouted to Randy. "If you're such a fabulous brain, why did it take so long to figure this out?"

"Just shut your yap and unlock us."

Myra gave him a hateful glare. Then, with a fumbling motion, she snapped open the locks.

I yanked my hand free, flexed it luxuriously, then considered making a dash for freedom. Not even Randy Alston could be nuts enough to shoot me in plain sight of a hundred multicultural theme park visitors.

"Mom!" Chloe's piercing voice carried above the din of music and the crowd. To my horror, I saw her break from a group of her friends emerging from the Alien Planet pavilion. She began skipping toward me.

"Get rid of her," Randy muttered in my ear. The gun barrel prodded my vertebrae. It occurred to me that maybe he *was* crazy enough to shoot me; and what effect would it have on Chloe's future development to have seen her mom gunned down before her eyes?

"Where's Daddy?" I called to her.

"He's still on the ride. He'll be out in a couple of minutes."

"Okay, I'm going to go on it now."

"You can't," she said adamantly. "They don't allow pregnant ladies."

"That's just a recommendation. I'll be fine."

"Then I'll go on again with you. It's an awesome ride."

"No!" I screeched. "Can't I even do one goddamned thing by myself without one of you always having to tag along?"

The look of hurt and shock on Chloe's round face was more than I could stand. Her two friends who had just come up beside her gaped with astonishment.

I turned abruptly and plunged through the turnstile leading into the attraction. My brace of Alston escorts followed close behind.

"That was cool," Randy commended me. "Now just keep moving."

We moved swiftly into an arcade crammed with props and cut-out figures from the movie. *Alien Planet* had been the blockbuster hit of 1982: a boy stowing away on an intergalactic fighter jet teams up with the rakish pilot to save the galaxy from the forces of evil. The film spawned three sequels, a billion dollars' worth of related merchandise and this seven-and-a-half-minute ride, which was still the most popular attraction in the park. The line of people waiting to get in snaked along a maze blocked out by satin ropes; above their heads, an electric sign declared the current wait to be thirty-five minutes.

I moved politely into place at the end.

"We don't have to stand on line," declared Myra, Queen of the Theme Park. She began elbowing and shoving her way roughly through, ignoring the mutters and cries of protest. Randy and I tagged in her wake.

The line had its origin at the Spaceport, a terminal that looked disconcertingly like a New York City subway station except for the color scheme: white-on-white with accents of titanium. Instead of the IRT express, every twenty seconds a Triscuit-shaped intergalactic fighter ship rumbled up with a passenger load of six. A pair of leggy young women whose skimpy, spangled uniforms marked them as Stewardesses of the Future helped the arriving crew off and bundled six new ones in. The movie's heroic theme blared at a migraine-inducing volume.

At one end of the platform, I spied Marcus sitting with his legs folded, while what appeared to be a genuine security guard hovered over him.

The three of us shuffled in tight formation over to him. "Hi, I'm Randy Alston," Randy announced, shouting over the din of heroic horns.

"Recognized you right off, sir." The guard bent his head, adding a third chin to the two already in situ. "I've seen just about every one of your son's movies. *Tricky Rick* I went to three times."

Just my luck: My only hope of rescue was a Jamie Alston groupie whose taste in movies had been arrested in the seventh grade.

"I'm so relieved you found this child," Myra simpered loudly. "We hold ourselves responsible for the school group, since we were the ones who bought the tickets. When we heard he was missing, my heart stopped."

"I'm not going with those people!" Marcus hollered, squinching himself up against the wall. "They're not my parents. They want to hurt me."

"Come on, up you go," the guard said, hoisting him by his arm. Marcus tried one of his patented shin-kicks, but the guard impressively managed to evade it.

"He's right," I blurted. "These people are out to harm this boy. He was a witness to a murder Jamie committed and they want him out of the way." Even to myself I sounded like a raving lunatic.

"Who is this?" the guard asked Randy.

I felt the gun jam painfully into the small of my back.

"She's with us," Myra said. "She just likes to kid around." She held her hand out to Marcus. "Let's go, young man, before everyone starts to get worried."

"No," he insisted.

A fresh intergalactic car had rumbled to a stop at the Spaceport platform and disgorged its occupants. A middle-aged Japanese couple were stepping decorously into the front two seats.

I suddenly reached forward and grabbed Marcus's hand. "Come on!" I yelled. I elbowed aside the two teenagers about to climb into the middle row and pulled Marcus into it. The teens settled into the seats behind us, and, with a jolt, the car began to pull away.

"Thank god!" I breathed.

With a second jolt, the car stopped again. One of the futuristic Stews sashayed up and mumbled something to the teens, who rather sullenly climbed out. They were replaced by a triumphantly grinning Myra and Randy.

Another lurch, and we rolled forward again.

Marcus stared up at me, his eyes huge with alarm. "Don't worry, they won't do anything with other people around," I assured him. I leaned forward and shouted to the Japanese couple in front: "You've got to help us! The people behind us are out to kidnap this boy!"

The couple beamed and bobbed their heads.

"Don't you understand English?"

More beaming and bobbing.

Then suddenly all six of us were shrieking at the top of our lungs as the car took a steep drop. I felt my stomach rise; the warnings to pregnant women thundered in my head. We leveled off and were surrounded by projections of a space war: our craft dipped and bumped and careened as colored lasers zapped around us and deafening explosions boomed on a soundtrack. Then we lurched sharply to the left, eliciting another communal holler.

"I hate these things!" Myra wailed.

"It gets a lot worse," I shouted over my shoulder. "Wait till we start doing loop-de-loops."

She gave a bleat of terror.

"Don't listen to her," Randy ordered. "This stuff is safe, or else they wouldn't let kids on."

Then, rather miraculously, we appeared to be floating through a vast and starry universe filled with breathtaking celestial events. "There's a crab nebula!" Marcus breathed, momentarily forgetting his terror. The Japanese couple uttered an "aaah" of delight.

We listed precipitously onto one side as we skirted a giant asteroid. From Myra's throat issued a sound like a death rattle.

The car righted itself, then dropped like an elevator in free fall as a shooting star streaked over our heads.

"I've got to get off this!" Myra shrieked.

"Be my guest," I yelled back.

"Relax, for chrissake!" Randy snarled. "It's nothing."

We suddenly appeared to be rocketing directly into a fiery sun. I found myself tensely gripping the safety bar. At the last minute, the sun exploded in a supernova. Our car rocked and shook as it traveled through the debris.

"You shouldn't have made me get on!" Myra screamed at Randy. In the unearthly light, she looked romantically wasted, as if she spent her spare time composing sonnets rather than plotting to abduct small boys.

"You're right, he shouldn't have," I shouted to her. "He's always making you do things you don't want to, isn't he?"

"I suppose you want that kid to get away?" Randy barked at her. "So he can blab to the whole world about Jamie?"

Marcus goggled up at me again. "What are they going to do to me?" he asked.

"Nothing," I said firmly. I turned my head again. "Listen, you don't have to worry about Marcus. He's not going to turn Jamie in. Tell them, Marcus."

"Jamie didn't do anything," he declared.

"You see?" I said to the Alstons.

We all shrieked again as our car plunged downward. Now we were skimming the surface of the alien planet. We dodged something that looked like an enormous soft ice-cream cone while tree-sized, and evidently meat-eating, tuliplike flowers snapped at us from both sides.

I looked back at the Alstons. "I told you. He's not going to squeal on Jamie."

"Jamie didn't shoot that lady," Marcus broke in. "He did." He pointed at Randy.

"What?" Myra squealed.

"He's a stinking little liar!" Randy bellowed.

The car whipped around another bend, and now we were sailing above an alien city. A Zeppelinish aircraft appeared behind us and gave chase through corridors of alien skyscrapers. I took time out for a whoop as we shot through a particularly narrow canyon.

Then our car touched down and began to cruise rather calmly on alien ground.

"Tell us what happened," I said to Marcus.

"Jamie and Kerrin had this gun they were fooling around with. He took it away from them." Marcus shot another over-the-shoulder glance at Randy. "Then later I went down the back stairs and saw Joyce. Then I heard this shot and she started to fall. I tried to catch her but she fell anyway. And when I turned around, I saw *him* running away."

"He's lying his fucking head off," Randy screamed.

"Come on, Myra," I said. "Which one of them are you going to believe?"

Her thin face was a perplexed blank. Our car had now entered the Plain of Monsters. Fabulous, vaguely prehistoric-looking beasts lumbered about us. A pterodactyl-type bird swooped overhead.

"Face it, you're married to a cold-blooded killer," I went on. "That's really who you've been protecting these last two years, not Jamie."

Myra's face suddenly twisted with intense hatred. "You shit!" she hissed at Randy.

"Hey, I did it for both of us," he hollered. "The bitch was going to screw us out of everything."

"You let me believe all this time my son was a murderer!" she shrieked. "I ought to kill you!"

"You ought to kiss my ass. You think you'd be living like a fucking queen if that bitch had managed to cream Jamie's career? You'd be back waiting tables, baby."

There was a deafening roar that made us all flinch. A twelve-foot-tall monster surged up beside the car, a beast with scales and pointed horns. It waved its claw-pawed arms at us with that rather arthritic motion of animatronics. The Japanese couple laughed and pointed, then turned to include the rest of us in their enjoyment—just in time to see Myra sock Randy in the cheek. Their smiles froze.

Whap! Randy cuffed Myra on the side of her head. The two Japanese swiveled to face front again.

"Wait'll this is all over," Randy was shouting. "You'll be sorry, baby. You'll be so sorry."

"You bastard," Myra shouted back. "I'm sorry already for ever seeing your ugly face."

The monster roared and reared menacingly on its hind legs.

"Hey, Randy," I yelled. "Did you know Myra is trying to get pregnant again?"

"That's none of his business," Myra declared, clutching the safety bar.

"You're her husband, aren't you? I should think it is your business. She knows Jamie's career is heading south. Even if his behavior doesn't put him out of work, he's going to hit puberty soon. So Myra's going to breed another little star, and this time you're out of the loop."

Aaaargh! went the monster, in rather happy synch with the *aaaargh!* that came from Randy.

We were rocking so hard it seemed as if we were about to tip over. Marcus's hand squeezed mine. The Asian couple resolutely faced front, obviously more willing to take their chances with the beast than the battling Alstons behind them.

"No way you're having a kid without me," Randy bellowed to Myra.

"Oh yeah? Well just watch me. And it won't be the first," she sneered.

"What's that supposed to mean?"

"Do you really think a kid as adorable as Jamie could possibly have any of your genes?" She gave a sharp laugh. "Get real."

"You frigging bitch, I ought to kill you!" he howled. He threw the safety bar up and made a movement to lunge at her. At the same instant, the monster's arms locked onto the side of our car and began rocking it violently. Randy gave a whoop as he lost his balance; he frantically flapped his arms, trying to keep from pitching over the side.

"Watch out!" Marcus yelled and reached to grab hold of his jacket.

A gleaming starship suddenly materialized from the maw of a tunnel directly ahead of us. There was an ear-splitting explosion as it fired on the monster, making us all jump in our seats, and causing Marcus to let go of Randy's jacket. The monster flailed feebly at the starship, reared once on its haunches and then, with a dying bellow, began to fall.

In all the commotion, I could never be absolutely certain of what happened next. But it seemed to me that I saw Myra lean toward her husband and give him a quick, forceful shove. Whether or not she did, Randy suddenly toppled with a shrill scream over the side of the car. As the mechanical beast came crashing down on him, I pulled Marcus close and pressed his face into my shoulder to make sure that this time he didn't see.

25

Brandon would have hated this, I thought.

The memorial service was being held in the assembly hall of the high school he had attended. Some hundred people dressed in their Sunday finery were squirming uncomfortably on folding chairs. A podium was bedecked with dyed carnations and baby's breath, plus an enormous crescent of flowers that looked as if it had come off the neck of a horse that had run in the money.

And outside, all the oppressive drip and dreariness of the Midwest in high mud season.

It was everything Brandon had tried to escape from, I reflected, and in the end had been delivered right back into.

A cousin with an unmusical soprano was ripping through a quavering rendition of "You'll Never Walk Alone." I stared out the silt-streaked window and let my thoughts wander.

It had been two and a half weeks since the riotous trek through the Alien Planet. After Randy had plunged over the side, the car had soared up into a tunnel of total darkness, then taken a sharp turn, and suddenly we were cruising back into the antiseptically gleaming Spaceport. Where, on the platform, we were met by Terry Shoe with a contingent of authentic security personnel.

The Japanese couple, who turned out to be a Mr. and Mrs. Shin-ryo from Nagasaki, on a honeymoon trip they had postponed for twenty-four years, had tottered off the car first, uncertain whether the crushing of an American man in the gears of a flipper-armed monster had actually been some sort of special effect and all just part of the show. Myra, in a state of florid hysteria, had had to be bodily lifted out of her seat, while Marcus would not release his grip on my hand until he'd been safely delivered back to his mother's care.

After everything had been sorted out and I'd had a chance to regain my bearings, it occurred to me to ask Terry how she'd known to be at the platform.

"I was kind of bamboozled by the way you took off in that security cart, leaving me cold," she said. "So I hitched a ride with the next one I saw and went after you. I recognized your daughter outside that Alien Planet ride. She told me you had just gone on it, which was a tip-off something was wrong, since I knew you wouldn't voluntarily jeopardize your pregnancy."

"I suppose she also told you how I suddenly turned into the Mommy from Hell," I said, with a guilty twinge.

"Yeah, which confirmed my thinking. You had to have a good reason, otherwise you'd never have treated your kid that way. You're too damned good a mother."

So it seemed that my Damned Good Mother credentials had been revalidated. To solidify them, I had a heart-to-heart with Chloe to discuss my strange outburst. I explained that I had pretended I wanted to be rid of her only to protect her from the crazy and dangerous person I was with.

"You know I'd never, ever really reject you, don't you?" I asked her.

"Uh-huh." She nodded.

"And I'm really sorry if I embarrassed you in front of your friends."

"That's okay." She shrugged. "They just thought you had PMS."

As a Damned Good Mother, I also checked back in with Dr. Ray Tetweiller Sr. Another ultrasound, another paternal reassurance that all was well. He prescribed a week of bed rest: "Just to keep us on the right side of safe," he drawled, practically snapping his red-striped suspenders. I dutifully spent the next seven days curled up in my quilts, watching Kate Hepburn movies and weird animations from the old Iron Curtain Czechoslovakia, talking endlessly on the phone to a recovering Valerie Jane, and thumbing through the popular press.

It was courtesy of the popular press that I learned that Annie Manzano, the cha-cha-cha-ing divorcée, had announced her engagement to a rakish former governor of Colorado with whom she'd been carrying on a flaming affair for over a year—meaning Kit had been telling the truth about the platonic nature of their own relationship.

I glanced at him now, sitting almost motionless beside me. When I had been debating whether or not to make the journey here, it was Kit who had urged me to go, insisting on coming with me in case anything went wrong pregnancywise, but tactfully allowing me enough space to grieve in my own way. Catching my glance, he gave me an encouraging little smile and I returned it. I thought of his indiscretion with the reporter from *Vanity Fair* those years ago—whatever lingering resentments I still kept burrowed within me, perhaps it was high time to let them go.

A particularly shrill note from the podium made me wince. For some reason it triggered a thought of that other Damned Good Mother, Myra Alston. It appeared she was going to emerge from the entire fiasco scot-free. She had maintained that she had been just another victim of the depraved Randy, claiming she had known nothing about his shooting Joyce Korshalek or Brandon McKenna until just that day at the theme park. She had proclaimed she had gone along with him in order to be able to protect Marcus Barnes—that, she swore piously, had been her sole motivation. And it was preposterous that she had pushed her husband out of the rocking car—she had actually tried to save him from falling.

Myra, in fact, was fast acquiring a rather heroic reputation.

Moreover, she was about to get even richer. From all reports, Jamie's career was back on the ascendancy. There had been a general outpouring of public sympathy for him: *Poor unfortunate boy! With such a brute for a father, no wonder he had been behaving so badly.* All his previous transgressions were forgiven—plum starring roles were once more cascading his way.

The soprano cousin hit a crescendo finale, then stepped down to light applause. Brandon's sister-in-law, Sharie, now tripped up to the podium to pay her last, and possibly first, respects to the deceased. In a feathery red-orange frock, she looked less like a canary and more like, say, a scarlet tanager. For her selection, she had chosen a particularly mushy passage from Kahlil Gibran which she began reading in her twittery voice.

I felt a nudge. Paul Lynch, sitting on my opposite side, made a pained face. "Brandon would have wanted Wallace Stevens," he whispered.

"Or Emily Dickinson," I whispered back.

He nodded ruefully. "These people know nothing about him at all."

They certainly didn't know about his budding relationship with Paul, who had presented himself as merely a friend. And naturally they had no idea I'd been anything to Brandon other than briefly an employer.

I remember how I had thought with frustration that I really had known nothing about him either. But there was at least one thing I was sure of. On the last morning of his life, when he had dropped off Chloe at Windermere and stood chatting with Paul, he had spied Myra in her limousine—and to his shock and horror, realized that her supposedly estranged husband Randy was sitting right beside her. At that point, he could have immediately jumped town.

But there was something he had to do first—he had to warn the

Barneses that Marcus was in mortal danger. Which is why he was in that deserted road in Topanga Canyon—it was the shortest route to the Barneses' house. Ensuring Marcus's safety had been more important to him than ensuring his own.

Because I could not stop for death, death kindly stopped for me . . . I had a vivid memory of Brandon reciting the Emily Dickinson poem to me in his shabby, roach-infested apartment in Morningside Heights. It might even have been the night we had tossed down so much Hearty Burgundy and first made love. I thought of how every girl hopes she'll lose her virginity to someone special, even extraordinary. It occurred to me now that I actually had.

Several people, I realized, had turned to me and were staring at me with frowns of disapproval. It must have been because I had manifestly the Wrong Expression slapped on my face.

I was grinning with broad delight.